CAPTURED
BY THE
ORC GENERAL

MONSTROUS MATES BOOK 2

CHARLOTTE SWAN

Kingdom of the Gods
Lastlight Forest
Moonbourne
Blackfire Castle
Myrkarvin
Home of the Dark Elves
Brakenbone Mountains
The Bridge
Merrywood Forest
Solys Castle
Lysan
Home of the Light
Old Stone Town

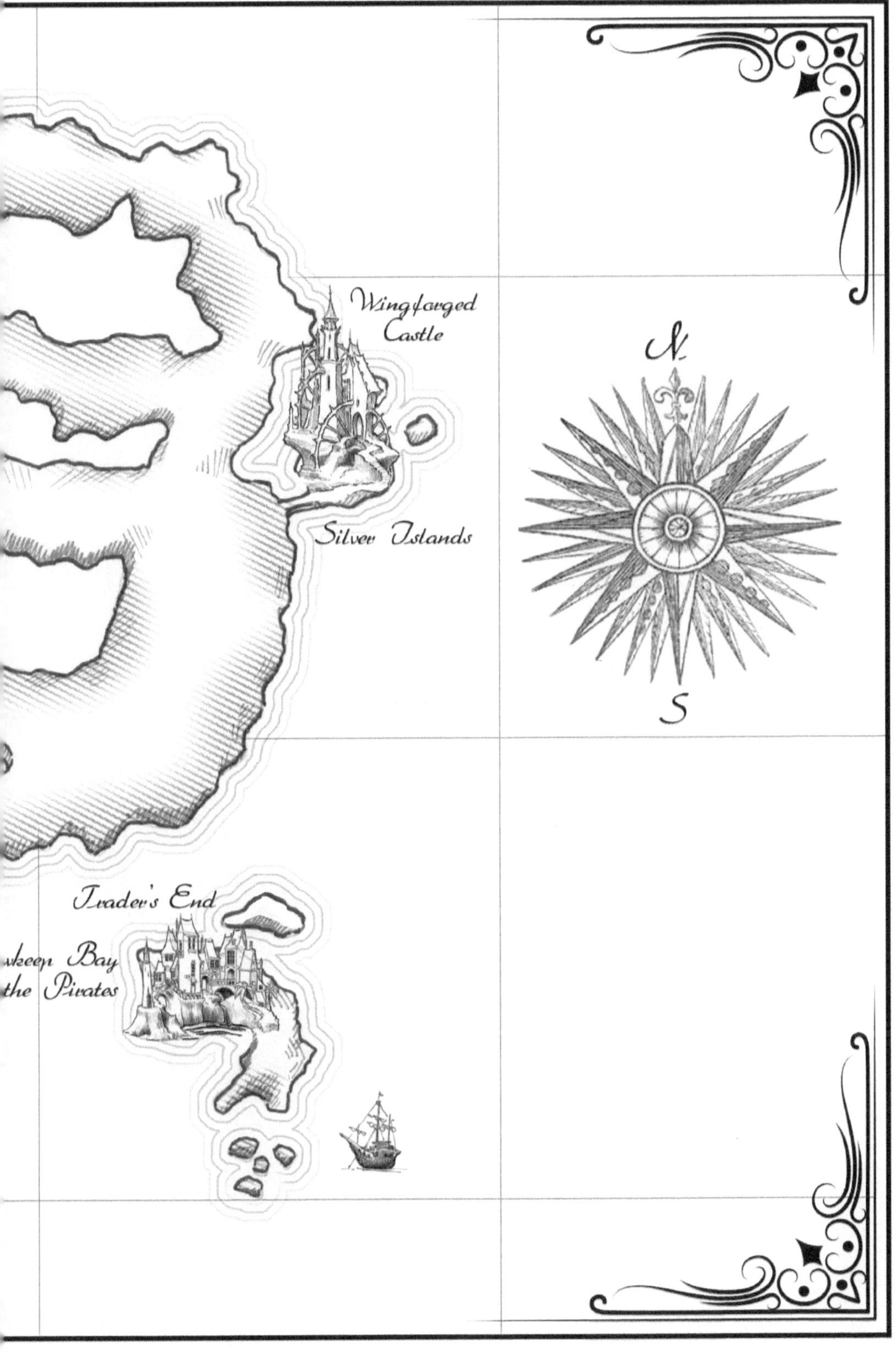

Wingforged Castle
Silver Islands
N
S
Trader's End
skeep Bay
the Pirates

eBook ISBN: 979-8-9870192-2-1
Paperback ISBN: 979-8-9870192-3-8

Cover Art by Magdalena Pietrzak (@barnswallow.art)
Cover Design by Haya Designs
Map & Interior Formatting by Qamber Designs & Media
Editing by A Taylor(ed) Edit

www.authorcharlotteswan.com

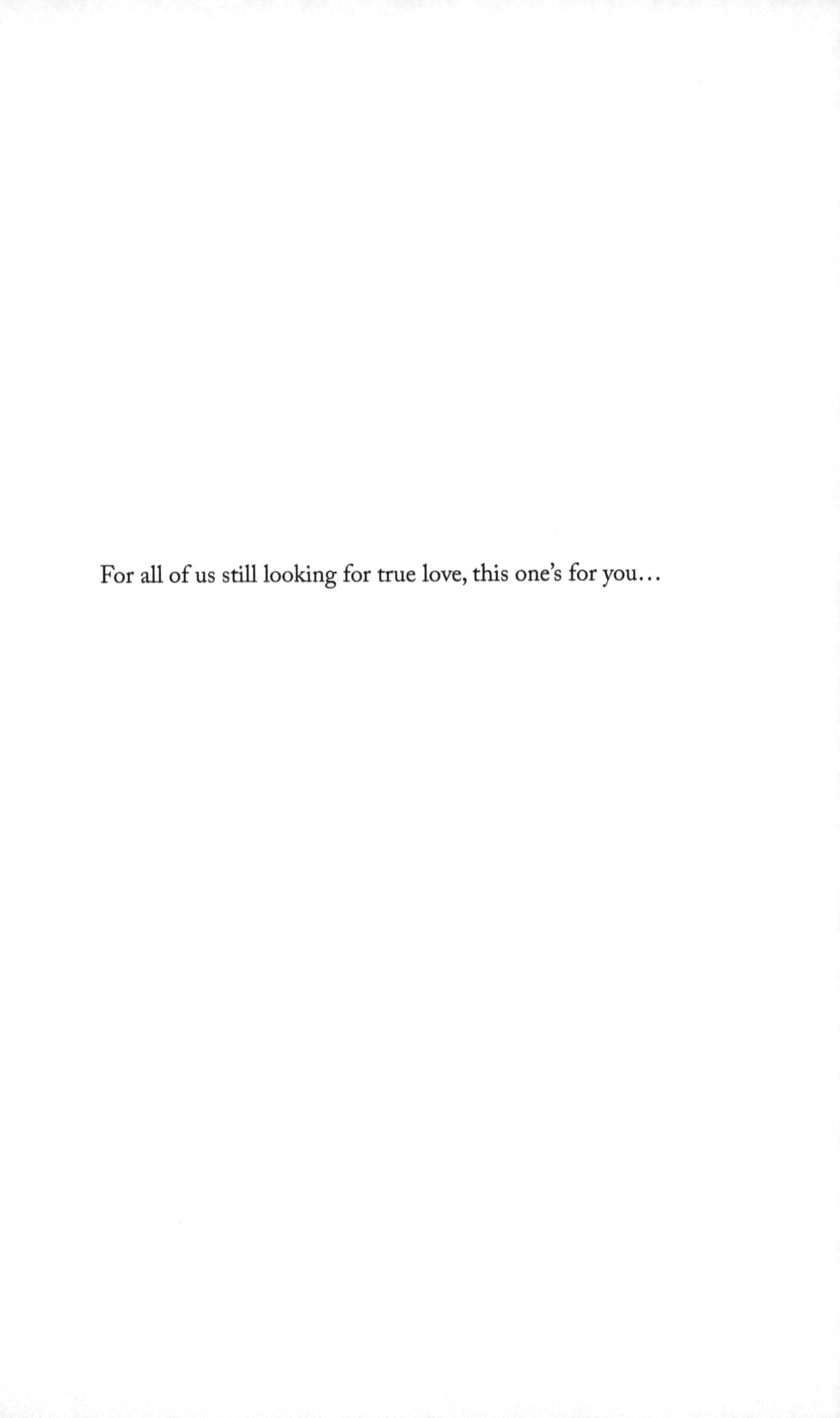

For all of us still looking for true love, this one's for you…

NOTE

Please see the author's website
for a detailed list of all content warnings.

www.authorcharlotteswan.com

CHAPTER 1

KAETHE

The innkeeper was a liar.

That was the only explanation. Or the people of Moonbourne have a very different definition than I do of a short journey. I guess I can't entirely blame the old keeper, perhaps back in her day this was a quicker journey. However, it's been two days since I left the inn, two days since I sent a letter back to Queen Elvie in Myrkorvin to inform her that I was still very much alive if only tired and cold.

Tired and cold has been the motto of this journey.

I had set out from Myrkrovin with so much purpose. Leaving behind the comfort of Blackfire Castle, my work, my friends…all in the hopes that a whisper of a rumor was true. I followed that rumor to this barren, frozen land so I could investigate it myself on the off chance that it would lead me to finding my brother.

As a woman of academia, I know there is no great likelihood that my brother is alive in Dread's Keep. While we have heard talk of humans living on Brokenbone Mountain, the chances of him being one of them are slim.

We were just children when our home was attacked.

Sometimes, in my dreams, I relive that wretched night. I can feel my mother's frantic hand on my shoulder shaking me awake and hear the front door to our cottage slam shut as my father went to investigate the strange noises coming from outside. The screaming, smell of smoke, and carnage unleashed on our village is what I remember most. My mother had done her best to shield my brother and I from the worst of the blood, the bodies. But I had still seen enough: orcs were raiding our town.

They each had a cruel gleam in their yellow eyes as they cut down another one of our neighbors. It was the same look one of them had as I watched him slice cleanly through my father's neck, his blood staining the front of his white sleep shirt. Being so young, I couldn't even process what I was seeing.

My mother understood though, and I watched the light in her dark eyes go out. She had twisted her ankle working in the field that morning and her limp would slow us down. She urged my brother and I to run quickly into the forest and hide until the morning. She made my brother swear to look out for me, a massive promise to elicit from an eight-year-old.

Then I watched her limp over to my father's lifeless body and sit beside it. I watched as the same orc who had cut down my father brandished his sword at my mother's throat.

We ran before I could see his blade make contact with her neck.

My brother's hand was clammy as it gripped mine, pulling me through the scattered bodies and roaring fires. Our blacksmith's house was in flames; his smoking corpse lay just outside the front door as an orc, its yellow-green skin shiny with blood, pilfered through his tools. The smell of burning flesh was indescribably awful.

I still remember the glint in the orc's eyes as he spied me and my brother. He picked up a hammer from the forge. It glowed molten red in the dark and even at a distance I could feel the heat it gave off.

Then the great creature gave chase.

Its thunderous footsteps sounded behind us as we ran. My legs carried me as fast as they could at six-years-old, the muscles burning with each step, my bare feet crunching on broken glass and sharp stones. The orcs had set so many fires that the air around us was heavy and choked us with all the ash.

We ran straight into another group of humans trying to flee.

They were shouting at each other, urging us all to make for the river. One of them, our town's woodcutter, was missing his left arm. The crimson stain on his shirt looked like the filling from one of mother's *moonberry* pies. Red and clotted and sticky. The woodcutter was a kind man, always carving me little figurines of bears. I had a whole collection back in our cottage that I wished I had remembered to take with me.

My feet snagged in the damp grass and my nightgown was soaked with sweat. It was me who stopped, who hesitated. Me who allowed us to be swallowed up by the hysteric crowd, and me who lost my brother's hand in the midst of it all.

All because I was going to ask if the woodcutter would be able to carve me some new bears.

That is my last vivid memory of that night. Once I realized I couldn't find my brother, panic began to set in and turned everything into a blur. The next thing I remember was waking up at the base of the river with a throbbing head and bleeding palms and knees from tumbling down into the embankment.

A few other survivors were with me, none of which knew where my brother could've gone. They said we needed to leave before the orc clan found us. Despite my pleas and protest, I was put into an old rowboat and sent down the river to a new town.

To start a new life.

I stayed in that village for a few years, taken in by an older couple who never had any children of their own. They were kind but were not very fond of my…experiments. One day, an older alchemist happened to be passing through when he spied me, tickled by my ability to transform clay into steel. Under his tutelage, I was taught the art of alchemy before being shipped off to the royal academy.

On our way to the academy, the carriage we took rolled through what remained of my old village. The older alchemist told me that orcs had raided it a few years back. I made no mention of my being there. He also said those who survive an orc raid are taken to Brokenbone Mountain, to live in servitude to their new king.

My stomach sank and I spent the rest of the journey silent.

Seeing the scorched remains of what used to be my home as our carriage rolled passed made me vow to myself that as soon as I could, I would search for my brother. Even as I looked at the barren earth, a part of me, a very small hopeful part, believed my brother had found a way out and was safe somewhere waiting for me to find him.

Even as I devoted myself to my studies and worked my way up to the top of my class, I held on to that hope. I kept my past a secret, even as King Arkain began to take notice of me and brought me to his castle to work on a secret mission of his own. He wanted me to find a cure to the *orc's teeth poison*, the same poison that had killed his father during the Orc Wars centuries earlier. I was more than happy to find a defense for those who were defenseless like me. Like my brother.

My life has been full of so many wonderful things and experiences. The self-blame I carried for losing my brother lessened over time, but my resolve to look for him never did. It's what kept me going for the last twenty years and now I am so close to finding out the truth, to finding out what happened to him.

Wait, have I passed this tree before?

I look up and see a familiar evergreen tree looming in front of me. There is an ornate carving at its base that looks like some type of flower, maybe? A bird? Who knows, but it was distinct enough for me to remember it when I first passed by it.

Two hours ago.

Groaning, I pull the map from my satchel but instantly regret it as I watch snow soak the thin paper. Survival skills were not taught at the Royal Academy of Alchemy and the Arts. I glance arounding, noting that the snow is beginning to fall more rapidly. Making camp before the last golden rays of sunshine are swallowed up by a fathomless night sky is now my top priority.

I'll figure out just how lost I am in the morning. The King of the Orcs is expecting me in two days-time, and I worry my visit will be denied if I am late. King Arkain, who I am sure was coaxed into doing so by his mate and my friend Elvie, wrote a letter stating my purpose in coming to Dread's Keep; to train their healers and alchemists as a peace offering between our two kingdoms.

That was as much protection as King Arkain could afford me and I will not blow it by being late.

I need to find shelter from the wind. Night means colder temperatures and more snow. More snow means my clothes getting more soaked and more soaked means I'm definitely at risk of losing a toe or two.

I regret not buying more supplies in Moonborne.

As I survey the scene around me, I realize my options are quite bleak. This close to the mountain everything is covered in snow and ice. Last night, I was still far enough from the summit that the earth was dry. In this snowy wasteland, however, my meager bedroll will be ruined in a matter of seconds.

How have I made it this far being so woefully underprepared? Maybe instead of twenty vials of *merc weed,* I should've packed another cloak. One that repelled water.

While I stand at the base of one of the great evergreen trees, I weigh the possibility of climbing it with all of my gear. However, one wrong turn in the night and I plummet thirty feet to the ground with only two feet of snow to cushion my fall. The bright, pine smell of the tree tickles my nose and the cold wind tugs at my hair while I continue calculating the climb.

Suddenly, a long, resounding howl cuts the air and my blood freezes. *Great, just great.*

Not only am I soaked, starved, and cold, I am about to be something's dinner.

Pivoting slightly, I glance over my shoulder only to spy the outline of a figure on the other side of the tree line. Whether it's an animal or a man I can't tell, but I can feel its eyes on me. Waiting for the moment to strike.

What did some of the guards tell me before I left? If it's a wolf I should play dead, or was that for a bear? Is it for both? No wait, one of them said to run if I could. Or maybe he was joking? I curse myself again for not being better prepared.

With all of my education, you'd think I would've remembered the cardinal rule to never go into a situation without knowing all the variables. It looks like the first time I don't heed that rule I will be paying for it with my life. *Okay, think. Play dead or run? Which one, which one...*

I decide on a third option: walk quickly.

It seems like a good middle ground. If I run, I become prey; if I play dead for too long, I'll freeze to death in the snow. This way I can at least put some distance between me and whatever is lurking behind my shoulder. Impressed with my sound logic, I take quick and measured steps away from the evergreen tree.

The smell of smoke is faint in the air as I walk deeper into the trees. Are my eyes playing tricks on me or is that…a fire? Just up ahead I can make out a faint orange glow. Perhaps there are other travelers who will allow me to seek shelter with them tonight. The innkeeper had said that this side of the mountain was the safest for humans since the orcs rarely come down this far from Dread's Keep.

I practically feel the warmth of the fire on my skin, and the prospect of having a warm, dry night's rest has my feet, rather clumsily, moving faster. Stray branches tangle in my braided hair, snagging on my clothing but still I move forward towards the light.

My foot snags on a branch and I hear a distinct snap. It isn't until I feel the net close around my body, simultaneously launching me into the air while a scream is being wrenched from my lips, that I realize the fire up ahead was likely meant to be a trap.

Suddenly being a wolf's dinner is the least of my concerns.

CHAPTER 2

BAZUR

ZAROD IS THE MOST FOOLISH orc I have ever met.

Even as children, when we had been forced to spar together at the Keep, I knew he would rather use his head for jokes than making wise decisions. On the day we first met, one of his eyes was already bruised, swelling shut, but he still wore that wide smile as he made some quip about my mother's cooking and him eating it. Truth be told, I don't understand most of his *jokes*.

It made the others around me laugh and that had been all the reason I needed to punch him, ending our round in one minute flat.

As children, I could tell Zarod was different from other orc males. Not only because of his humorous disposition but because most younglings would've sulked and cried after a defeat like that. Zarod only laughed, smiled through the blood in his mouth that dripped onto his fledgling tusks, and said he'd rather be my friend than ever receive a blow like that again.

Here we are almost thirty years later, and he still wears that ridiculous grin. One that has not faded even after all the horrors we've seen and inflicted over the years together. He joined my clan after I was named general and moved with me into the Black Claw Village—remote and as far away from Dread's Keep as possible—without question.

He has become my best soldier and a dear friend through it all.

And now he was going to die.

This was supposed to be a simple mission, one King Vorgak had given to me with glee, knowing I would have no choice but accept it. Despite how degrading it was. As general of the Black Claw Clan, my soldiers and I are the strongest orcs on this mountain and he had us scouting out each and every western outpost to make sure they were in good shape and stocked for the winter. This was simple work, far below the standing of my clan.

Not to mention, the king hasn't sent a scouting party west in decades. This whole mission is just his way of exploiting his control over me. Whatever he demands, I have to obey it, no matter how much I hate it.

I'd kill him if I could, but then that would leave ruling to me and I have no desire to be anything except general to my clan. I've seen what power does to the orcs in my family and I have no desire to follow their fate.

In two days we will be back at the Keep, assuring the king that the outposts have been surveyed and replenished. Another day after that I will be back in my village where I can watch over my people and train our newer soldiers.

Zarod groans at my feet as he rolls onto his side and throws up the contents of his stomach. Liquidy, half-digested vegetables from our meager stew earlier today fall into the snow.

"You are a fucking idiot, Zarod," I say, his white tusks gleaming in the fire light as they break into that familiar smile.

"I prefer the term *reckless thinker* because I did think about those berries before eating them. I thought maybe they would be a tasty afternoon treat. But *recklessly*, I didn't consider that they could be poisonous."

"Your *reckless thinking* is going to end in your death."

"Gah," Zarod cries, "you are morbid. Our great general Bazur is so sullen and morose."

"Morose?" I raise a brow.

"Morose," Zarod says again, a dreamy look washing over his face. "Mornga taught it to me. Says she likes it when I use sophisticated words like that. Especially when we're both naked."

Despite myself I chuckle. Once.

"She'll like it a lot more if you return alive. Which given your current state…" I trail off, motioning toward his vomit.

"Ah, cheer up Bazy, I'm strong, I'm young. Able-bodied, witty, charming, and I have a massive co—" Zarod cuts off to throw up more of today's lunch.

I grimace and look around our bleak campsite.

Despite our roaring fire, the chill in the wind is rapidly becoming unbearable. My fur lined cloak barely keeps me warm and my traveling clothes are already damp from the snow. The soldiers around me share the last of our meager rations. This journey was long and grueling; we packed only what we could carry. I never anticipated the storms being this bad or the wildlife being this sparse.

My men had gone to bed at night with growling stomachs. Each time one sounded, my teeth would grind, shame curdling my stomach. It is my job, as their general and leader, to protect them and provide for them. And I haven't

Zarod shouldn't have been so hungry that he ate those yellow spotted berries. I am angry with him for eating them but I'm furious with myself for letting my soldiers down.

Targoc approaches Zarod and I slowly. He is the youngest among us at nineteen and has never set foot on a battlefield. His light green skin is not marred with scars like mine and Zarod's. Targoc's green eyes take in Zarod's paling complection, the perspiration on his brow and the reddish tinge to his vomit. Blood. Not a good sign.

"What are we going to do with him, General?" Targoc asks me. "We are two days from Dread's Keep. My mother treated a male who had eaten those berries and he didn't last the night."

"Why is everyone in this clan so set on my death? I'll be fine, it's a little fever, nothing more."

Even as Zarod speaks, his eyes become more unfocused. I try not to recoil when I press my hand to his forehead. He is burning up.

"What did your mother do to treat this?" I ask.

Targoc's mother is a wonderful healer. I remember how proud she was of her son when he was selected to come out for this mission. She thanked me for choosing him, thanked me for all that I had done for her family.

If she could see how he has labored in my care I doubt she would be so grateful to me.

"It was a long time ago; she used some type of herb. The most important thing is to get the fever down. If we can lower it and keep him cool until we reach the Keep, he may survive."

"Easier said than done, friends. I'm a hot-blooded male," Zarod says, his words slurring slightly. "That's what all the females say. You know, my charming disposition, which is in sharp contrast to the two of yours, is what makes me irresistible to them. It's how I got my beautiful Mornga. Oh, Mornga…"

Zarod sighs again and that dreamy loving expression overtakes him once more.

"Stop talking," I growl, picking up fistfuls of snow and holding it against his hot skin. Zarod thrashes, resisting the icy temperature but quickly stops his protest. The snow meets his flesh with a disheartening sizzle. Targoc and I work to bury him enough so he stays cool for as long as possible.

"He needs food and water," Targoc says once we cover Zarod's feet.

"Everyone needs food and water."

Targoc blanches at my harsh words. It is not the youngling's fault. It is mine. I am harsh with him because I am being harsh with myself.

"I can try and "— A thunderous snapping of branches followed by a shrill scream reaches my ears. Targoc's eyes widen and the soldiers around the fire perk up. Even Zarod manages to make an excited sound despite his snow covering.

Hunting in this climate has been abysmal. We've set traps at every camp and every night we wait for that familiar sound. That sound meant food, that sound meant not going to bed hungry.

My mouth is already watering as I rise from Zarod's side.

"Watch over him," I direct Targoc. "I'll go and see what our trap caught for dinner."

"I hope it's a great, juicy beast. My belly has been empty for far too long," calls one of my soldiers from the fire pit. I grab my bow, strapping it across my back, then do the same with my quiver of arrows. I pick up my battle ax and loop it through the hook on my belt.

Trudging through the snow and away from the warmth of camp I make the quick journey to the trap. My capture is oddly quiet. The whiny, pitiful sounds the *frostelks* usually emit once caught are absent, and I quickly become apprehensive. I quiet my steps, not wanting to announce my presence until I know what I've caught.

The trap comes into view, the old net fraying but holding as it dangles from the strong branch of an evergreen. I reach for my arrow fifty feet away and ready to strike this creature in the heart and bring it back to camp to feed my soldiers.

What color fur is that? Is it...*pink?*

Blinking rapidly so my eyes adjust to the darkness around me, it comes into view.

Not an it, I notice with some alarm. A she. A female, a human female. With brightly colored pink hair. The same magenta as the *darksky* roses that grow on Brokenbone Mountain. She can't see me hidden in the tree line like this. Human ears aren't as sensitive as an orc's so I know she didn't hear me come upon her either.

I watch as her brown eyes scan the area around her, frantically searching for something, anything to free herself with. It's clear she is unarmed, or she would've already tried cutting through the net.

I can hear her muttering to herself quietly. Chastising herself in some way but I can't make out the words. What is she doing out here? Humans are weak, prone to injury, and risk becoming dinner to any number of predators lurking in the tree line. Yet this tiny human, shivers and shakes inside my net, all alone?

Her traveling party must be around here somewhere—she must've gotten separated from them.

The thought of leaving her does cross my mind. Humans are trouble. Especially ones that look as fragile as her. Thin traveling clothes, a soaked cloak, no gloves to keep away the chill in the air. If something doesn't eat her out here, she'll freeze to death.

Where is her traveling party? I haven't heard anyone close by.

I consider returning to camp and explaining to my men that the trap was accidentally triggered. Their sounds of disappointment are already ringing in my ears as I imagine the scenario. I can't come back with nothing. But the only thing I have caught in the last two weeks is this pink-haired human.

This human who I can hear beginning to weep softly. *Mother of the Mountain, spare me…*

Emerging from the tree line before I properly think this through, I make as much noise as possible. I step on a few fallen branches, the crack echoing in the night air, and brush along the low hanging limbs. It's enough to startle her and make her aware of my presence.

I watch as she frantically wipes at her eyes and tries to sit up straighter in the net.

"Hello," she calls out, "who—who's there?" Her voice is soft, gentle. It strokes over my skin like a caress, and I realize how long it's been since I've enjoyed a female's company. After being around so many gruff orc soldiers I forget just how soft voices can be.

This pink-haired human speaks the elven language of the west, like most of the humans I run across. Mornga was the one who taught it to me years ago. It made my job a lot easier once I learned it. However, almost all of the humans in my village use our language, *orcish*, so my knowledge of the words are a bit rusty. But I can still understand her.

There is enough light from the moon that I know she can see me as I emerge from the tree line. Her pale skin grows even whiter, her eyes rounding in fear. It's the type of response I'm used to getting from humans and orcs alike. It's a response I enjoy getting; I am larger than the other males in my clan. In any of the clans really. Stronger than most, deadly in battle. I should be feared and respected.

However, I find her stench of fear mixing with her earthy scent displeasing.

I should try to make myself look like less of a threat, but I'm not sure there's a way to do that. Countless battles have rendered my face anything but handsome. It is scarred and hard and I can't help the scowl that's formed at finding her instead of dinner.

Being armed to the teeth with an assortment of blades, I'm sure, isn't helping the situation either.

"Oh my, gods," she says, almost breathlessly. I grit my teeth. If she's this scared of me, I doubt she'll accept any of my offers to help. She looks close to fainting as is. This has been such a colossal waste of time. Zarod is dying back at camp and here I am wasting his last moments silently watching this human.

"What are you doing here?" I ask, my voice sharp and she cringes.

"Who are you?" she asks instead. I try not to roll my eyes.

"An orc."

She swallows. "I can see that. I thought your kind didn't travel down this far?"

"Clearly we do." *Why am I answering her questions? Cut her down and be done with it.*

I watch her brows furrow, they are dark brown like her eyes, despite the vibrant color of her hair. I've never seen a human with that color of hair...maybe she is from the Southlands? Strange that her eyebrows wouldn't be the same color.

It doesn't matter what color her hair is, leave her out here and return to camp!

"What is your traveling party doing this far up our mountain?"

"I'm not with a traveling party." Despite myself I feel a smirk carve my lips as I watch her eyes widen in shock. She didn't mean to share that bit of information with me. "I mean, I'm not alone. I'm meeting someone."

Who is she meeting? Why do I wish to know? It has nothing to do with me. Again, I think back to Zarod. I need to end this conversation with this human and return to him.

"I'm going to lower you down from the net."

The pink-haired human looks shocked again.

"Will you let me go?" she asks, and I nod.

"I have no need to keep a human."

"You won't eat me?" A humorless laugh booms out of my chest. This human, who seems to know nothing of our territory, has still managed to hear those stories.

"You wouldn't make much of a meal."

Before she can respond, I grip the rope tied around the base of the tree I'm standing next to. Gently, I pull apart the knot and hold it firmly as I absorb the weight in the net. She's a small thing, barely weighs more than a baby frostelk.

Landing on the ground with a soft thud, she wrestles with the net for a few moments. I should offer to cut her free, but I'll need use of this net once we move to our next location.

Watching her struggle, her clear exasperation makes me want to smile. I don't.

I need to get back to camp.

Finally, she is free and the color has risen on her face, matching the pink of her hair. That vibrant colored mane of hers is pulled back in a braid, revealing every freckle that dots her nose and cheeks. Trudging over to her in the snow I take her in fully. She's dressed in a dark black cloak that is too thin to make a difference against the wind and a wool dress the same dark green as my own skin, stitched with a fine gold threat. A large satchel is slung across her body with papers and plants sticking out of random pockets. There's also a large metal trunk she's carrying that rattled when she fully stood up.

This human is tiny compared to me. Her head barely reaches my chest. She's all soft curves and round features. Round eyes, round face, round hips. Not that I should be looking at those.

The fragility of a human has never appealed to me when it came to looking for a lover.

This one though, she makes me think she could take what I have to give. She'd offer enough softness for the both of us to handle the rough pounding I'd like to give her. She's shivering in her wet clothes, obviously needing a male to keep her warm and safe. I shake myself from that thought.

Mother of the Mountain, I have been on the road too long.

"Who are you meeting?" I ask, noticing with some disdain her take a step back from me. Her expression is guarded, wary. Smart of her but I don't like it at all. She'll trip and fall and crack her skull open and then I'll have a dead human and a soon to be dead orc to deal with.

"It is not for me to say."

My brows lower, unease pricking the back of my neck. The human takes another step back, still shivering. She makes quite a sad sight and despite the unease I feel, something else is making my chest feel funny.

"Thank you, for freeing me. I should go now."

Pivoting on a heel, I watch her battered brown boots take one step. Then another, the snow making her sink all the way up to her knees. With a silent curse, I rub my forehead.

"Wait," I call out, watching her small frame freeze. "Come back to my camp and warm yourself. The storm is too strong now, you'll never be able to build a fire."

Turning back to me, her wide brown eyes are wary.

"Oh, that's okay. I'd rather—"

"You'll freeze to death before the sun rises."

A gasp escapes her full lips. I don't like the blue tinge to them. I know she wants to deny it, to find some excuse to flee my presence but if she wants to live, I am her best chance for survival.

Stowing my ax, I try an approach that has always worked the best for me when dealing with scared humans.

"Look, I'm not going to hurt you." I hold up my hands, palms out so she can see they are empty. Just tough green skin decorated with callouses and dark raised scars. She takes a cautious step forward.

"You have two options: either you trust me and come back to my camp where I promise you, you will not be harmed, or you can set out into this storm and freeze. It's up to you."

"But ..." she trails off, looking around herself. "You swear you're not going to try and eat me."

"Believe me, I'd rather fill something other than my stomach with you," I say in our orc's tongue. Her dark brows furrow and that confirms my suspicion that she doesn't know our language.

"What?"

"Nothing. I swear I won't try to eat you. Now as for my soldiers..." Her spine straightens so fast I fear she may snap in half. I laugh once and shake my head. "They won't try to eat you either."

"That's not so funny," she says, taking another step toward me, this time close enough to touch that soft skin of hers. She must realize it too because her breathing kicks up, her heart pounding in her chest. Her fear is even stronger up close. I really don't like her being afraid and I really don't understand why I care.

"Here," I say, digging into my pocket and pulling out a small paring knife. I hold the hilt out towards her and watch as her small hand closes around it. "To make you feel better."

Her brown eyes look up at me, still wary and unsure.

Watching as she grips the knife, I lead her from the tree line and back up to camp. The journey is quiet, only the sounds of her boots sinking into snow remind me that I have a companion next to me. Soon though, I can hear the voices of my soldiers. Their bawdy laughter carries on the wind. The human begins to breathe rapidly again, nervously twitching and gripping the knife harder.

I find myself wanting to ask why she is so scared but I already know.

She's a human woman, who's heard tales of our kind. Some true, some not but that makes little difference. The image of us portrayed in songs and legends has worked on this human female. And based on some of the stories I've come across in my travels she is well within her rights to fear us.

I'll make sure none of my soldiers give her any more reasons to.

As we pass through the edge of camp, the energy inside of it shifts. Pairs of glowing yellow eyes focus in on us, dark eyebrows raised. All of these orcs have seen humans before, lived and worked beside them, but seeing one out here like this is a shock.

"Not the type of dinner I was expecting," one of them jeers. The others laugh but I silence them with a look. This human pales at the words she doesn't understand.

"I found her in the trap. She is warming by the fire then she will go."

"Vorgak will want to know—"

"I don't care what Vorgak wants. She's a lost human, nothing more," I growl at all of them. Motioning the human toward the fire, I watch as she lifts her delicate hands towards the flames. "There will be no more discussion on this."

"Warm yourself, *akorzag*," I say, quietly so only she can hear over the roaring fire. I don't need any of my soldiers watching her too closely. Their attention on her makes her nervous and their focus needs to be on the storm we are preparing to brace for.

The human nods and opens her mouth but is cut off by Targoc.

"Bazur, it's Zarod, he's...something's happened."

I curse and stomp over to him. My stomach flips when I see his face devoid of that grin. In the short span of time that I was gone, his color has faded from a vibrant green to a pale yellow. The color of death amongst our kind. His eyes are closed and he moans and shivers. Despite being deeply compacted in the snow, sweat still slides in rivulets down his temple.

"These appeared just after you left." Targoc wipes away some half-melted snow to reveal Zarod's chest, which has broken out with hundreds of red bumps and welts that throb and pulse before my very eyes. Letting out a groan that rattles his chest, I curse again. Emotion closes my throat.

This is my fault. All of this is my fault. If I hadn't pissed off Vorgak, he never would've sent us on this mission. Zarod would be home now, laughing and causing problems. My soldiers would not be half starved.

What kind of leader am I?

"Put more snow on him," I respond. "We can only hope his fever breaks."

Targoc and I pick up more handfuls when there is a sound behind us.

"No!" cries the pink-haired human, charging right at us with the knife extended.

CHAPTER 3

KAETHE

MAYBE RUNNING AT TWO VERY large, very armed orcs with a knife wasn't the best decision.

Both of them reflexively reach for the weapons on their belts, looking at me with shocked yellow eyes. Their muscles are bunched so tight under their sturdy wool shirts and pants, it's amazing they don't rip clean through them. Under any other circumstance, those muscles would be nice to look at.

However, knowing they are attached to two orcs who could snap my neck with half a thought makes them lose some appeal. I can tell they view me as a threat and my throat will be slit just like it was done to the people of my village. It's in their nature.

I've come all this way just to fall victim to the same fate as my parents.

The younger of the two, jumps to his feet first and unsheathes his weapon. I realize I'm not even going to get a chance to get the words out to explain myself. I shouldn't have reacted, I should've stayed at the fire and let the sick one get sicker.

I suck in my last breath on this earth and prepare for the blow that never comes. The older one who found me, halts him with a growl of authority. Whoever this one is, he seems to be their leader.

"Wait," I say, holding up my hands after tucking the knife into my bag. "He's been poisoned?"

The question is rhetorical. From his moans, the sickly yellow of skin, the rash, and how I can see the sweat pouring off him despite being covered in snow, poison is the only thing this could be. It would've been so easy to keep my mouth shut. Perhaps I should've kept my mouth shut and let the warmth of the fire sink into my bones while I let one of them die in the background without giving them so much as second thought. Just like they didn't give slicing my father's neck a second thought.

But I couldn't do that. Blame it on the training from the Royal Academy. I need to save those who have fallen ill, and to hear the cries of someone in pain when I have the means to treat it? Elf or orc, friend or foe, it doesn't matter. I have a duty to save them. I took an oath at the academy to save and render aid and that is what I am doing now.

Nothing more, nothing less.

"Yellow spotted berries that grew by a frozen lake," the orc who found me says. The orc who trapped me is more like it. He was kind enough to let me go but I am still uncertain of his motives. Orcs are dangerous, not to be trusted. Once I have met with their king and my safety is guaranteed, I will be able to relax a bit more. But my survival at the Keep hinges on Vorgak keeping his word to King Arkain.

As soon as I heal the sick one, and warm myself I will leave at first light. I have delayed this journey long enough and I cannot risk offending their leader.

"*Dawnsrays berries*, very poisonous," I mutter under my breath, kneeling in front of the sick orc. Pulling my trunk from across my body, I pop open the lid and take stock of my supplies. He is much larger than a human or an elf so I do some quick calculations to get the right amount of antidote made.

"What?" asks the orc from the woods.

"How many did he eat?"

"Five," murmurs the sick one, his breath rasping out of him. His inhale makes a disheartening rattling sound in his chest. Not a good sign. "I would've eaten the sixth but, Bazy here told me to hurry up."

The orc who found me, Bazy I guess he is called growls something at him in their own language. It dawns on me that all three of these orcs speak the elven language. After the Orc Wars, the new generation must have learned it.

I'd have asked about it if I thought I was going to be spending extended time in their company.

"Well, it's good you didn't eat the sixth one," I say, plucking out a vial of riverhearts.Four seeds should do the trick. "That amount would've killed you instantly."

The sick one laughs meekly. "I guess you were right, Bazy. Reckless thinking was almost my downfall."

"Are you a healer?" Bazy asks.

"In a sense." Better not reveal who I am fully just yet. King Vorgak was clear in his letter that his orcs may not take too kindly to a lone human woman, and it would be regrettable if some unfortunate fate would befall me by untraceable perpetrators.

"You," I say, pointing to the younger one, "boil some snow and bring me a cup. I need to steep these seeds and then we'll need to force him to drink the tea."

The younger one hesitates but Bazy nods and he scurries off to retrieve the supplies.

This is science and medicine. These are the things I am the most comfortable with. Using logic and my training to tend the ailments of others allows me to fully sink into my role as a simple healer wandering around the mountain side. I let muscle memory take over me. In this state I am not afraid or wary of the company around me.

I am focused on the problem at hand and how to solve it.

"Is this safe?"

I look up at Bazy; even on his knees he towers above me. I bristle at his tone.

"Well, I don't see how I could possibly poison him more, if that is what you are asking."

"I don't know you, human. In my experience humans can be deceiving."

"In my experience, so can orcs." We stare at each other, locked in a battle of wills. This orc captured me.And when I offer to help his fellow orc, he questions me? I should grow nervous under his stare, but instead I find I am…insulted? He is questioning my integrity and that has my back up. Shuffling footsteps sound behind me as the younger one approaches with the boiling water.

I narrow my eyes one last time at Bazy before breaking his yellow stare.

"Thank you…" I trail off and the younger male shuffles from foot to foot.

"Targoc," he says. "My mother uses those seeds too. Gave them to me when I was sick last winter."

"Your mother is wise, Targoc." I try my best to emulate the gruff way he pronounced his name. Picking out four of the blue colored seeds, I place them in the cup with the boiling water. They begin to steep, the water turning a cerulean blue and emitting an herbal scent that tickles my nose. "*Riverheart seeds* made into tea will cure almost anything."

I venture a glance up towards Bazy and meet his yellow gaze. He's got a serious staring problem. Among other problems: his gruff nature, setting up traps in the middle of perfectly good walking paths, but staring is at the top of my list.

A few minutes tick by and the tea is ready.

"Okay, now this is the hard part." I hold the cup in my hand, the warmth from it soaking into my cold palms. "Since he's had a fever for so long, that rash has most likely spread to his mouth and tongue."

"And?" asks Bazy.

"And, drinking this is going to feel like swallowing hot iron. He must drink it all, or it won't work." I look between the two of them. "Can you both hold him while I pour this down his throat? If you can keep him still enough, I can get it done in a few moments."

Bazy looks at Targoc, then over his shoulder. He yells out to the other orcs in their language and they rush over. So many of them are close to me, crowding around me as I'm hunched over the poisoned one. *The blood, the burning, the fear…*

Taking a deep, steadying breath I push past those memories. I have a job to do, one that needs to be done before the seeds lose their potency. Otherwise he will die, and I will have wasted four of my seeds.

"Hold him steady, keep his mouth open, and pinch his nose. I've only got enough seeds for this one dose."

More orders are barked from their leader, Bazy, and the other males spring into action. The sick one groans at the contact, the welts from the fever I'm sure are protesting as his arms and legs are pinned down. His shoulders and lower body are pinned as well. Bazy wraps a hand around his jaw, leveraging it open and pinches his nose.

"Good, good, okay now sit him up. Gently." Like a well-trained unit they do what I ask, moving in tandem until he is in the right position. I stand up in order to get the right angle. His mouth is open and I can see the angry red welts lining his mouth and tongue. A few of them are starting to secrete white puss. He doesn't have long; I have to act now.

Saying a quick prayer to the gods, I dump the contents down his throat.

"Cover his mouth!" I order and Bazy does so immediately, locking a hand like a band of iron around his lips. The orc screams through the agony. His whole body shakes and the males holding him are straining to keep him in position. They manage it somehow, their strong muscles tensing and flexing.

I watch his mighty chest rise and fall, his throat work in one powerful swallow that tells me the tea has been ingested. The poisoned orc sags with relief, and his bloodshot yellow eyes close. The last of his fight leaves him as he sags against Bazy, and the other males release their death grips.

"What happens now?" Tagoc asks me, his expression odd. They are all looking at me and I try not to fidget under their stare. I was so focused on the task that I was able to distract myself from the situation for a moment but it's all roaring back to me.

"Now, he sleeps. In the morning, he should be fine, if a bit groggy."

Already the tea is having an effect. The red welts on his chest begin to go down and it no longer rattles with each deep breath.

Their stares have gone from guarded and curious to impressed and…thankful. Are my eyes playing tricks on me?

"His fever is gone," confirms Bazy. He is wearing the strangest expression out of all. It is tinged with an emotion I can't name.

"The tea works fast. Especially with that strong of a dose."

Bazy nods and the other males rise, giving me thanks and returning around the fire. Standing there in the snow, I feel the shift in this situation. Before, I was a lost human, warming myself by their fire. They were disappointed I was not the dinner they were looking for, but now, now I am something different. I am the human that saved one of them. I am a human deserving of thanks and respect.

Perhaps I could use this to my advantage.

"Thank you, human, for saving him," Bazy says quietly next to me. It is just me and him at the sick orc's side.

I smile slightly, unwilling to meet his yellow stare. The look he's giving me is far too intimate and open. I liked his look of disdain more—it was easier to match with one of my own. This look of gratitude though has me thinking he is a kind orc.

A dangerous thought.

"Sitting by while someone else suffers isn't something I can do." It's the best nonanswer I can give him.

"I owe you a debt," he says quietly. I look up at him now, meeting his stare. This is my way in. I'm a realist, I know I'll never be able to make it to Dread's Keep in time without some help. These orcs know this mountain. I'm sure they know the fastest way to the Keep.

I don't have to tell them who I am just yet. However, only a fool would dismiss this opportunity. Despite my wariness and unease, I can't let this go to waste.

"There is something you could help me with."

"Name it, and it will be done."

Taking a deep breath, I square my shoulders.

"I need you to escort me to Dread's Keep."

Bazy rears back as if I had slapped him, shock coloring his already hard features.

"Take you to Dread's Keep? Why?"

"My reasons are my own," I say dismissively.

"It is no place for a human, especially a human female."

He's right about that at least.

"Will you take me or not?" I ask. "Someone is expecting me and I must arrive in two days' time."

"Who is expecting you?"

"That is none of your concern," I say again, straightening my spine. There is a chance he will deny me, but I can't risk exposing myself until I am in front of the king. I saved their fellow orc and earned their respect, but if they find out I am an emissary from another kingdom they may not look too favorable at that. Again, I throw myself at the mercy of King Vorgak in the hopes he will assure my safety.

It's the only option I have.

"Fine," he says, after a moment. "We can make it there in two days. It will be a hard ride."

I nod, relief flowing through me.

"You can keep your secrets, human, for now at least." Bazy turns from me and walks back toward the fire. A few paces from me he halts again.

"Thank you," Bazy says again.

I wave him off, heading to the opposite side of the fire to put some distance between me and the other orcs.

"You've already thanked me, you all have."

"Zarod isn't just any soldier." He pauses, his eyes looking down at the snow. "He is my friend, and he became ill because of me. Without you, he would've died, so thank you."

I almost ask what he means by it being his fault. The berries are easily mistaken for their sister plant *moonray berries*, which are safe to eat. I've cured many people who've accidentally ingested them like Zarod.

The question is on the tip of my tongue, but his eyes wipe the thought of asking from my mind. They wipe any thought from my head. I see the earnest thanks in them and the gratitude too. But the thing that paralyzes my legs from moving me any closer to the fire is that emotional look I couldn't name before. Now I see it with such clarity.

Reverence.

CHAPTER 4

KAETHE

I AM EXHAUSTED THIS MORNING AS I prepare for our departure.

Thanks to my ability to save their fellow soldier last night, the group was generous enough to give me a meager bowl of stew and a spare fur to put under my bedroll to prevent it from getting wet. They even let me sleep closest to the fire. Even with these small comforts, I still only managed an hour of rest.

With every groan of a male, every breeze that rustled the branches of the evergreen trees, every crackle of the fire I jolted awake. I slept with the knife Bazy gave me, curled tightly in my hand. Upon waking at the first rays of dawn, I felt the warmth of the hilt pressing against my chest.

My only source of security should someone come upon me in the night.

They are all still thankful, smiling around their white tusks and nodding toward me. The sick orc, Zarod, has made a full recovery. He rose from his bedroll looking haggard, but dark green once more. The other soldiers came over to check on him and to bring him another bowl of measly stew that was provided as breakfast. They spoke in their own language so I couldn't make out what they were saying.

When they started nodding and pointing at me it was easy enough to surmise they were discussing me.

I'm rolling up my bedroll and securing the last of my packs when I see two boot clad feet next to me in the snow. Looking up, I find Zarod looming over me with a wide grin on his face. For an orc, he is quite handsome. He doesn't possess that severe, authoritative look like Bazy does.

No, his features can only be described as jovial, almost child-like.

His face is scarred as well and one of his white tusks is chipped and devoid of the deadly sharp point.

"You must be my savior," he says, kneeling down to help secure the loose tie on my bed-roll.

"I am." We stand and he holds my pack out towards me, his eyes dancing with amusement. His expression, his body language is too relaxed to cause any fear to spike through me. How strange. "I guess I don't have to tell you to never eat *dawnsrays berries* again, huh?"

"Never again, I swear! I thought they were *moonrays berries*; Mornga makes the most delicious pie with them."

"Mornga?" I ask.

"Don't get him started," another orc groans from behind him.

"They're just jealous, pink-haired human, that I have the most beautiful female and they do not. Mornga is my mate. And she makes the best pies. The best *anything* really."

"Oh," I say, feeling heat rush to my face. I am not used to such direct outbursts of affection. Sure Elvie and Arkain make no secret of their obsession with each other but I know them. Elvie is my friend and talking about that sort of thing doesn't make me feel shy about my own lack of experience. I'm not the best when it comes to men and how to navigate conversations regarding love and intimacy.

"Lovely." That's the only response I can think of.

"That she is. Lovely…I shall call her that word when we are back."

"Make sure to drink water today. Your body is still recovering," I say, desperate to get off the conversation of Mornga. His eyes have gone dreamlike, and I suppose if I were his mate, I would be pleased to know he spoke of me with such reverence.

However, I am not his mate, and I'm eager to begin this journey so I can be one step closer to completing my mission.

"Don't worry, Bazy has already lectured me about drinking more water this morning."

I look over to where their leader stands, our eyes locking, and I quickly look away.

"You speak the elven language well. Your accent is almost unnoticeable."

"Mornga taught me." Oh *gods*, and we are back to this. "Bazy wasn't as good of a pupil though, that's why his sounds so ruggish. All hard constantents and chewed up vowels, as Mornga would say. That or our general's grumpiness does not suit the words."

A small laugh escapes me and that seems to please this orc, his smile deepening.

"I'm Zarod by the way. What's your name?"

"Oh…" I hesitate. Do I tell him? Is this safe enough to reveal yet? I'm sure it will be fine. "It's—"

"We're setting off," Bazy says in a gruff voice. He has moved quickly from the other side of the camp to stomp between me and Zarod. While Zarod is a large male, Bazy is massive. Being their general makes sense; he moves with an air of authority. He's a good half a foot taller than Zarod. His shoulders are broader, his arms and thighs are made up entirely of corded muscle. His large body is covered in thick wool clothing and a heavy fur cloak. His tusks are dangerously sharp and glint in the morning sun. His black hair is pulled back from his face, long enough to be secured in a low bun at the back of his head.

I am cataloging his features to give a description to the king if he tries to kill me. No other reason.

Bazy lets out a sharp whistle, cutting through the snowy land. It echoes around the trees and shakes the ground. No—the whistle didn't shake the ground, but the ground is shaking. I plant my feet to withstand the sudden disturbance until they come into view.

Massive beasts with silvery-white fur as pale as the snow approach our camp at an alarming speed. Black lips peel back revealing sharp teeth and red tongues. As they draw nearer, I note the way their muscles bunch and flex.

No one around me is panicking as these beasts approach. Do they not see them? We are about to be attacked by *icewolves*! Massive creatures that can eat you in one bite. Well maybe not eat an orc in one bite but me, surely.

They're about ten feet off when a scream threatens to crawl out of my throat. But suddenly they halt. The great beasts bow their heads and for the first time I notice what's on their backs: saddles made of tough brown leather. Each saddle is carved with an ornate design. It looks to be a pattern of sorts but as my eyes focus, I see a few repeating symbols. It takes me a moment to realize they're names. Carved on each saddle is the name of their rider.

Of course orcs would ride these monstrous beasts.

"You can ride with me, human. My beast is the gentlest," Zarod offers. Before I can respond, Bazy growls, the sound making the hairs on the back of my neck stand up.

"The human is with me." Zarod only laughs and shakes his head. They speak briefly in *orcish* as I eye the *icewolves* warily. Am I really about to climb on the back of one?

Zarod and Bazy end their conversation and Bazy steps in front of me.

"Let's go," he grunts, motioning me forward. He walks me toward the first *icewolf*, the alpha of the pack. He's larger than the others, his all-white fur brighter and his claws sharper. His yellow eyes appraise me as I approach. Hopefully he sees I am with his rider and doesn't think I'm some sort of morning snack.

Wait a minute.

I do some counting and see there are just enough mounts for each of the orcs present. Meaning...

"Hold on. I'm not sharing a saddle with you," I say, blood rushing to my cheeks. It's way too intimate to do with someone I barely know. Let alone with this orc who may decide I actually would make a nice meal for him. I mean, that stew couldn't have been filling for someone of his size.

Despite what I just said, Bazy stows my packs in one of the great saddle bags along the beast's side.

"Can you ride one by yourself?" he asks.

"I'm sure I could—"

"Even if you could manage to figure it out, which you couldn't, do you see one here for you to ride?"

"Well no, but—"

"But what?" He cuts me off.

"I thought maybe I could find a horse or something."

"Horses freeze to death out here."

Oh, well…

"I'm sure there is some other way—"

"There isn't and now you're wasting time." Bazy leans down, so that our faces are close together. He smells of pine and fresh snow and something spicy I can't name. The scars on his face are raised and dark, a puzzle of imperfect pieces fitting together to create his serious expression.

"Just like last night, you have two choices. One, get on that saddle with me and head toward the Keep before the temperature drops again. Or two, walk behind us making our journey ten times as long, keeping in mind you'll freeze to death before we even make it halfway to Dread's Keep. Do you understand?"

I did, unfortunately. Nodding only once, Bazy grunts again. Without warning, his giant hands grip me around the waist. They span my entire midsection and his thumbs come dangerously close to grazing the underside of my breast. There's nothing sexual about his touch, but still give a girl a warning before you grab her!

"Hey! What are you—" He sets me down in the saddle before jumping up behind me in one leap.

"You complain a lot, *akorzag*." There's that word again. I grit my teeth against it. Calling someone a name in a language they don't know is very rude. Even for an orc. "Makes me wonder how you came to make this journey alone. This terrain is unforgiving," he continues.

"It makes me wonder why you think it is okay to just grab me without warning!"

I spread my cloak out behind me, creating a barrier between our two bodies. It's not enough but it's at least something. Sitting with my spine locked straight, I can still feel the heat of his body behind me. The thick muscles of his leg brush against my own in my dress.

Gripping the reins, he calls out to the others and we shoot forward into the snow. We move at a furious pace. Snow shoots up along the sides of our company as the icewolves cover the land in powerful sprints. I grip the front of the saddle to keep myself upright and off Bazy's massive chest. Thankfully I redid the lacings on my gown this morning as the impact of each step has my breasts jostling.

I wish I had brought something with more support.

We are silent as the beasts cut through the deepest piles of snow. When the snow is no longer past their knees, our pace slows to something more manageable. We have cleared out of the frozen valley and are now on flat land. The evergreen trees here are thicker, holding most of the snow in their branches, so it's not so deep.

"Relax, human. You won't make it an hour sitting up that straight, and we will not stop to accommodate a sore back."

I grit my teeth. He's right, my back muscles are already straining, but to relax would mean to touch him. Can I really do that?

"I know you're scared of my kind. Which makes your desire to go to Dread's Keep all the more strange."

I glare at him over my shoulder, disliking his astuteness.

"I promise not to touch you again without asking. Try and relax, the journey is long."

Once again, what choice do I really have here? Our eyes lock and I notice his yellow eyes are flecked with green. They're not so much yellow as they are gold, like warm honey.

I shake myself out of that train of thought.

"You promise?"

He nods, the muscles in his strong neck flexing.

Reluctantly, I lean back and find myself in quite a predicament. This is way closer than I was planning on being with any orc. It would take nothing for him to hold me to his massive chest and crush me. Or reach down and slit my throat without his *icewolf* even missing a step.

Worse still, I find myself more comfortable than I should be.

His smell, more intense now that my back is against his muscled chest, invades all my senses. My head rests squarely at the center of his chest and looking up I can see the hard set of his jaw. He's warm, oh gods, so deliciously warm. I almost throw caution to the wind and bury myself under his fur lined cloak. The warmth seeps into me, thawing some parts of my body that haven't fully recovered from last night.

It feels good, but I can't let my guard slip.

"What is your name, human?" he asks, the sound rumbling from his chest and vibrating along my back.

"Kaethe," I say.

"Strange name."

My mouth pops open and I look up to glare at him.

"That's bold coming from someone called Bazy," I counter. He laughs once, his breath tickling my face.

"Only Zarod calls me Bazy because he knows I hate it," he explains.

"So, what is your name then?" I ask.

"Bazur." I huff my own laugh at that.

"Oh, yes I see, massive difference between the two. Bazur is clearly the least ridiculous one."

"Are you—" he pauses, "making a joke?"

I roll my eyes. "If I have to explain it, it must not have been a very funny one."

"I don't get jokes. Especially Zarod's."

"Really? That's shocking."

"No, it's not." His face is serious as he looks down at me. "I can never tell if—"

"That was sarcasm, Bazur." His name tastes funny on my tongue. The sound of it is so different from that of my own. His jaw tightens. Whether it's because of my interruption or how I said his name, I can't tell.

We travel in silence for a while. Beneath the trees, the sun is blocked out enough to where we are shaded. This chill in the air only gets more pronounced the higher up the mountain we go. I wrap my cloak more fully around my body. My teeth begin to chatter as my shivers become more incessant. Bazur grumbles something under his breath before opening his own cloak and draping it around me.

I have to swallow down a moan at how warm it is.

"Thank you," I say softly.

"Don't need you freezing before we get to the Keep. I'm sure whoever you're meeting won't want to see you half-frozen."

I nod, burrowing deeper into the cloak.

"Who are you meeting there? I know most of the orcs, especially the ones in the Keep."

The sudden bliss I felt at being so warm is gone. I can't share that I'm meeting with their leader—that will only invite more questions. I have to keep the deceit going until I am at the Keep.

Come on, think of something, give another nonanswer.

"Someone I haven't seen for a very long time."

"How long?" Gods damn this orc and all his questions. The trick to a good lie is to have some truth in it. I'll keep as close to the facts as I can and then change the subject.

There's no need to reveal fully who that person is.

"Oh, gods it has to have been about twenty years since I've last seen him."

Bazur makes a choking sound, his hands tightening on the reigns.

"Twenty years? Surely you couldn't have come of age that long ago."

"What does my coming of age have to do with me meeting someone?"

"You couldn't have taken a male to your bed twenty years ago. You barely look twenty now."

My face heats and my mouth pops open. Oh my gods, oh my *gods*! He didn't just say that. He thinks I'm reuniting with my orc lover? I suppose it would be a good cover but I'm afraid if I say that's why I'm here he'll only ask more questions.

Gods forbid he asks me the orc's name.

"This male didn't," Bazur hesitates, swallowing once. "This male didn't force himself on you when you were young, did he?"

I groan and shake my head. There is genuine concern in his voice, which does cause my stomach to warm, oddly enough.

"No! No, nothing like that. I'm not going to the Keep to be reunited with someone I was...in a relationship with." My face feels like it's on fire.

Some of the tension leaves his features, and he seems relieved by my answer. To his credit, he seemed appalled at the idea I had been assaulted in some way, so it makes me believe that, at the very least, that won't happen to me while I'm in his care.

"How old are you?" he asks suddenly.

"Twenty-six." I look up at him. "You?"

"Thirty-six." His dark brows lower over his honey eyes. "You seem younger."

"You seem older," I counter. He laughs, at least I think it's a laugh. It sounds more like he's just expelling a puff of air.

"When you've seen all that I have, Kaethe, it ages you." He faces forward, his eyes looking into the distance but unfocused as if he's remembering some half-forgotten memory. "It's good to see the world hasn't robbed everyone of their youth."

CHAPTER 5

BAZUR

T HIS HUMAN IS...FRUSTRATING.

Like all humans she is incredibly weak. But Kaethe, as she calls herself, seems unluckier than most. Oblivious too, not noticing the predators who track her movements from deep within the tree line. I can feel their eyes on her, salivating over an easy meal.

When we stopped to make camp she slid off the back of my *icewolf* so fast to avoid me touching her again, that she did not consider how deep the snow would be. It came up past her knees and she trudged through until she got to the clearing. The bottom half of her dress was soaked and clinging to her legs.

Before she even made it to where the snow leveled out, she stumbled twice. Both times I had to reach down and pluck her from the snow, her cheeks red with embarrassment. All I could do was grunt and lead her forward.

It's exhausting keeping this human alive. Given the chance, I'm sure she would set off on her own. However, she knows she wouldn't make it to the edge of camp before the starving beasts of the woods decide to take a bite out of her.

I wonder for the second time since stopping to make camp if she is worth the headache.

Yes, she is, a small voice whispers to me. *She saved Zarod, and she is nice to look at.*

Kaethe did save Zarod, and I owe her for that. She's checked on him at each stop, to which he responds with jokes that make her small smile appear. It is a pleasant expression and yes, it is true that she is nice to look at.

The time on the road has been long and I can't remember the last time I was with a female. I've never been with one like Kaethe though. Tiny and soft, supple and smooth. Her big brown eyes dance as she takes in the sights before her with timid wonder. When she was nestled between my thighs earlier it had been nice to share in her warmth. As it would be nice to share the warmth of any woman or female.

Regardless of her pleasantness there is the matter of her secrets.

Anyone who keeps secrets is dangerous, and her situation is extremely odd. A human female, one clearly not used to camping and navigating barren terrain, has set off alone to meet someone at Dread's Keep.

I make a note to keep watch of this human.

But what she doesn't have in brute strength, she makes up for in intelligence. With what's in that kit of hers I suppose she could poison all of us. The apprehension I see in her as she keeps her distance from our group makes me believe the thought has crossed her mind.

Vorgak will want to know all about her. There will be no way to escape him in Dread's Keep. Whoever she is planning on meeting there has to know that.

And whoever it is is not her lover.

As much as that knowledge pleased me, for reasons I don't quite understand, it also adds to her mystery. Why come all this way if not for someone you love? Dread's Keep has very few humans, so it is unlikely she is meeting another one there. She has no orc in her, I'd be able to smell it.

All of it leaves me baffled with the same questions I've had since finding her in that hunting net.

We've stopped at an old outpost. The clouds above are dark, meaning they will bring in more snow this evening. The outpost we are at should provide enough coverage. The wooden roof extended past the entryway of the building and provided enough protection from falling snow. However, that means no fire while we sleep.

A small one is built away off to heat up dinner; another meager stew that is basically hot water and hard root vegetables. Kaethe gives thanks for her portion and goes to sit closer to the fire. The elements have taken a toll on her. Her pink braid is in tangles, her skin is pale and looks icy. And the purple bags under her eyes make her look sick.

I pull my eyes away from her as I hear footsteps come up beside me. Zarod clasps his stew in his hands and downs it in one gulp, wiping his mouth with the back of his hand.

"She is very pretty," he says in *orcish.* "I see that you've noticed."

"I doubt Mornga would approve of you noting another female's beauty," I say, raising a brow at him. Zarod only shrugs.

"Mornga used to be partial to females herself, if you recall."

"You think she'll leave you for this one, given the chance?" Zarod laughs and I am confused. I was genuinely curious. I don't know much about having a mate, I just have the primal urge to find mine, wherever she may be. Surely mates would not be shared with someone else?

I can't imagine ever wanting anyone to touch mine.

"No, Bazy, she likes my cock too much."

Shaking my head, I look back at Kaethe. There is tension in her neck and shoulders, I can tell by the way she is holding herself. Sitting apart from everyone as they chat and laugh. Her eyes survey the crowd. No one is speaking in *elven.* In fact, no one is speaking to her. She looks lost and afraid and more than a little sad.

Her small hands grip her soup bowl, and our eyes meet as she looks over toward me.

As if in a daze I turn my body toward her.

"Sit with her, she must feel awfully lonely among us," Zarod urges me. Would it really be that simple? Would she welcome my company? Her eyes drop from mine to her bowl. My body wants to walk over to her. To sit beside her and ask her more questions.

But talking and sitting with her could lead to dangerous thoughts. Thoughts that would be no good for anyone. Least of all this human.

"No," I say, turning away from her, from all of them. Zarod calls after me but I ignore him. This human is not my problem. My job is to get my men back home safely. We will take her to Dread's Keep and we will leave her at Dread's Keep. And there she can spend her days talking to whoever she came all this way to meet.

But as the sunsets and I finish setting up where we will be sleeping, I return to the fire to see Zarod engaging her in conversation. He's telling some horrible joke and she laughs quietly. The tension from her body gone, her guard not down but relaxed, if only for a moment. A few of the others chime in and I watch her smile at them softly. Answering whatever they ask her.

In this moment, I wish I was the reason her body was less tense, and she felt safe. I hate this ugly emotion worming its way into my heart. It isn't something I've felt for a while and as it settles in my stomach, it tastes an awful lot like jealousy.

Walking over to them, I clear my throat.

"Time for bed. Targoc will take the first watch. The sun will rise before any of us are ready for it."

Targoc grumbles but nods while everyone else makes their way to the overhang to set up their bedrolls for the evening. Kaethe walks past me with Zarod, both still locked in some sort of conversation.

"I unrolled your pack for you."

She stops short and looks up at me, surprise shining in her dark eyes. I add, "No fire tonight."

Mother of the Mountain, I sound unpleasant even to my own ears.

"Oh, thank you," she says, a reluctant smile curling her lips. I want to puff my chest out as if to say, *see I too can make you smile.* All my pride quickly diminishes when Zarod snags her by the elbow.

"Put your bedroll next to mine, Kae. I want to hear more stories about the king and that saucy queen of his."

My face twists. He touches her and she doesn't recoil. He gives her a nickname and she doesn't scoff. Zarod has always had a way with females. Easily approachable in a way that I'm just not. I've never minded before, but to think Kaethe prefers his type of male makes my teeth grind.

"She will sleep in the center where it is the warmest."

Zarod looks over at me, mouth in an easy grin that means he's about to make some remark. Whatever expression he sees on my face has his brows lowering. I hold his stare for a moment until he nods.

"Right, of course," he finally says.

Kaethe glances between us with a questioning look but I turn and walk away, retrieving my own bedroll. The camp is dark with no fire. Even with my good eyesight, it's hard not to trip over anyone.

Everyone sets out their bedrolls, and I make my way as close to Kaethe as I can near the center of our formation without arousing suspicion. Everyone settles under the wooden awning extending out from the main part of the outpost. The night is quiet and before long I can hear the soft thuds of snow falling against the roof above us. The wind kicks up and I burrow deeper under my cloak.

Closing my eyes, I try not to think about how close she is. How perfectly she fit against me while we rode today. These thoughts serve only to complicate hers and my life. Complications I don't need. I already have enough problems to worry about.

The wind whips through the trees, shaking some branches, and a few flurries are blown in under the roof. Rolling on my side I wait for sleep to claim me. I'm bone tired, uncomfortable, and I want to savor the few hours I have before we have to set off again.

I can hear a few of the males snoring around our camp. But mixed in among the deep breaths and wheezes are feminine whimpers of pain.

Flipping onto my side, I look over to Kaethe. Her small body, nothing more than a bump under her cloak, is shaking from the force of her shivering. Her teeth rattle as they snap together; the cold air is seeping through her thin cloak.

I groan and roll to my knees. Haven't I survived worse with less before?

Trudging over to her shuddering form, I throw my cloak down on top of her. I grit my teeth at the moan she lets out before she shoots upright. Her eyes look around frantically in the dark.

"Your shivering is keeping me awake."

"Oh, s—sorry, th—th—thank you." Her teeth are still chattering. I grunt, not trusting what I might say to her and move back to my own bedroll. I brace myself against the chill of the wind. My clothes will keep me alive through the night, that is all that matters.

"Who knew you had a soft spot for pink-haired human females?"

I hadn't even realized Zarod had set his bedroll up next to mine until I hear his voice in the dark.

"Shut the fuck up and go to sleep," I snap at him in *orcish*. Zarod chokes on a laugh, but I hear him over the whistling winds.

"Oh Bazy, never did I ever think I would see the day."

I close my eyes and pretend I have no idea what he's talking about.

CHAPTER 6

KAETHE

Dread's keep is, well...dreadful.

Built directly into the side of the mountain, the Keep's metal doors shine in the morning sun. At this high altitude, the wind whips through my hair and kicks up the snow around me, blowing it into the unmoving faces of the orcs guarding the door. They are dressed differently than the orcs I traveled here with. Both guards are fitted in leather lined with fur, and a gold emblem on the right side of their chest sparkles in the light. They both death grip sharp spears and clutch wooden shields in front of their immense torsos.

They look ready to spring into action should we prove to be a threat.

Once again, I reluctantly find myself thankful to have found this orc party. Especially as Bazur speaks gruffly to the two guards, who begrudgingly open the door after a few harsh words are exchanged. No way could I have commanded them in such a way. It becomes clear to me as we make our way through the door that I could've traveled all this way just to be turned away by them.

Entering through the metal doors, we step into a new world. One consisting of dark stone, cold metal, and the dank smell of earth. The entry is carved from the mountain itself, and polished marble floors are illuminated by sconces and torches along the entryway. More guards wearing uniforms like the ones at the door greet us, standing in two lines that bracket the walkway into what seems to be a throne room.

Stalactites hang from the ceiling above. I spy a few openings along the roof that lead me to believe there is some sort of tunnel system in here. It would make sense; King Arkain often remarked the tunnel system inside Brokenbone Mountain made it incredibly hard to infiltrate.

The orcs in my company have assembled in their own formation as we make our way forward. As expected, Bazur leads his company forward. I walk just slightly behind his left shoulder with Zarod taking point on his right. They move in step with each other, and I try my best to keep up.

Ever since we reached the front gate my traveling party has remained quiet. Even jovial Zarod didn't have a funny comment for me this morning when we dismounted our *icewolves*. Bazur looks the most severe of all. His face is harder than I have ever seen it. A cold fury settles in his honey-colored eyes.

"Kae," Zarod, whispers beside me. I turn and look over at him. He's still facing forward, not missing a step. "I don't want to be the one to tell you this, but whoever asked you to meet them here stood you up."

Indeed, my lie really doesn't seem plausible now. We are so close to my cover being blown anyways, what's the harm in telling him?

"Well, I'm—"

A clap interrupts me. Then another, and then thunderous applause is heard from in front of us. We push into the throne room and immediately I regret my decision to come here. Despite more torches illuminating this cavernous room, this place feels dark and unholy. The throne room is lined with paintings depicting war and violence. More torches light up this cavernous room. The orcs with me form a line behind Bazur and I.

The hairs on the back of my neck stand up as my eyes land on a figure.

He's an older orc, his skin not the rich green of Bazur and Zarod. His eyes are dark, beady and cruel as they take us in. There are metal caps on his tusks, making them even sharper, and he wears head-to-toe armor that gleams in the dim light. The metal radiates a power that, even just looking at it, makes my head throb.

It's magical in some way, that is more than evident.

The crown of bones resting above his brow matches the ones of the throne he is sitting on. I try not to focus on how human the skulls look. Or how small some of them are. Bile rises in my throat. This can only be one person.

Vorgak, King of the Orcs. The creature that my brother may be toiling away in service to right now. The one who may have given the order to destroy my village. The one who now holds my future here on this mountain in his clawed hand.

He claps once more, an evil gleam in his eyes, before letting his hands fall to the armrest of his throne. He playfully twiddles his fingers around a massive skull with a metal band around the forehead; that was once an orc of great importance. Perhaps even an old king.

The thought makes me shiver.

My traveling party bows slightly, and not wanting to be disrespectful, I do the same. I dip into a courtesy as I stare at the floor. When I rise and look up, I see there are a few more orcs scattered behind Vorgak. They all rake me with gazes that make my knees lock.

The larger of the three makes no effort to hide his stare but lingers on my chest and hips before licking his tusks hungrily. There are supposed to be humans here, the king's own alchemists and healers, but I see none. Perhaps they are wise and stay hidden. Something I too will be doing when I begin my stay here.

Vorgak calls out to Bazur in their language. Bazur nods and responds to a smug Vorgak. They chat for a moment, while I try to ignore the other orcs's gaze on me.

I've just about worked up the courage to interrupt when Vorgak's eyes fall on me. He says something to Bazur who narrows his eyes, before pushing me slightly forward. I take a step and bow again.

"Well, it looks like you found something interesting at the outposts after all." Vorgak's words are swallowed by his thick accent. His *elven* is choppy and cold. I lock my spine and remind myself I didn't come all this way just to be scared off by his presence.

I slip my hand into the pocket of my cloak and produce a letter stamped with the royal crest of Myrkorvin. Holding it out to Vorgak, I feel Bazur turn toward me. I don't have to be looking at him to see his surprise. Willing my voice to be even, I clear my throat.

"I am Kaethe, Royal Alchemist to King Arkain and Queen Elveena of the Dark Elves. They have sent me here as an emissary so that our people may be united in the ways of science and medicine. I have come to help train your healers and alchemists, at my king's orders."

One of the orc guards snatches the letter from my hand and brings it to Vorgak. The silence stretches, I can hear a few of the orcs whispering behind me. Apprehension trickles down my spine as more silence passes.

Vorgak reads the letter, turns it over in his clawed hand and chuckles.

"We did enjoy the last gift your king sent our way."

The orcs in the hall chuckle, something evil lighting in their eyes. Wylan always gave me a bad feeling, and what he did was treasonous. I never gave much thought to what happened when he was dumped at their tunnel but now I can't stop myself from asking.

"What became of Wylan?"

The orcs snicker even harder, Vorgak's scarred mouth twists into a smirk.

"You are a woman of science, are you not?"

I nod once at his rhetorical question. "Let's just say, we did our own experimenting on him."

I shiver, knowing that whatever that means, it can't be good. Vorgak sits up straighter on his throne, crushing Arkain's letter in his hands.

"Your arrival has come at a poor time," Vorgak says. I lower my brows in confusion.

"King Arkain wrote months ago saying I would arrive on this day. I—"

"In our kind's experience, the dark elves don't always keep their word. I had no reason to believe your king to be trustworthy. To send us one of his most trusted alchemists, after decades of silence? You under-stand my wariness."

Not a question, a statement and I nod, feeling dread sink my stom-ach. He's going to turn me away. All of this was for nothing. I can't bear making the journey back. Not ladled with failure and limited supplies.

"In fact, my own healers and alchemist had been sent away from the Keep weeks before the first letter from your king arrived. I could've called them back, but again, why disrupt their studies when it was not certain you would turn up."

"I can conduct my own research here, if no one else is—"

"Don't," his voice snaps like a whip, "interrupt me."

Swallowing, I nod my head and my knees begin to shake.

Vorgak falls back onto his throne, letting my letter from King Arkain drop to the floor. "But seeing as you are here now and have traveled all this way, I cannot simply turn you away."

He chuckles again. "Conduct your own research? Do you see where you are, human? This Keep is not safe for your kind. The creatures that roam these tunnels will have you for dinner. Or worse."

I can only nod my head, my failure weighing on me. Vorgak looks over his shoulder to the orc who has been staring at me this whole time. The orc has moved closer and I can see a prominent scar that runs along one cheek. His yellow gaze appraises me like a rare fruit, and I avert my eyes.

"You'll need a chaperone while you're in my lands to keep you... *safe*. Can't have King Arkain's prized alchemist go missing on my watch." Somehow, I don't believe he's concerned about my safety. Vorgak nods at the leering orc. "He will take you up to Wolf's Teeth Clan, they have few humans but your skills will be welcomed there."

My head feels dizzy. Going to a clan? That wasn't part of the plan. I was meant to stay here, to find out what I could from the humans living in these walls. They would surely know where all the humans who get captured are kept.

"King, I—"

"You are welcome human, I'm sure they will be thrilled with your company."

The orc starts walking toward me and suddenly I am six again and there's no running. I have to go with the orc who looks at me like I'm his next meal. Whose eyes promise to inflict pain as soon as he is free to.

My hands tremble, my vision blurs—I'm going to faint. *I'm going to faint.*

A growl erupts from beside me.

"That won't be necessary," Bazur says. "I'll chaperone the human."

I snap my head to the side. Something powerful glows in Bazur's eyes as he stares up at Vorgak. An unspoken conversation takes place between the two males before me. After a moment, Bazur raises his hand, gesturing at the orc that was approaching me.

"Mazgark will eat her before they make their first camp. Then we will have war with the elves." I sway on my feet at the thought of that.

"Perhaps war is what I wish for. Our kind is built for it, and we have known peace for far too long." I watch as Vorgak cuts Bazur a sneer. "You most of all should know what years of peace can cost."

Bazur responds back in *orcish* and I can no longer understand what is being said. Whatever it is, the orc who was supposed to take me, Mazgark, grows more and more tense. His eyes like yellow fire blaze at Bazur, his muscles tense and his fingers dance along the hilt of the sword strapped to his hip.

Vorgak says one last thing before looking back at Mazgark. With a wave of his hand Mazgark is dismissed, growling as he retreats to the far corner of the room.

"Fine. The human shall remain in your care Bazur. I trust you will keep an eye on her." Vorgak leans forward, baring his teeth at me. "He will let you train the humans in his clan until the summer. I will issue this warning only once, human. Bazur will watch you day and night. If I get a whiff of you doing anything other than what your king stated in his letter, I will be very angry."

I nod, my voice wavering but somehow I manage to say, "Thank you."

Vorgak waves me off. "Go, it is a long way back to Black Claw Village and I'd hate to change my mind before you leave."

My feet seem glued to the stone floor. Luckily, Bazur's aren't. His warm hand curls around my upper arm and pulls me from my trance. My booted feet scuff along the smooth floor. I twist to look over my shoulder and up at Bazur, my mouth open to…explain myself? To ask why he volunteered to take me with him?

All of it is at the tip of my tongue but he lets out a low growl at me. "Be quiet and keep moving."

"Human," Vorgak calls, my feet are just about to cross over the threshold out of the throne room but his rasping stops our whole party. I turn slowly to look at him; those beady eyes zeroing in on me. "The punishment for spies found on Brokenbone Mountain is death. Remember that."

Bazur's grip on me tightens and I shake my head.

"Y—yes, King." My mouth begins to water, my vision goes blurry. *I'm six, I'm running on cut feet, the bodies are burning, my parents are dead, and I'm going to be dead soon too. I have to keep running, I have to—*

"Move, Kaethe. Now," Bazur snaps in my ear, and I somehow manage it.

Bazur's strong grip on my arm is the only thing that keeps me up right as we make it through Dread's Keep. Once we're past the guards and I can feel the morning sun on my face, the snow and cold wind stinging my cheeks, Bazur releases his hold on me. My knees buckle and my head spins and I plunge into a waiting darkness.

I feel nothing as I land face first in a pile of fresh snow.

Chapter 7

KAETHE

DESPITE MY FAINTING SPELL EARLIER, there is no time for breaks as we travel one more day on wolf-back to Black Claw Village.

The journey was uncomfortably quiet. I had regained consciousness just as Bazur had wordlessly pulled me from the snow mound and dragged me onto the back of his *icewolf*. In a trance-like state, I leaned back against his chest and stared out at the terrain in front of us. Each forceful step the wolf took shook me but I barely registered it.

The adrenaline I felt when we first arrived at Dread's Keep has left me and now I am exhausted. The days of traveling are catching up with me. At least tonight I can find lodging somewhere and sleep on a warm, dry bed.

We will be a day's ride from Dread's Keep and despite my initial hesitations about being so far away from where I believe the best chance at locating my brother is, I can't help but welcome the distance. I won't have to stay there alone. I am grateful to Bazur for volunteering to take me but I know I have to remain on my guard.

Vorgak's warning still rings in my ears. If it were discovered what my true purpose for coming here was, Bazur would have no choice but to do as instructed. I won't risk that. Being on this mountain has brought me closer to finding my brother than I have ever been. Wherever Bazur's village is, Vorgak said there are humans. Perhaps one of them has heard of my brother or knows someone that was captured twenty years ago and what may have happened to them.

That golden thread of hope glows in my chest once more as the *icewolves* carry us forward.

We haven't stopped once to rest. The urgency I felt from Bazur as we left the throne room continued as we made our way up the mountain. It was as though Vorgak was on our heels and it was only a matter of time before he caught up with us.

I'm still deep in thought when Bazur lets out a yell.

A great groaning sound is heard and my eyes focus on what's in front of us. When we left the Keep, I expected us to go deeper into the mountain, perhaps through one of the great tunnels we passed. Instead, we rode further around to the other side of the mountain. Traveling over a few hills and valleys to where we are now.

It's mostly flat here. Rows of evergreen trees make a path in the snow that leads us toward two great wooden doors carved with the symbol of a wolf's paw. There are two orcs manning the door, but unlike the ones at the Keep, their attire matches the orcs in my company.

The stiff snow crunches beneath the *icewolves'* massive paws, and the guards call out to Bazur in *orcish* before bowing their heads in respect. As soon as we push through the doors, there is a flurry of excitement. Bazur's name is shouted from every corner of the village, and shock renders me even more speechless. Humans and orcs alike are congregated together to welcome Bazur and his company. Old and young, male and female. Some are dressed like the soldiers with me, while others are more plainly clothed. One woman, around my age with dark hair, cradles a baby with pale green skin close to her chest, while an orc male rests a hand on her shoulder. My mind spins, questioning what I am seeing in front of me.

Bazur nods at a few of them, his stoney expression still in place. Black Claw Village is quaint and much larger than the one I grew up in. Rows of wooden homes and shops line the snowy street. There's a baker, an orc male wearing an apron covered in flour , taking fresh loaves out of a hot oven. The smell of baked bread makes my stomach growl. An older human woman with tan skin and tightly curled brown ringlets drapes muted color fabric in her window. She nods as we pass.

Bazur receives many looks of respect but I catch a few of curiosity and a handful of disdain from a few of the younger human and orc females alike. Being their leader, I would assume Bazur is quite a catch to any female in the village. For all I know he may even have a mate, though he is not as vocal about it like Zarod.

Not that there is any relationship between me or Bazur; he is my warden. I'm hoping there's an inn that I can stay at. I need some time alone to get my thoughts together and devise my next plan. But mostly, I am desperate for a warm bath.

Maybe I can convince Bazur to let me stay with a human family, one I can pepper with questions that hopefully won't arouse any suspicion.

Most of all I am desperate for a warm bath.

We continue down the main street, as the sun begins to set. One by one the soldiers peel off, heading toward their own homes. The buildings become less dense indicating we've left the heart of the town.

We pass a wooden row house that is painted the most beautiful shade of blue. The glow from a fire inside warms me even at this distance. I lean my head back to watch the thick smoke from the chimney curl into the darkening sky. The front door swings open and emerges an orc female. She is breathtakingly beautiful. Sharp features, thick black hair that flows in a soft wave down her back. Her frame is willowy, all long limbs and sleek muscles barely hidden beneath her wool dress. Her ears are slightly more pointed than the orcs' that I've seen, and her eyes glow a familiar red.

She's part dark elf, I think with a start.

The female orc narrows her eyes at me and Bazur for a moment, a questioning look lowering her brow. That is all forgotten when Zarod lets out a howl and charges toward the house.

"Kaethe it was wonderful to meet you, thanks again for saving me," he calls over his shoulder. "Now both of you fuck off and don't disturb me for at least a week. I'll be busy."

Zarod jumps down from his *icewolf* and marches up the front steps. No sooner is the female, who can only be the infamous Mornga, within arm's reach, that he has her pressed against his chest. She laughs up at him before his mouth swoops down on hers. Her fingers move to his cloak untying the knot and letting it fall off his shoulders.

"My lovely Mornga, I've missed you." Zarod's voice carries on the wind.

"Lovely? I don't think you've called me lovely before," Mornga chuckles.

"A travesty." Zarod kisses her once more. "Now let me get you naked so I can call your pussy that as well."

Mornga hits his chest and then they push through the front door and into the warmth of the town house. We can hear their laughter all the way from the street.

My cheeks heat at such a display of affection. Bazur mutters under his breath as we push forward. For a moment I wonder what it would be like to have someone so obsessed with you like that. To be the reason they smiled and looked at you like you were the center of their entire universe?

I hope to find out one day, but it won't be anytime soon. Not when I'm on a mission. Not when I'm going to be staying in this village.

We continue to the end of the road until we reach another house. It is a humble home, built into the base of an evergreen tree. The front steps lead to a porch with a desolate flower bed, and the upper levels of the home are tucked into the branches of the tree. I've never seen anything like it.

Our wolf stops in front of it and Bazur slides off. He looks up at me with his hands raised in silent permission. I nod once and he plucks me off the saddle and sets me on the ground. Off to the side is a training yard with wooden swords lining a simple wooden fence. Stone cairns in the snow designate fighting circles.

Bazur clears his throat and I look back at him. The journey has taken a toll on him as well. Snow clings to his dark hair and frost coats some of the light stubble on his face. My fingers itch to touch it and I don't understand why.

"This is my home." he gestures toward the tree house.

"It's very nice," I say, furrowing my brows. "Where will I be staying?"

He nods toward his house.

Oh, gods why didn't I consider that? So much for alone time.

"Surely, it would make more sense for me to stay with one of the human families in town. If I am to teach them my skills—"

"You stay with me." I fight the urge to stomp my foot. I was really looking forward to getting away from this orc and collecting my thoughts.

I need to walk through all the variables of this situation and devise a plan. I can't do that when he is so close.

He unsettles me.

"You interrupt me a lot," I mutter. "Is that something all orcs do?"

"You say a lot of nonsense I don't have time for."

Bazur pinches the bridge of his nose. "Vorgak told me to watch you. So, I am going to watch you. I take this job very seriously."

"Why?"

"Why?" he snaps. "Why would I not want to watch you closely? You have secrets, secrets make you dangerous."

"Look at me," I say, gesturing down my body. "I am no threat to you."

"Maybe not physically, but you're smart. That's why I agreed to let you come here. Your knowledge will help my people." He crosses his arms over his massive chest, the fabric at his arms bunching around his thick biceps. "Why didn't you tell me you were a royal emissary?"

I sigh, pulling my cloak around myself. "Before I left, King Vorgak made it very clear that my safety on the mountain could not be guaranteed until I made it to Dread's Keep. He informed my king that any orcs I came across may not take too kindly to a lone human woman." I let the sentence hang there and Bazur nods, understanding what I'm not saying.

"It's obvious to me now," I continue, "that he never thought I would make the journey and that I would perish along the way."

"Did your king force you to come here?" Bazur asks. I pinch my eyes shut. *Remember the secret to a good lie. Stay as close to the truth as often as you can.*

"No, I volunteered."

Bazur shakes his head at me, disbelief coloring his golden eyes.

"That's what I don't understand. Why would you volunteer to come here with your obvious aversion to my kind?"

"I don't have an aversion—"

"You don't need to tell me another lie."

"You don't need to keep interrupting me!" His incessant staring and his constant interruptions are dueling for his worst trait.

He grumbles something under his breath, uttering that word he called me two nights ago after I saved Zarod. I bristle upon hearing it, knowing it can only mean annoying, or liar, or *very-difficult-to-deal-with-I-should-just-eat-her*. He motions for me to walk into the house, but I plant my feet in the snow.

"What's the problem now?" I can hear his teeth grinding together. Good.

"I'm waiting," I say, lifting my chin.

"For?"

"An apology."

"For what?" He raises his dark brows.

"A plethora of things—"

"Plethora?"

"But mostly for constantly interrupting me." Bazur blinks. I hold his stare not moving a muscle. We lock eyes and I wait for the fear to creep in, to lessen my resolve and make me retreat into myself. It never does. For some reason I know I can hold my ground with Bazur and he will not harm me.

Not over this at least.

He exhales and rubs his forehead.

"I am sorry," he growls so harshly that I barely make out the words.

"What are you sorry for?"

"*Mother of the Mountain.*" He rolls his eyes. "I am sorry for interrupting you."

"And you won't do it again?" A muscle in his cheek twitches but he nods.

"I won't do it again."

"See, was that really so hard?" I brush past him and up the front steps.

The house is dark but even without adequate light I can tell it doesn't have much furniture. Bazur moves to the fireplace off to the side and quickly gets one going. He returns to light a few candles and I take everything in.

A simple kitchen with a metal oven and stove. An old kitchen table with two chairs, both carved with some ornate design. There are a few shelves littered with bags of flour and some other spices. Simple metal cutlery sits in a pile on the counter next to a couple of wooden bowls.

"Tomorrow, I will take you to see Lady Myren," Bazur calls to me from the fireplace, holding his green palms over the roaring flames. I join him by the fire, the heat warming me enough that I can finally slip off my cloak. I let the flames warm me through the thin wool of my green dress.

Bazur is quiet and I turn to look at him only for him to shift his gaze away from me quickly. Strange orc.

"She will show you how to teach the other humans your healing gifts."

"I'm an alchemist, technically, not a healer."

"We have no need for gold here. More gold doesn't keep the *Frost Cough* from coming every winter," he replies, moving away from the fire.

"*Frost Cough?*"

"A sickness that comes after the first freeze. It infects the lungs and decimates our humans here, the old and the young especially."

How can I argue with that? I nod my head and he grunts. His favorite reply. Sufficiently warm, I also take a step back from the fire and survey the room again. There are very few personal touches. The walls are made of simple cedar wood, decorated with a few massive *frostelk* heads. Their magnificent horns curl upward toward the wooden beams of the ceiling.

Noticing my stare, Bazur inclines his head.

"This is the kitchen," he says motioning to where the stove is with the small table. "That takes you up to the bedroom." I follow him toward the short wooden ladder that separates the two floors. The smooth wood is polished and cool to the touch as I grip the sides and climb up the rungs.

It leads to a landing with a small door at the back. The only things up here are a bedside table made from the same tan wood the rest of the furniture in the house is, and a massive bed covered in furs and thick wool sheets. An array of pillows decorates the headboard. The heat from the fire rises up here making it deliciously warm. A yawn sneaks up on me.

Oh, how I'd love to collapse in that thing.

"Back through there" —Bazur points to the small door— "is the washroom. This house is set up to catch melting snow. There are metal pipes that heat the water for the bathing pool." He leads me to the washroom and the sight is magnificent. A large steel tub takes up the entire center of the room and is built directly into the wooden floor. It was obviously built with an orc in mind because it is easily six feet deep. There is a toilet and sink off to the side, as well.

Wordlessly he shows me how to turn the faucet and heat the water, and I say a silent prayer of thanks to the gods for not making me have to collect buckets of water in these icy conditions. There's a small drain at the bottom of the pool which allows the dirty bath water to escape. The bathroom becomes steamy from the hot water, and I can't wait to be out of these clothes and in the tub scrubbing the road from my skin. He shows me where he keeps his towels before we exit the washroom and are once again standing in front of the massive bed.

I look around with a raised brow. Above us is a glass roof that reveals some of the snow covered branches of the tree we are in as well as glimpse a few stars. During the day I'm sure it provides an ample amount of natural light. There's a small landing along the steepled roof. It's narrow but I'd be able to lie on it. Perhaps that is where I will set up my bedroll? The only problem is there is no ladder leading up to it.

My palms begin to sweat as uncertainty seeps in.

"So…where will I be sleeping?" When he raises a dark brow in confusion I suppress my groan, somehow already knowing what he's about to say.

"There's only one bed, *akorzag*."

CHAPTER 8

KAETHE

ONE BED. SURELY HE CAN'T *be serious.*

Sharing a home is one thing. Sharing a saddle out of necessity is another. Sleeping in the same bed as someone I barely know, not to mention an orc who sees me as his annoying ward, is something else entirely. Needlessly intimate, I'd rather sleep on a bedroll in a barn.

In theory at least, I can't deny that the bed looks deliciously comfortable.

"I'm not sharing a bed with you," I splutter, Bazur shrugs his massive green shoulders.

"This isn't an ideal arrangement for me either."

"Then let me find lodging with some of the humans in town. You rule over this village, surely you can find a nice family to take me in while I'm here." Before he can protest I press on. "I promise, I'll check-in with you every day so you know what I'm doing at all times."

"No, I will watch you." He speaks with such finality that my cheeks heat.

"I'm not sharing a bed with you," I repeat. He scrubs a large, calloused hand across his brow. A gesture he seems to be doing a lot in my presence.

"That is fine, *akorzag*. I will sleep on a bedroll in the front room." *There he goes, calling me annoying again right to my face.* "That way I can hear if you try to escape."

My mouth pops open and my face is heating for a different reason now. Indignation.

"I wouldn't try to escape. I gave my word, besides where would I even go."

"I don't know you, Kaethe." His use of my name has my eyes narrowing on him. "All I know about you is the lies that you've told me. Why would I give you even an ounce of trust? Until I know for a fact that you are not a danger to my village—to my people—I will be keeping you under my roof, where I can keep my eyes on you."

Crossing my arms over my chest I glare at him. He has a point godsdamn him. "Fine."

Bazur meets my steely glare until my stomach rumbles. He mutters something under his breath and my irritation grows further.

"What did you say?" I ask but he merely raises a brow.

"I hope you like stew. It's the only thing I can cook." I cringe at that statement, not wanting to be an ungrateful guest. Then I remind myself I am not a guest here. I am a captive. Captured by this orc general and made to stay under his roof, in his bed, albeit without him in it.

"I can't say I'm the biggest fan of it," I admit. Bazur's face is blank, before he turns and makes for the ladder.

"You better start liking it."

"I can always cook something." Bazur's whole body freezes on the top rung, something unreadable passing through his golden eyes. He shakes his head as if to clear it, a few dark stands of his hair escaping to tickle his cheeks. I roll my eyes at his dismissal. "I won't poison you with my cooking."

"Based on all those herbs in your bag, you can't blame me for thinking you've considered it."

My teeth grind at that statement. They continue to grind as I tuck into my bowl of thin meat stew, that's more water than broth. *Poisoning him?* I look over towards my trunk as I spoon the last portion of weak stew into my mouth.

Now that's an idea.

The night had been strange to say the least.

Bathing in the warm pool was luxurious, as was slipping under the wool sheets and furs. I almost felt bad for Bazur sleeping on his thin bedroll downstairs. But sinking into the warm softness of his mattress, dressed in my thin, clean nightgown almost made me moan with comfort. The bed smelled of him; rich pine and spice lulled me to sleep.

And then a gruff voice startled me awake.

Bazur looked tired. The dark green circles under his honey-colored eyes caused guilt to creep up on me again. Until I reminded myself that he volunteered for this position. As grateful as I am that I'm not stuck at Dread's Keep, I'm not so grateful to let him share a bed with me.

I dressed quickly and together we ate another bowl of thin stew before setting off to Lady Myren's.

There is so much...*life* in this village. I noticed it as Bazur and I walked through the town this morning. Children run through the street, human and orc offspring alike, throwing snowballs and tackling each other. Human and orc couples hold hands. A few of the males rub the round stomachs of the human women they are with.

Bazur dropped me off at Lady Myren's front steps, exchanging some words with her in *orcish* before switching back to *elven*. He said he had soldiers to train, and that he would be back for me this evening to escort me home. There was a thinly veiled warning about what would happen if I tried sneaking off or if I didn't listen to Lady Myren. I'm trying to block it from my mind, or I will be just as vexed as when I first walked in here.

Why does his distrust annoy me so much? Because if he trusts me, the more freedom I will have. And with more freedom it will be easier to find out where my brother could've been taken to. I've kept my eyes peeled in town in case I see anyone baring his coloring but so far no one looks even remotely similar to my brother.

Lady Myren is an older woman, with deep crow's feet along her bright green eyes. Her long black hair is streaked with gray and silver secured in a long plait down her back.

There is an intelligence in her stare, a worldliness only someone who has seen things many others have not. Living in this village, I can't even imagine the things she's seen and heard.

If I am going to be working with her for the time that I am here, she is the best option to pump for information on the whereabouts of other humans. Her home alone indicates she has lived here for a long time.

Her longhouse is a single level and extends nearly to the edge of the wood. The front door opens into a kitchen where the stove and fireplace are situated. Beside the hearth is a small cedar table and two matching chairs. Both are ornately carved with pictures of Brokenbone Mountain. Just to the right of the door is a long work table, cluttered with all types of jars and cataloging supplies for the various herbs that decorate the windowsills on the front wall of the house. There are massive wooden bookcases filled with rows upon rows of herbs, ointments, tools, and books on the art of healing.

As I walk further into the house, I notice between the front room and the bedrooms toward the back are about ten cots lined up in two rows separated by a walkway. Clean white linen sheets are stretched tightly over each one. Lady Myren isn't just the town healer but seems to run an infirmary here as well.

"Bazur says you are from the Royal Academy in Myrkorvin?" Lady Myren cuts through my thoughts and I turn to look at her. A smile curves my lips and I nod. I need to get off on the right foot with her.

"Yes, I studied there for seven years."

She nods once. I think she is going to ask me questions about the academy or at the very least give me some indication that she is impressed. Instead, she walks over to one of the bookshelves and plucks a leather-bound book from the shelf. She settles it down in front of me with a thud, dust flying up and tickling my nose.

A tray of vials is placed next to me as well. All filled with unmarked seeds.

"Good, then cataloging should be something you are familiar with."

I raise my eyebrow at her. Cataloging is a necessary task, sure, but it's meant for a novice. It's low man's work.

Which in this village, I guess means me.

"What are these for?" I ask, picking up a vial of seeds. Brown and unassuming, they could be anything. There are hundreds of seeds that look like this.

"If I knew that, I wouldn't need you to catalog them for me, would I?"

My cheeks warm and I nod my head.

"They're local herbs, brought to me by one of the farmers. That's all I know."

Lady Myren isn't very chatty. This work is tedious, and I feel like an hour has passed since starting but when I glance up at the clock, I find it's only been fifteen minutes. Gods, this is going to be a long winter.

Just then the front door opens. A young orc male comes rushing in, his tusks smaller, less pronounced on his lower jaw. Lady Myren jumps up and goes to the child's side. There is a deep gash along the top of his hand, and crimson blood drips from the wound onto the floor as Lady Myren examines it.

"Get my kit by the door, we need to clean this cut," Lady Myren shouts at me. I grab her bag and bring it over to where she is sitting on the cot. The young male sits beside her, his yellow eyes assessing me with curiosity, and I set the bag of supplies at their feet.

"How did this happen?" Lady Myren asks. Popping open her healing bag, she hands me a glass bottle of antiseptic. The strong scent singes my nose.

"It wasn't my fault, the ax just slipped, Lady Myren. I swear!" Lady Myren takes out some clean clothes and lays them on a tray next to the bed. She hands one to me and I coat it with the antiseptic.

"Here, put that on his wound to cleanse it. You know how to tend to wounds, yes?"

I nod. I've had some wound training, especially living at the palace where a guard or two was known to need some stitching up after sparring.

"What was Zarc thinking, letting you chop wood all by yourself. That lazy woodcutter." Her words clatter through me and suddenly I'm back in my village, the smoke is choking me, and I'm looking up at our woodcutter. The one who carved me figurines. *My hand leaves my brother's. The woodcutter's arm is missing, red blood, sticky and clinging to his—*

"Kaethe!" Lady Myren's voice cracks like a whip and pulls me from my thoughts. Quickly, I put the cloth to his skin. The burn causes the child to jerk but Lady Myren holds him firm. I wipe away at the wound, then apply pressure to stop the bleeding. My hands have gone sweaty, my eyes unfocused.

"Don't tell me you're squeamish around blood."

All I can do is shake my head no.

The bleeding stops and we find the cut isn't deep enough to require stitches. Lady Myren tightly bandages the child's hand and sends him off with a stiff warning and a threat to tell his mother he shouldn't be chopping wood unsupervised.

"You want to tell me what that was all about?" Lady Myren asks, turning from the door. I sit down at the work bench and pull the vials of herbs closer to me. I need to lose myself in my work. That has always helped when my memories threaten to pull me under. A distraction in the form of a mundane task will help the smell of smoke leave my nose.

"Just a bad memory, nothing more." Lady Myren looks like she wants to ask more but doesn't push. In fact, the rest of the day we barely speak, both of us quietly absorbed in our own tasks. We only talk when villagers come in for healing.

An hour after the orc child left an older orc came in with a slight cough. Lady Myren made him tea and sent him on his way. A few hours later a young human male came in with a sprained wrist. I helped Lady Myren bandage it before sending him back to work. Next, there was a pregnant human female with wildly curly red hair and a smattering of freckles that came in complaining of a sore abdomen and cramping. Lady Myreen applied a thick ointment to her stomach and sent her home with a jar of it, telling her that her mate needs to rub the cream on daily.

We set broken finger bones, we brewed tea together, but we never spoke, not even casual small talk. By the time the sun began to set, my back was throbbing from being hunched over and my eyes are dry from staring at the small print in her herb catalog. I finish labeling the last vial when Lady Myren approaches me with a cup of tea. The steam curls over the lip and it smells of peppermint.

I take a sip as she looks at my handiwork. Wordlessly, she collects the labeled containers and places them back on the shelf. Returning, she sits across from me at the worktable appraising me under thin dark brows.

"Thank you for doing that," she says. "Tomorrow a few of the women in the village will come to help make tonics for *Frost Cough*."

I nod my head, trying not to look too relieved that we will have company. Maybe one of them will be more receptive to me and I can get some information out of them.

"You are a very talented healer," I say. Lady Myren shakes her head, a secret smile gracing her pink lips.

"It is the least I can do for being brought here. To be allowed to live here."

I'm puzzled by her response and seize the opportunity to ask another question.

"Have many humans been brought to live here?" Her eyes narrow. I quickly include an explanation and vow to be more subtle in my questioning going forward. "It's just that people looked shocked to see me when I arrived yesterday."

Lady Myren chews her bottom lip and I try not to wilt under her hard stare. After a long, uncomfortable silence she says, "We get new people, from time to time."

A non-answer if I've ever heard of one. Great.

I open my mouth to say something when the door slams open. Targoc appears, sweat staining the front of his wool shirt and his green forehead glistening. He unties the sword tied around his waist before toeing off his boots by the threshold.

"Mother, you won't believe what Bazur let me try today!" There is so much excitement in his green eyes. Green eyes…the same exact shape and color as Lady Myren's. My mouth falls open.

How did I not piece that together sooner? Bazur stands behind him in the doorway, his eyes finding mine as if to make sure I didn't disappear during the day. He rests a meaty shoulder against the doorframe and crosses his muscular arms over his chest as he turns and smiles at Lady Myren. She returns it with the most pleasant expression I've seen her give all day. Her body is relaxed, her eyes bright and happy.

Not at all like the body language she showed me today.

"How was my boy today, General?" she asks. Even the timbre of her voice is softer.

"Targoc is showing great promise." Bazur nods to me, signaling it's time to go. I rise, grabbing my cloak from the hook on the wall, the chill from the open door already seeping through my blue dress. This is my last clean clothing item; I'll have to find a way to procure more here shortly.

"Please, won't you stay for dinner?" Lady Myren asks, a courtesy that was not extended to me.

Bazur shakes his head. "Not tonight, thank you. It's best I take her home now."

My glare at him apparently doesn't go unnoticed as Lady Myren frowns at me. She looks between us for a moment before speaking to him in their orc language. Bazur responds and she nods. There is a familiarity between them that is hard to miss.

They stare at each other for another moment, something unspoken passing between them.

"I will bring Kaethe back at the same time tomorrow," Bazur says in *elven*, and I turn to look at Lady Myren.

"Thank you for today. I look forward to seeing you tomorrow."

She only nods. We both know it is a lie, but it seems we each have our roles to play. Lady Myren may prove to be another obstacle while I am here. I will have to keep my guard up around her so she doesn't turn me into my orc warden.

With that thought in mind, I step over the threshold and walk into the chilly night air.

CHAPTER 9

KAETHE

THE NEXT MORNING, I REPORT to Lady Myren's house once again.

Bazur drops me off with a grunt, saying he will be back again to collect me in the evening before stomping off in the snow. I sigh and try my best to put on a smile as I walk through the front door of Lady Myren's home.

There is a buzz of chatter as I make my way inside, but all conversations cease when the door clicks shut behind me. Five other women from town are here. A few are around the same age as Myren, and the pregnant redhead from yesterday is closer to my age.

"Good morning," I manage to say in a small voice. Lady Myren nods at me, turning back to her conversation with one of the women at the fireplace. She stirs something in a heavy metal kettle, the scent of peppermint and honey dancing in the air.

"Sit next to me, Kaethe."

I look over to see the pregnant woman patting the bench next to her. I smile gratefully, removing my cloak and settling in beside her.

"I remember being new. It's a small village, people like to talk, but their curiosity will wear off soon enough."

Her blue eyes sparkle and her nose crinkles when she smiles.

"Thank you…" I trail off and she smiles even wider, a soft flush staining her cheeks.

"Oh goodness, where are my manners? My name is Jessica, I live next to the butcher's." She giggles softly. "Well, my mate is the butcher so that's why I live there. It's convenient for him. I used to help him in the

63

shop but after about the third month I couldn't stand the smell of raw meat."

Her pale complexion begins to turn a little green, and she covers her mouth as if in danger of throwing up just thinking about it.

She said mate, not husband. That means she is with an orc. Of her own choosing? I have no reason to believe otherwise but still—I file this information away. Perhaps it will be helpful to me in the future.

"How long have you been with your mate?" I ask, trying to subtly gauge her age. Jessica has an openness about her that makes me believe I'll finally learn some information about this place.

"Hmm…five years now? I came here when I was twenty. Pardak's family took me in and well…one thing led to another as you can see." She rubs her swollen stomach, love shining in her eyes.

My heart pangs. I never gave much thought to children and family. I was a late bloomer having been shipped off to the academy at sixteen. Sure, there were men and males in my classes, but I never paid them much mind. And they never paid much attention to me either. We were all so absorbed in our studies that by the time I left at twenty-three I felt behind other people my age and confused when it came to relationships.

Secretly, a small part of me always thought it was too late for me. Foolish, I know. I'm young with plenty of years ahead of me to find some-one and settle down with. But seeing Jessica caress her stomach makes me long for that sort of connection.

But I won't be finding it in this village.

Lady Myren brings over the hot liquid from the stove and instructs us on how to fill up the jars. The base of *Frost Cough* tonic is peppermint and honey, like I smelled earlier. I also smell a dash of ginger root as well. All good for soothing sore throats.

Jessica works beside me, carefully spooning the hot concoction into the labeled containers.

"Did your family come with you?" I ask and Jessica looks at me. A sad expression colors her features.

"Oh no, it was just me." She doesn't say anymore, and I don't push. I understand too well that far off look in her eyes. I've glimpsed it in the mirror a hundred times.

We continue working in silence, but I notice Jessica begins to slow at her task. Her hand isn't as steady and pouring spoonfuls of the elixir becomes a greater effort. Lady Myren notes it too, her eyes always watching us.

"Was there anyone else with you when you came here?" I ask Jessica, lowering my voice. A yawn sneaks up on her and she tries covering it with her hand.

"What do you mean?"

"When you were brought to this village, were any other humans with you? Do you know if they go somewhere else?" Jessica and I are off to the far side of the work bench. Hopefully no one else can overhear our conversation. I know I'm getting ahead of myself but I'm desperate for a lead.

"No, I was found alone. Usually—"

"Jessica," Lady Myren's voice interrupts. She walks over to us, throwing me a stern look. "I think it's best you head home, before you fall asleep and burn yourself with the liquid."

Jessica nods her head, yawning again, before rising to her feet.

"Yes, being this far along I hardly have any energy anymore." Jessica smiles down at me. "It was wonderful to meet you, Kaethe. I hope we will get the chance to chat again."

I smile and tell her I would like that. She quickly retrieves her cloak from the door and heads into the late morning sun. Lady Myren's eyes pin me to my seat from across the room. A few of the other women cast curious looks at me but quickly turn back to their work.

"You are very inquisitive, Kaethe." Her lips are pinched into a thin line, and I try my best to smile but can feel how brittle it is.

"My teachers at the academy said the same thing. It's what advanced my studies."

"But not here," Lady Myren says, adding, "in this village inquisitiveness can be seen as nosiness."

Our eyes lock and my body goes rigid. Godsdamn me I was too obvious with my questions. I overreached and aroused suspicion, which is going to make my life ten times harder than it already is. Lady Myren looks ready to say something else when the front door slams open.

I let out a sigh of relief, but it is short-lived when I hear Lady

Myren call out to the visitor.

"Mornga, it's been a while since you graced us all with your presence."

"I'm not here for you, Myren, I'm here to see this new human."

My skin prickles as I look up and lock eyes with Mornga. Her red stare is unblinking, assessing and frank, the way all dark elves stare. She stomps toward me and I grow more rigid in my seat.

"So, you are the alchemist the dark elves sent us?" she asks. Her long hair drapes around her like a midnight curtain. Her pale gray dress hugs her body and accentuates her slim frame. All elves have a similar build, tall with long limbs. Orcs are as well, but they are more muscular and stout. Only humans seem to come in a wide variety of shapes and sizes.

"Yes," I say, trying to project confidence in my tone.

"Why have you come here?" Her scarlet gaze grows more severe. Perspiration begins to form on my brow and on my palms. I can't be so nervous, surely she can smell it. With a calming breath, I formulate my reply.

"King Arkain wanted to demonstrate how serious he is about peace between the two realms. He sent me here in the hopes that—"

"You are lying."

Breath is stolen from my lungs, my face on fire. The women around me freeze in the middle of their work. Lady Myren's head snaps up. I've been found out. Any moment now she is going to get Bazur and he is going to send me off to Vorgak for execution.

"I . . ." I try formulating some sort of response. "No, it's true."

"Why would your king send us his alchemist? He had to have known how treacherous the journey here is?" She raises a brow. "Unless of course he wanted you dead."

"No, no. King Arkain sent me here to find a way for our two kingdoms to learn from each other."

"Learn what exactly? Alchemy and healing are not high priorities for King Vorgak."

"He sent me here to learn something specific." It is risky to admit this, but it is the only explanation I can think of that will make unsuspecting sense. Mornga waits for me to continue and I swallow. "The king is seeking an antidote for *orcs' teeth poison*. He thought I would be the best candidate to send here because I am the most familiar with it. I have been searching for a cure for him for the last few years."

Mornga purses her lips, as if tasting my answer.

"Then he sent you on a fool's journey. There's no cure for it. Orc's blood carries the antipoison but it cannot be used as an antidote. We've tried," Lady Myren says quietly. Mornga looks over her shoulder and nods. Something softens her red gaze, and her mouth cracks into a wide grin as she turns back to face me.

This answer has passed her test. For now.

"Zarod said you were adorable when you blushed," Mornga says, as if that explains it all. "You can relax. My interrogation is over, for now at least."

I nod, turning back to my task, trying to hide the trembling in my hands.

"I'm sure I don't have to tell you," Mornga says from across the room, "but Bazur has zero tolerance for spies. Even ones that blush adorably."

Just like that, I am on edge again, my stomach flipping as I nod. Mornga and Lady Myren speak to each other in *orcish*. It's disheartening to know everyone here can speak it except me. With time hopefully I can persuade someone to teach me, it's too risky to ask for that now.

Mornga and Lady Myren stop chatting, and Mornga walks over to where I sit at the workbench. She takes the seat across from me and pours some of the elixir into a labeled jar.

"So, tell me about Myrkorvin." Mornga doesn't ask, she demands. There is an air about her that will not be questioned.

"It has changed a lot as of late. King Arkain took Princess Elvie as his wife and mate, she's a light elf. He found her during the Night of a Hundred Faces." Mornga chuckles and shakes her head.

"They still do that?"

I nod. "This was the first one held in quite some time. The bridge is open between the light and the dark elves, and the two people are united once more." We are silent for a moment before I venture a question. "How long has it been since you were last in Myrkorvin?"

"Not since I was a child." Mornga fills another glass jar, her red eyes focused solely on her task. "My mother was a she-elf noble and my father a displaced orc soldier. They met right after the end of the Orc Wars."

I nod, not sure what to say. Her scarlet gaze lifts to me and she smiles slightly.

"It was quite scandalous, but mating bonds can't be denied. No matter how illogical they seem at the time. My mother had me in secret, leaving her noble house once I was born, to live a quiet life with my father on the mountain." Emotion lights a fire in her red eyes. "Dark elves live longer than orcs, so when my father passed, she went with him. I was around sixty at that time and flitted from place to place until I found my way here."

There is a sadness to her words. Even with an immortal life, living through the death of a parent is never easy.

"I'm sorry," I say gently.

"Don't be." Mornga's smile is wistful. "I'm happy they had each other and had such a long life together. They couldn't live without each other. I didn't understand it then, but I do now."

"Because of Zarod?" I ask, though the answer is obvious.

"Yes, because of Zarod. When it is time, I will go with him to join the *Mother of the Mountain*."

Just like earlier with Jessica, something pangs in my chest. That look of love and adoration is so strong I have to turn away.

"Are there any more halflings like you?" I ask. Mornga shakes her head.

"No, in my one-hundred-and-fifty of being alive I've never met another half-dark elf, half-orc before. Humans and orcs are the more common pairings." My unease at that knowledge doesn't escape Mornga's notice.

"Kaethe, you are safe here. Humans are safe here. Whatever stories you have been told about orcs don't apply to the ones here. Not all the stories are true."

I so desperately want to believe that, but I can't let myself. I'm not here to change my outlook on orcs, I'm here to find my brother.

I smile weakly at her.

"Unfortunately, I know first-hand that some of those stories are true."

CHAPTER 10

BAZUR

Aɴᴏᴛʜᴇʀ ᴇᴠᴇɴɪɴɢ ᴍᴇᴀɴs ᴀɴᴏᴛʜᴇʀ ᴜɴʙᴇᴀʀᴀʙʟʏ quiet dinner.

I used to look forward to the silence after spending the whole day shouting and training my soldiers. Dinner was a chance to collect myself, to unwind and relax before getting up to do it all again the next day.

Now, dinner is just half an hour of uncomfortable silence. Sitting in this shared silence unnerves me. Especially since the person sitting across from me is who I spend most of my day thinking about.

Lady Myren reports her movements to me every evening I go to collect her. Beyond being inquisitive and asking the other humans about life here, nothing really stands out. She does her work, keeps to herself, and stays in line.

Kaethe wanting to know the cure to *orc's teeth poison* isn't surprising. It killed the dark elf king's father. If it were me, I'd want to make it so no one else fell victim to it too. It's honorable, the king's desire to avenge his father's death.

My relationship with my own father isn't quite so noble.

Kaethe clears her throat, dragging me from that train of thought.

"I met Mornga today."

I nod, Lady Myren told me she had stopped by, but Kaethe doesn't need to know that.

"How was she?" I ask, slurping down another spoonful of stew. It's weak and watery; I need to get more vegetables before the ground freezes over. I have another person to feed for the rest of winter now.

"She was interesting." Kaethe sets her spoon down. "I've never met a half-dark elf before. Never really met anyone beyond dark elves and humans."

She pauses before continuing.

"Except for Queen Elvie, she's a light elf, but there are more similarities than differences between the two kinds."

I grunt at that as I have no experience with either kind beyond Mornga.

"How did you become friends with the queen?"

Kaethe smiles slightly, her full lips tipping upward.

"I had planted *riverhearts* at the base of this old tree. The king held a ball the night before and some of the party goers stomped right over my seedlings." She looks genuinely devastated. Perhaps where she's from humans have strong affection for their herbs? "Elvie found me upset over them and used her magic to help regrow them. She worked with me every day, helping me regrow plants for my experiments. I think she was avoiding the king in the beginning, but they found their way to each other in the end."

Her cheeks turn the same color as her magenta hair. The reaction confuses me but I don't ask about it.

"We heard he had taken a bride. I was there that day at the Keep when the western scouts emerged from the tunnel carrying a dark elf male. Proclaiming him a peace offering from your king."

Kaethe's eyes widen in shock before she responds. "Wylan was… not a good male. I always steered clear of him. He tried to have King Arkain killed. His treachery almost killed Elvie." Her dark eyes get a far off look in them before speaking softly. "The king loves Elvie very much. Wylan's plot had put her in harm's way, King Arkain wouldn't stand for someone endangering her like that. They are mates after all."

Mates. The word clangs through me. The king of the dark elves found his mate, the other half of his soul. Joined with her in a way that is primal and permanent. Kaethe doesn't say any more and we resume a familiar silence.

Dinner with my mate wouldn't be held in awkward silence, I tell myself.

The love and lust that thread through the mating bond would be instantaneous, like it was for my parents. Like it was for Zarod and Mornga. It would be world altering and immediate. The primal urge inside me would be freed and I would carry my mate off to fuck her for a week straight.

I should not be thinking of fucking when Kaethe is so close. When the worn wool of her pale dress hugs her breasts so perfectly. It makes me itch to see them naked. Makes me contemplate what color her nipples are and how they would fill my mouth perfectly. Those are things I can't think about even as my cock hardens under the kitchen table.

Grunting, I point to a bag Myren gave me when I went to collect Kaethe this evening.

"There are fresh clothes from Lady Myren in there. She noticed you've been wearing the same dress." I liked the way her earthy scent deepened the more she wore it. Growing richer and sweeter over time. My cock pushes painfully against the tie to my breeches.

Mother of the Mountain, spare me.

Kaethe smiles, wrinkling her nose as she looks over toward the bag. "I'll have to thank her tomorrow. Truthfully, I didn't think she liked me all that much."

This confuses me. Lady Myren is the kindest human in the village.

Before I can question this, Kaethe rises from the table. She places her used bowl and spoon beside the sink and collects the bag of clothes on the counter.

"If you'll excuse me, I'm going to bathe."

I suppress my groan as I watch her head for the ladder, her dress showing the subtle curve of her hips, her backside. Something I shouldn't be looking at. Something that is only making my hard cock harder. Especially as my advanced hearing picks up the sound of her shuffling around in the washroom upstairs. I can practically hear her wool gown gliding along her soft skin and the sound it makes as it pools at her feet. My ears twitch at the sound of her light footsteps on the floor as she makes her way into the tub and moans softly as she sinks into the warm water.

I don't even realize I'm biting my lip until my tusks break through the skin, the metallic taste of blood coating my tongue. I need to fuck someone. Badly.

That will surely ease this ache. It has been too long since the last time and living with a female, human or otherwise, is taking a toll on my sanity. But the thought of someone other than Kaethe, with her soft skin and big eyes, underneath me makes my chest hurt. To think it won't be her full lips I kiss, or her breasts bouncing as I pound into her, or her sweet little pussy on my t—

Enough of this!

A tiny voice screams at me and I shake myself, not even realizing my hand has drifted to my cock. I run my palm up the length of it and suppress a groan. It's too risky. Not just with her being so close, but if I make myself come while thinking of her, it will change things.

Which can't happen.

I need to scratch the itch so I can continue viewing Kaethe as a job. A potential spy who has come to infiltrate what I have built here. My hard cock wanes slightly. She is too secretive and no matter how sweet she looks, underneath it all could be a viper ready to poison me.

Kaethe will help Lady Myren through the winter when the *Frost Cough* comes and then she will be gone.

Why does the thought of her leaving make my heart race faster?

A soft splash from above catches my attention. A few minutes later light footsteps pat over to the bed before the lantern upstairs grows dim. I listen to her deep breathing from my seat in the kitchen. I look over to the thin bedroll I've been sleeping on and groan.

This is going to be a very long winter.

CHAPTER 11

KAETHE

I'VE BEEN IN BLACK CLAW Village for just over a week and I am no closer to finding a lead on my brother than when I first arrived.

Jessica is the one I try coaxing information out of the most. Since that first day we met, she has come to help make the *Frost Cough* medicine three times. We work together at the table, and I see her grow a little more comfortable with me each time.

During her last visit, she shared about the life she had before she came here. Her father had died when she was a baby, and her mother had tried her best to keep a roof over their head but she soon fell ill as well. Jessica was sixteen when her mother died. After her mother's death, she worked odd jobs in different towns until a man approached her with a position doing housework.

It was a great distance away, but the pay was unbeatable.

It was also a lie. He stole Jessica, tied her up and put her in the back of a wagon to take her up the mountain. She said she nearly froze to death on the journey. When they arrived at Dread's Keep, Bazur was there and saw what was about to happen to her. He had been able to convince Vorgak to give Jessica to him and Bazur brought her here.

That's it, that's the whole story.

A few of the women, some of the other town healers, tell their stories in similar ways. There was their life before they came to this village and their life here now. Both are tales they are willing to share but *how* they got here is never revealed. Just that Bazur saw them and brought them here. Simple, straightforward.

But none of them can quite meet my eyes when they say it. Lady Myren gets a sharp look on her face whenever one of them even mentions coming here. There is something more to their stories, but I will have to be patient and wait until they let whatever it is slip. If only I could convince one of them to teach me *orcish*. I've picked up a few words here and there but nothing substantial that would clue me in to what they are saying when they whisper to each other and cast glances my way.

Jessica is close to giving birth and said she won't be around much anymore. The temperature has been dropping as the first true frost approaches. Because of this, a lot of the other women have started staying home too to tend to their own patients on their side of the town.

Their absence leaves me and Lady Myren together for endless hours a day in stiff silence. She respects my skills and capabilities, but she has no great fondness for me as a person. Regardless, she has given me some trust this week when she leaves me alone in her home while she collects supplies in town. Obviously these *errands* are tests—ones designed to see if I'll flee.

I don't. And each time she returns I get the sense she's disappointed that I'm still here.

In her absence I have started tending to patients who walk in on my own. Soothing sore stomachs, resetting bones, tending to scraped knees has helped me become more familiar with the orcs and humans who live here. And they are all so kind and grateful to me for helping them.

Most surprising to me is that I haven't been dragged down by an old memory since the one last week.

Although I'm still wary of everyone here, Mornga may have been right: these orcs aren't at all like the ones who attacked my village. That much is evident and my stomach sours thinking about how I categorized them in the same way. In truth, Bazur is the most unpleasant of them all, but even so, he treats me with his own form of kindness. Despite the distrust that shines in his golden eyes.

Bazur. He is the most interesting orc of all.

A week has passed since the start of us sharing a home and we still barely communicate. Sometimes I catch him staring at me, a funny look on his face. One that is quickly replaced with a glare. He still calls me that name, *akorzag*, though it's uttered under his breath. I guess his annoyance with my presence is understandable. Bazur is a young male, unmated I have learned, and he has a human female he can't stand being around living in his home and sleeping in his bed.

Him scurrying off after mealtimes started at the end of our third dinner together. I'd hear the front door close after I had turned out the light and crawled into bed. Where he goes at night, I don't know. But if I had to guess, it is to visit one of the females in town.

I'm not blind to the looks they give him. Human and orc females alike bat their eyelashes and flash demure smiles at him every time he leads me to Lady Myren's.

Bazur can do what he wants with whomever he pleases.

I suppose I should be grateful he doesn't fuck them on the first floor. That would be awkward, and upsetting to some very, *very* small part of me. A part that demands we get a glimpse of him when he's in the bathing pool.

A part that I will ignore the entire time I'm here.

Quite suddenly, the front door blows open, the wind whistling through the house and chilling my back. I'm standing at one of the tall oak bookcases shelving a thick leather bound herbology book. Lady Myren has taken my advice on planting some *riverheart seeds* before the frost hits and has gone into town to retrieve small ceramic bowls, which they grow the best in.

She hasn't been gone very long so I'm surprised she's back already.

"Do you want these cataloged too? Bronwyn dropped them off while you were—"

The sound of large, shuffling footsteps steals my attention from the bookcase. The glass jar of seeds I'm holding almost slips from my hand as I take in the sight before me. Lady Myren isn't back. It's Bazur. His massive frame is leaning against the doorway and his large hand is pressed against his side, a crimson stain soaking through his wool shirt. His dark hair has escaped from the leather strap at the base of his neck and clings to his sweaty forehead.

"Oh my gods," I cry, hurrying to him. "What happened?"

He winces as I sling his arm over my shoulders. Bazur is heavy, too heavy. Trying to support his weight is near impossible. Together we shuffle to the nearest cot. As gently as I can, I sit him on the edge while I assess the damage.

"Training." His response is barely more than a grunt. I collect the necessary supplies to treat the injury: Lady Myren's antiseptic, clean cloth to bind the wound, and a needle and thread are all placed on a clean tray that I take over to Bazur. The amount of bleeding alone tells me it will need a stitch.

"Why didn't you have someone send for me?" My face heats and I distract myself by pulling up a stool. "I mean Lady Myren. You may have agitated the wound by walking all the way over here."

"It's just a scratch," he says, and I can't help but roll my eyes.

"Well, I need to see this *scratch*." Reaching for a pair of scissors I gently cut along the side of his shirt. My mouth goes dry. His injury is gruesome to be sure but that's not what my eyes linger on. He's so…burly. Hard muscles stack on top of each other under tough, green skin. There are raised scars along his abdomen and along his pectoral muscles. How many ab muscles does he have? Eight? That's an obscene amount.

Totally medically unnecessary if he wants my expert opinion.

My fingers itch to trace them, to lick them, to feel them press into the softest parts of me. His scent tickles my nose and my thighs grow damp.

I took his shirt off for a reason. What was it?

"Kaethe," Bazur bites out my name and my eyes flutter shut. My face is burning with fire. Be a professional. He is a patient. Nothing more. This is a male body. I've seen the male body. Many, many times. Bones, skin, muscle, and tissue.

"Sorry, your heinous wound gave me pause." This time he rolls his eyes, but I notice them dip to my mouth as I speak. That does nothing but make more heat curl in my stomach.

Taking a clean cloth soaked in antiseptic, I knock his hand away and press it against the open wound.

He barely winces as I clean the gash. After a few moments the bleeding stops long enough for me to begin stitching. Orc skin is thick, tougher than human or elf skin so it requires a special needle. I pierce through his green flesh and sew it back together as quickly as possible. Again, Bazur gives very little reaction.

"The scar from this will be prominent," I explain, trying to keep my mind on my task and not on his muscles.

"I've had worse before," he says, using his free hand to gesture towards his face. Thankfully the wound was deep but not long. I sew the final bit of skin together and slice and snip the thread, before securing it in a knot.

"This'll add to your whole *battle-hardened-warrior* look you have going on," I say, wiping my hands off on a clean cloth. Bazur lowers his brow, appraising me from head to toe.

"Was that—were you making a joke?" he asks quietly. He's so serious, so literal. That alone makes me chuckle softly.

"Yes," I say.

Bazur smiles slightly at my laugh, his tusks pressing into his upper lip. He should do that more often, it's a pleasant expression. I would die before I suggest such a thing to him. Besides, he'd probably think it was some poorly executed seduction tactic to get him to lower his guard long enough for me to make off with the great secrets of this town.

Or whatever he thinks I'm here to spy on.

"You are good at jokes," he states, wincing slightly as I help him sit up. "Zarod has always been better at them than me. Better at recognizing them too."

"You're funny in your own way," I say, placing a bandage at the wound and reaching around his midsection to secure it. It is quite the feat, given how bulky he is. My cheek presses against his side as I secure his dressing. I try not to breathe in too deeply, acutely aware of my breasts pillowing up along his side.

Is it my imagination or is he more rigid than usual? It's undoubtedly my imagination. He's shown me no interest in that way. Not that I want him showing me interest in that—it would needlessly complicate things and fighting off romantic advances is not something I've ever had to worry about. Having that become a problem here and now would hinder my mission. And I already feel like I am falling behind on that front.

"I don't think a female has ever called me funny before."

"I wonder why that is."

"It's because—you're joking?" Bazur asks. I nod, wrapping the bandage around him one final time and securing it in place with a fastening. "You confuse me, Kaethe."

The hairs on the back of my neck stand up when he says my name.

"You confuse me too, Bazur," I confess. We're so close to each other. Closer than we've been since sharing a saddle. I can feel his warm breath ghost over my face. I watch his eyes dip to my mouth again before snapping back up to my eyes as if he were embarrassed. "Is that why you think I'm annoying?"

His eyes widen. "I don't think—"

The front door opens and Lady Myren walks in. I am grateful for the interruption. Why would I ask that? I don't care what he thinks about me. Do I? This is why I don't like being around him. He distracts me from my mission, and I can't allow that.

Lady Myren lets out a gasp and I spring back from Bazur, standing off to the side of the cot as she rushes over. A bag of plants and herbs lay forgotten in the entry way as she takes in the scene.

Bloody shirt, bloody sheet. Her eyes snap over to me, wild with anger.

"What happened? Why didn't you come and get me from the market?"

"I—"

The way she is inspecting his injury is almost *accusatory*. Like I'm the one who hurt him. She starts asking him questions in *orcish*. She says a word I've overheard her and Mornga use when they talk about Bazur.

Bazur shakes his head and rises from the cot.

"I'm fine, Lady Myren. Kaethe stitched me up."

Lady Myren eyes me once more and looks like she wants to argue. She swallows whatever reply she wants to give and walks over to the shelves. She pulls out a large jar of brown liquid and hands it to Bazur.

"Drink this twice a day for the next five days. It will kill anything that could cause the wound to fester."

I roll my eyes at her obvious attempt to accuse me of not cleaning his wound properly. Even if issuing that tonic is a good idea.

Bazur nods and Lady Myren finally relaxes.

"You better take him home; he'll need to rest. And take these. His dressings will need to be changed twice a day." She hands me a stack of cloth and a whole bottle of antiseptic. Way more than necessary, but I don't argue. I stuff it all into my bag and collect my cloak. I sling Bazur's arm over my shoulder, bracing my feet to absorb his weight. He's so warm, I don't mind the weight because he'll block most of the cold wind as we make our way back to his house.

"Remember, twice a day!" Lady Myren calls to us as we make our way down the snow-covered street.

The walk takes us twice as long, but eventually we make it up the stairs and into his house. The inside is cold and dark. I deposit him on the chair before lighting a log to start a fire. As I make my way back into the kitchen, I notice the limp bedroll on the ground.

He can't sleep on that, not with fresh stitches. He'll rip them open.

"You sleep in the bed while your side heals." Bazur's head snaps up at me. The shocked look in his eyes makes me avert his gaze. "I'll sleep down here."

There is a beat of silence and then Bazur shakes his head. "No."

"You'll tear your stitches lying on the floor," I explain.

"Then you're sleeping in the bed with me."

My mouth falls open.

"Why?"

"I still don't trust you, Kaethe. I still don't trust that if I give you the freedom to make a run for it, you won't." He rises from the table, grunting slightly, and turns toward the stove.

"Why don't you trust me? Lady Myren's been leaving me alone during the day and I haven't once tried to escape."

"I'll trust you when you tell me why you're really here." His golden eyes bore into mine. The hard set of his stubbled jaw is unflinching. I cross my arms over my chest and meet his glare with one of my own.

"Why? So, you can kill me? Is that what you've been waiting for? Me to fuck up so you finally have an excuse to kill me?"

Bazur's head rears back as if I smacked him. Whether it's my use of foul language or my blatant accusation I don't know, but how dare he act shocked. How dare he act offended by my outburst when all he does is suspect me.

Maybe I lied about my purpose here initially, but I'm not a threat to anyone. I would never hurt these people. If he can't see that then I don't need to explain myself to him.

"You're trying to distract me," he says, turning back to the stove.

If he wants to be obstinate, fine. Two can play this game.

But as much as he annoys me, as much as I want him to be uncomfortable and suffering down here on the bedroll, Myren will kill me if she finds out I let him sleep on the floor. She's the last person I want to feel the ire of.

"We will share the bed," I announce, dropping into the kitchen chair. "So you can rest assured I will not make off like some spy in the night."

I've faced distrust since I've stepped foot in this village. From my first moments walking through the doors, to the women who came to help at Lady Myren's. I understand their wariness. I'm from a different kingdom. I ask them questions but offer very little about myself. It's understandable they'd be apprehensive toward me. And as much as it annoys me, Bazur is right: I am keeping secrets. They won't hurt him or his people, but I can't explain that to him.

He sits another meager bowl of stew down in front of me and I spoon the thin liquid into my mouth. There is one thing I don't understand as I look over at Bazur digging into his own dinner: why does his distrust hurt worse than theirs?

CHAPTER 12

BAZUR

Sharing a bed with Kaethe is a mistake.

I have missed my sheets, my pillows, my mattress and despite it being a hundred times better than the bedroll downstairs, I knew it was a mistake as soon as I slid under the sheets. I'm enjoying the way Kaethe's scent is mixing with my own.

Her smell arouses dangerous thoughts again. Thoughts that are causing my cock to stiffen under the sheets.

Luckily, she's turned on her other side, awake but pretending to be asleep. I know she's still seething over my comment about not trusting her. Why should I trust her? Everything about her is a contradiction. A contradiction that, if it was just me, Bazur, a simple orc without a village to look after, I would happily ignore if it meant getting her naked and sweating underneath me.

It's not that simple for me. No matter how much I want to trust her, I can't risk it. She's been here a week and I still know very little about her. She doesn't share much about herself, even to the other human women. And from what Lady Myren says, she's more interested in asking the other humans where they're from then sharing her own experiences.

Is it just pleasantries? A way to connect with the humans here? Or is it something more dangerous? If she truly has questions about this place, she should ask me. Does she not know that?

I glance over beside me to her hunched form. Even in the dark I can make out her stiff shoulders as she faces away from me. Her long mane of pink hair spreads out on the pillow beneath her head. The roots of her hair are darker, the same shade as her eyebrows. Interesting.

"I know you're awake," I say, watching her shoulders tighten even more.

"You should be asleep."

Her voice is quiet in the dim room. The moon from the skylight illuminates us in pale blue light.

"It shouldn't be a shock that I don't trust you. You don't trust me."

Her shoulders slump a little bit. I watch her small fingers play with a loose thread on the wool blanket.

"I have my reasons," she says quietly.

"I have mine too." I don't have to see her to know she's rolling her eyes.

"Then perhaps we will remain at an impasse until I leave in the summer."

My muscles tense. The thought of her leaving, of watching her walk through the oak doors of my village knowing she's never coming back, unsettles me.

It shouldn't; her leaving is inevitable.

The bed shifts slightly as she rolls onto her back and then on to her side to face me. I have to look away as the low neckline of her nightgown shows the ample swells of her breasts. My cock is hard, but she doesn't need to know that.

It's been hard since she emerged from the washroom. Dressed only in that thin shift of hers, her nipples pebbling against the front of it. In the dark, the material was so thin I had to tear my eyes away from the shadowy place between her thighs as she climbed in beside me. Kaethe's body is perfect, from the soft slope of her belly to her wide hips that beg me to grab them. I'm always thinking about it.

Then there's her voice. While we barely speak, the conversations we have replay in my head. Every word that passes through her pink lips, every expression flits through my mind on repeat.

Everything about her is tempting.

I'd think she was sent to torment me and lure me to my doom by using her body and her voice if she didn't seem so shy half the time. Surely she knows what she looks like. Surely she notices the stares human men and orc males give her as we make our way down the road. Surely she notices the stares *I* give her and understands what they mean.

It was true what I said at Lady Myren's: she does confuse me. She intrigues me, but all of that must be set aside. I can't risk being blindsided by her. I owe it to my people.

"Don't you think," she says, interrupting my thoughts, "that if I wanted you dead, I would've let you bleed out earlier today?"

"You don't have to want me dead to be a spy."

She huffs out a humorless laugh and begins to turn back over. A piece of her pink hair tickles my arm and without thinking I grab it. The soft strands snag on the calluses of my thumb.

"What are you doing?" she asks, eyeing me nervously.

"Why is your hair this color? I've never seen it before."

She turns back to look at me, and I let the strand of hair drop. I roll onto my good side and look into her dark, brown eyes, flecked with gold and green. Her scent fills my lungs, so earthy and sweet.

"I color it with *darksky roses*." Her nose crinkles as if she is remembering something unpleasant. "Though, I haven't seen any since I've been here. I don't know how I'll maintain it if I can't find any."

"Why?" I quickly ask. This is the most we've ever talked and I'm eager—no greedy—for more information about her.

"I don't know. A way to stand out maybe?" She shakes her head, her small hands twisting into the blanket. "I did it shortly after I graduated from the academy. I just felt so different from everyone else around me, I wanted to reflect how I felt inside on the outside."

She giggles softly, wrinkling her small nose again.

"Maybe I was just tired of looking boring and unremarkable."

I lower my brows at that statement.

"There's nothing unremarkable about you."

Kaethe is many things. Obstinate, difficult, secretive, a pain in my ass…beautiful in a way that makes me angry. Angry because my brain tells me to be wary of her, but my body wants nothing more than to hold her close. Someone unremarkable wouldn't have the power to do that to me.

"Tell that to human men," she says. "The last time one showed me any interest, I was ten. He kissed me under an old oak tree and then ran off, never to be seen again." Kaethe smiles slightly in the dark, an emotion passing in her dark eyes.

I want to tell her no males or men are worthy of her. That if they can't see how appealing she is then the problem is with them. There are so many things I want to say but none of them would be wise.

"Human men are idiots." It's the only response I can think of.

"They are," she agrees, her hand resting under her head on the pillow. "But I think before I didn't want anyone to take notice of me. I was hiding. But now I'm finally ready. I want to be seen."

I see you, even when my eyes are closed. I silently curse at myself. What would confessing that solve? Kaethe is here to help during winter. Whatever her motives for coming here, it's obvious it's not out of a great fondness for my kind. When summer comes, she will go and with time I will forget about her and she will forget about me.

It is for the best.

Silence stretches between us before Kaethe breaks it.

"What does *prognazoc* mean?"

My whole body tenses. Ice gathers in my veins and my palms turn sweaty.

"Where did you hear that?" I grit through my teeth.

"Lady Myren always uses it when she speaks about you to the other women. Especially when she chats to Mornga…" she trails off, noting my rigid posture. "Is that your word for general?"

I grunt, not trusting what I would say. She's picking up our language. I'll have to warn Lady Myren to be careful with the words she uses around her. Glancing down at Kaethe's soft face I see more questions dancing in her eyes.

Questions I'm not willing to answer.

"You should go to sleep; the morning will come soon." I turn away from her to lie on my back and stare at the ceiling. Closing my eyes, I hear the bed creak as she also turns away. When her breathing begins to deepen, I let out a sigh.

Prognazoc. She is an observant one. I hate lying to her. It doesn't sit right with me, but I'd rather lie than admit that word means prince.

CHAPTER 13

KAETHE

I CLEAN BAZUR'S WOUND THE NEXT morning before we set off for Lady Myren's.

As we make our way through the snow-covered streets there's something different in the air. A shift has taken place over the night between Bazur and I. The distrust is still present from both sides but there's a closeness now too. A tentative understanding that wasn't there when we took this routine commute yesterday.

There's nothing unremarkable about you.

That sentence rings in my ears as he drops me off. What did he mean by that? What did I want him to mean by that? Why did I turn even more slippery between my thighs when I glimpsed his muscles yesterday? My lack of experience with men and males once again makes me unsure. He probably was just being polite. I was oversharing and he was uncomfortable.

Something tells me that's not it. I caught him looking at me several times throughout the morning. First, while he pulled his dark hair away from his face. Then again at breakfast before he tucked into his meal of broth and bread. And now, as we make our way down the road I can feel his eyes on me, taking in my face, even my body. Before, his staring annoyed me but now I find I rather enjoy it. It makes my stomach tingle in an odd yet not wholly unpleasant way.

We make it to Lady Myren's house, typically this is where Bazur growls his *I'll-pick-you-up-this-evening-don't-try-anything* speech but he's strangely quiet. I turn and crane my neck to look up at him, the morning sun illuminating his hard face. There's something pleasant about it. He's not handsome, not in a classical sense, but the hard set of his jaw covered by a short, dark beard does something to me. His tusks, deadly and sharp, don't seem so threatening to me anymore. Even with the knives and swords strapped to his hip, I don't fear him.

Now that I think about it, I've never feared him.

We stare at each other for another moment. Whatever this change is that happened last night makes us both uncomfortable. It is unsettling as much as it is intriguing. I wonder if Bazur feels the same.

I gesture at his injured side to break the silence.

"Take it easy today. If you rip open your stitches, I won't be happy." I narrow my eyes in mock-sternness. "More importantly, Lady Myren won't be happy."

"I wouldn't mind having you stitch me up again." The skin under his eyes turns a darker green and . . . oh gods is he blushing? My lips tip into a small smile. His face hardens in an instant. "I just mean you have gentle hands."

I nod, my own cheeks warming, not trusting the words that would come out of my mouth.

Bazur shakes himself slightly, strands of black hair escaping his tie.

"I will collect you this evening. Don't—"

"Try anything and listen to Lady Myren," I finish for him, rolling my eyes. He lowers his dark brows and tips his head to the side.

"You have a bad habit of interrupting me." My mouth falls open at his serious expression. Before I can stop myself a laugh bubbles out of me. Bazur offers his own small smile.

"Did you just make a joke?"

"If I have to explain it was a joke, it obviously isn't very funny."

I smile and bite my lip.

"Okay, now you're just mocking me," I say, crossing my arms over my chest. I'm still smiling. Bazur's face grows serious, returning to its stony frown.

"No, I'm not, I wouldn't—"

"Bazur," I stop him and reach out to touch his arm. "I know you weren't actually mocking me. It was funny, your joke. With some time, you may actually become good at them."

"I doubt that."

We both stand smiling at each other. That is until we both realize I'm still touching his arm. It is the first time I've touched him when it wasn't necessary. We stare at my hand on his forearm, so small in comparison.

I drop my hand and look away, my face warming once again. Bazur clears his throat and I hear his feet turn in the snow. Is it just me or does it seem like he can't get away from me fast enough? Males are so confusing.

Or maybe that's just Bazur.

"I'll see you tonight," he calls over his shoulder. I turn myself and stomp up Lady Myren's front steps. Something makes me pause and look back. Bazur is much larger than everyone else, so spotting him is easy. He cuts through the crowd of villagers, and each one nods a greeting at him as he makes his way to the training yard all alone.

This new comfortability between us is confusing but it could be useful. If we can form some sort of mutual respect, he could help with my mission to find my brother. The more he trusts me the more freedom I will have.

There is nothing to our relationship beyond that, there can't be.

At least that's what I tell myself as I push into Lady Myren's house and hang my cloak by the front door. Lady Myren is sitting at the work-table, a steaming cup of peppermint tea beside her. A fire is roaring and I soak in the warmth before joining her at the table.

"Good morning," I say. She nods at me, looking up from her book.

"There are more seeds that need to be cataloged this morning. Then, we'll make some more elixirs for *Frost Cough*."

I pull the tray of unmarked seeds towards me as well as the large leather-bound cataloging book. Another day of tedious work. None of the other human women are coming until later this week so my quest for information about this place will be halted until then.

I had just cracked open the book and grabbed the first jar of unmarked seeds when the front door slammed open. Expecting it to be someone needing some healing I barely look up. But then I hear breaking glass. My head jerks up. Lady Myren's face is as white as a sheet, and the cup of tea she was drinking was in shards on the floor.

I look toward the door and see a young woman standing aghast in the doorway. I recognize her as one of the other healers in town who helped make tonics. Her dark curly hair is pulled back from her face with a scarf. She's wearing a gray dress with a white smock. And it is covered in blood.

"It's—it's Jessica." Her voice is shaky. Both Lady Myren and I rise at the same time. "Her baby, it's stuck. It's—"

"Kaethe, grab as much clean cloth as you can carry. Antiseptic and clean thread too. We don't have much time." Lady Myren's voice is quiet, but I move quickly. I package up everything we could need to assist with a birth. I stuff a bag with linen cloths, numbing herbs, and a few sharp knives that Lady Myren keeps for bloodletting.

When both of us are packed, we follow the other healer down the snowy street. I've never been this way before. We pass several shops and vendors selling the last of winter's harvests. A few passersby take one look at us, at the blood on the midwife's apron, and their faces pale. Moving quickly down the road, my boots crunch loudly on the snow and the hem of my dress is soaked.

The butcher's looms up ahead, an old wooden sign proclaiming it as such, with a closed sign hanging in the front window. We follow the woman through the front and enter the cold butcher's shop. There are a few rows of fresh meat laid out behind glass panels and I can see a carcass hanging in the backroom that still needs to be carved up. It's eerily quiet as we enter.

Until a scream pierces the air and the three of us look up the old stairs in front of us.

"Quickly, this way," the healer says, our feet creaking on the steps.

"How long has she been in labor?" Lady Myren asks.

"A few hours. She called for me just after dawn."

We make our way to the second level of the butcher's shop and barge into chaos. There are four other healers here. Two of them are kneeling at the foot of the bed wearing identical white smocks smeared with blood. One of them is steeping herbs in a bowl of water, while the other soaks clean cloth in the concoction.

Old sheets cover the wooden floor and the bed has been stripped of blankets and pillows. In the center of it is Jessica, sweating, her red hair braided down her back with stray pieces plastered to her forehead. At her side is her mate, Pardak, his own green skin pale as he holds her hand and rubs her back. His eyes meet mine and his look of despair and desperation makes my knees buckle.

Whatever the situation is, it's clearly not good.

"Have you given her something for the pain?" Lady Myren asks, setting down her bag and getting out fresh supplies. I do the same, unpacking my own linens and finding a clean tray to put the knives and herbs on.

"Yes," says one of the midwives on the floor. "The baby is breech. We've tried turning it but it's stuck."

The bowls of water on the floor are pink in color. This much blood isn't unusual but if the baby isn't delivered soon, it could prove fatal. Pardak kisses Jessica's forehead and whispers something in her ear. Jessica's kind face is twisted in pain, her chest heaving.

"Is this," Lady Myren pauses, "is this like the others?"

The others?

The midwife on the floor nods, her face grave. "Yes."

"Please," Jessica wails. "Please, I just want my baby."

Leaning down with the other midwives I assess the problem. Jessica is dilated as much as a human can be, and leaning in closer I can just glimpse one pale green foot. Much larger than a human baby's foot should be and therein lies the problem here. Jessica is too small to deliver a half-orc child naturally. They all must know that! It is a strange practice to even try this approach in the first place.

"You need to push Jessica," Lady Myren says. "Lest you both die."

Jessica does indeed push but it's of no use. Tears run down her cheeks as she uses all her strength to force her child through the birth canal. Her moans echo through the room, and her blue eyes are wild as they land on me. I don't think she even knows I'm here.

This is madness, there's no need for all this pain. In Myrkrovin this would've already been dealt with at the first sign of the baby being in the improper position for delivery.

I watch Lady Myren retrieve one of her own sharp knives. I breathe a sigh of relief. Except I seem to be the only one as everyone's faces pale. The midwives between Jessica's legs lift them up and lock them into a bent position, leaving her completely exposed.

That's not at all the proper positioning to accomplish. . .

Lady Myren isn't about to perform the birth technique that I was trained in at the Royal Academy. I know this to be true when I watch her kneel between Jessica's legs, knife angled to slice through her there.

"Wait!" I shout. Lady Myren freezes with her knife centimeters away from flesh, and all heads whip toward me. "What are you doing! You can cut the baby from her."

"I just want my baby," Jessica cries. "I don't need anymore, please just let me have this one. Please!" Tears roll down her cheeks and Pardak whispers something to her again.

"That's what we are doing, Kaethe. Now bring more sheets, the blood will come fast."

"No, you need to cut the baby from her stomach."

Shocked cries erupt in the room adding to my confusion even more. Pardak's eyes harden as he looks at me.

"We," Lady Myren growls, "do not kill women in this village."

Kill women? This saves women.

That's when it hits me. They don't know the method used in Myrkorvin. I rush over to Lady Myren and kneel beside her with my tray of supplies, grabbing her hand and pulling the knife away from Jessica before she can make contact. Lady Myren's green eyes blaze with fire as she rips her hand from my grip.

"Listen to me," I say carefully, "there is a way to cut the baby from her stomach that will not kill her. In Myrkorivn, this problem is common. Dark elf males are much larger than their females, therefore their offspring do not always fit through the birth canal. Especially when the baby is breech. They solved this issue over a century ago."

"Myren we need to act now—" I hold up a hand at one of the midwives. I am the expert here, not them. If they don't listen to me Jessica could very well die. Or be left in unnecessary pain for the rest of her life.

"We need to give her these." I pluck a few white oak seeds from my tray and place them in a jar with hot water.

"Those are poisonous to children in the womb," Lady Myren spits. I grit my teeth.

"The baby isn't staying in the womb. This will slow down her heart, slow down her blood flow enough for me to make the incision, remove the child, and sew her up without her bleeding out." I gesture around the room. "She's already lost a lot of blood, so we have to move fast."

"I'm not sure that—"

"We don't have time for this!" I snap at her. I'm done with her questioning. Every moment that passes is precious. "Your method will end in death for the mother or the child. At the very least, you will damage Jessica in a way that cannot be undone."

"Please Kaethe," Jessica murmurs from the bed. "Please save my child."

I look at Lady Myren and she nods once. That's all the approval I need. I spring into action, handing the jar with the steeped seeds to Pardak.

"Make sure she drinks this, all of this."

He nods and tips the glass to Jessica's lips, watching as she consumes every last drop. While I wait for the medicine to start working, I shove back the sleeves of my dress and scrub my hands and fingernails in warm water with soap. Next I douse my hands and forearms in antiseptic and pluck the tools I need from the tray. I grind a paste together of numbing herbs that will numb the area of incision and help protect the wound from infection.

"Lie her on her back. And get a sheet to cover her lower half, she won't want to see this." The midwives and Lady Myren move as a unit. Jessica moans a little at the discomfort, but they prop her back with a pillow as she lies on the bed. A fresh sheet is hoisted over her lower half.

"Heat up a knife, I'll need it to stop any internal bleeding once the baby is out."

I peel up Jessica's sweat-stained nightgown and take in her pale, freckled stomach. My hand with the knife is steady. Lady Myren comes to my side, holding fresh cloths and warm water. Truth be told I am nervous, it has been a while since I performed this procedure. But I can't let Jessica suffer, not when I can help her.

"Try and keep her still as best you can. Once I remove the baby, I will need to act fast to get the incision sewn back up." The healer who collected Lady Myren and I stands with a needle and thread on a tray in her hands. I nod at her and at Lady Myren.

With a prayer to the gods, I sink my knife into Jessica's lower stomach and begin. The crimson color is such a sharp contrast to Jessica's fair skin and blood oozes from the wound as Lady Myren wordlessly wipes it away. I find myself succumbing to muscle memory once more. My mind is blank, focused squarely on the task at hand. I recalled where my instructor had placed his hands, where to check for bleeding, where to cut to make this as efficient as possible.

I barely register what I am doing as I cut through layers of skin and muscle. I make sure to avoid her protective organs and it's not long before I see it. With another gentle slice I cut through the last barrier separating me and the child in her womb. I don't register what I'm sticking my hand in—if I do my knees will fail me. I feel for the child's leg and I grip it gently, pulling it through the incision.

After cutting it free from the cord and removing the afterbirth, I hand the child to one of the midwives. There are things I'm willingly not registering as I go about the last steps in this procedure, especially as I am handed the hot knife to seal the wounds. The smell of burning flesh should swamp me with old, horrible memories but it doesn't. I'm too focused on getting this done.

My mind isn't registering anything beyond the next task. The next step to finalize this procedure. The ringing in my ears drowns out all other sounds around me. The world is a blur, what my hands are doing is a blur, but somehow I know everything is going right. By the time I realize what's going on around me, I'm finishing the last stitch of Jessica's incision and smearing it with antiseptic.

A baby's wail reaches my ears and suddenly I'm sucked back into the room with everyone else.

Pulling her shift back down, I motion for them to lower the sheet. Their baby, a small half-orc male, has a good set of lungs. He cries with gusto as he takes in his surroundings. He's wrapped in Jessica's arms, and she coos at him softly as Pardak, still a little pale, kisses her forehead and tickles his son's cheek. Lady Myren hands me a cloth to wipe my hands and I nod at her in thanks.

Jessica and Pardak's eyes find mine, shining with so much gratitude.

"Kaethe, thank you doesn't seem to be sufficient enough for what you've done for us," Jessica says softly, tears shining in her blue eyes. My smile is small, and I nod my head.

"The incision will scar, no way to avoid it, I'm afraid," I explain, gesturing toward her lower stomach. "But it shouldn't be a problem if you want to have more children."

Jessica and Pardak's heads snap up, as does everyone else's in the room.

"More children?" The words tumble from Jessica's lips. My brows lower.

"Yes, we can use the same incision sight a few times but if you want to have more than four, we may have to open a new one. The scar tissue can be hard to cut through."

Jessica begins to cry softly, a wide smile gracing her lips.

"Thank you, Kaethe, thank you, thank you, thank you." I nod, feeling like I'm missing something. In fact, I know I'm not understanding the full scope of this situation when Pardak rises and walks toward me. There's so much respect and adoration in his eyes. So much hope that it should make me uncomfortable, but I don't balk from it. I don't balk when he places a warm hand on my shoulder, either.

"You saved my mate's life. My child's life. I owe you a debt."

"It was nothing, I'm just happy I could help."

He squeezes my shoulder again, his yellow eyes soft. He makes his way back to the bed and gathers Jessica and their baby to his side. I advise Jessica on wound care and one of the healers says she'll check in on the incision later today.

As Lady Myren and I make our way from the bedroom, my shoulder is patted, and many thanks are given by those we pass. In truth, I'm still a little high on adrenaline and don't really grasp what's going on around me. It isn't long before we are back at Lady Myren's house and I collapse in a chair by the fire.

My energy leaves me in a rush and now all I am is tired.

"Would you like tea?" Lady Myren asks from the stove.

"Yes, thank you." My voice is scratchy. A warm cup is placed in my hand and I take a sip of the hot liquid. Lady Myren and I both stare at the fire, the flames licking the side of the hearth, snapping and popping every few seconds. The silence is welcome after all we just went through.

"What you did today was a miracle," Lady Myren says after a while. "It has changed everything."

I shake my head while taking another sip of peppermint tea.

"It was science and training. I can teach some of the other midwives the procedure while I'm here." Lady Myren shakes her head, staring into the fire for a long moment.

"It was a miracle."

I have nothing to say so I take another sip of my tea. I think we will remain in our usual silence together, but she surprises me when she continues.

"Human women who mate with orcs are given one chance to have a child." Lady Myren's voice is barely above a whisper. It is laced with such devastation I have no choice but to turn and look at her. "The size difference between mother and child makes it so that either the mother dies in labor, and we save the baby after she bleeds out, or we make cuts that damage the birth canal beyond hope of her having another."

Lady Myren's eyes return to mine and for the first time since I met her, she actually smiles at me. "I wish you'd been here when I gave birth to my son."

It all clicks. The devastation on the women's faces today when they asked if Jessica was like the others. The blood, telling her to keep pushing…how many women have they lost here? How many orc males have children with no mothers? There're so many children of all kinds, but now that I think about it, I've never seen a human and orc pair with more than one child. Now I know.

My chest tightens as understanding dawns on me.

"Targoc is your only child then?" I ask softly and she smiles wistfully.

"Yes, what happened to me in my childbed is what would've happened to Jessica." Lady Myren reaches out and lays her hand on mine. Her long fingers curl around my palm and she gives it a gentle squeeze. "Thank you, Kaethe, for what you've brought to our village. We are lucky to have you."

My heart tightens and my own smile is watery. This would be the time to ask more information about the humans and where they come from. To seize this opportunity when Lady Myren feels grateful toward me. Perhaps grateful enough to not report my questions to Bazur.

But as I sit there, her hand cupping mine, I find I don't want to ask. Not today. Today I was Kaethe, the healer. Someone with no secrets and no agenda, just there to help others in her village. Tomorrow I will refocus on my mission, but today I need rest.

We stay like that in front of the fire for a few minutes, the warmth from it making my eyelids droop. Lady Myren squeezes my hand one more time and takes my teacup from me.

"You're exhausted. Why don't you head home for the day? We can pick up tomorrow."

I yawn as I rise from the chair, nodding at her, and putting on my cloak. So many things have happened in the last day. If I felt changed from my conversation last night with Bazur in bed, now I feel like a completely different person. Who I was when he dropped me off is not who I will be when he gets home.

My feet crunch along the icy path as I stagger back to his house.

It's chilly inside when I arrive but I don't even bother with a fire. I'm half delirious as I climb up the rungs of the ladder, solely focused on getting under those warm sheets. I shed my dirty clothes and shoes until I am just in my shift and slip beneath the blankets.

I am asleep the moment my head hits the pillow.

CHAPTER 14

KAETHE

IT IS DARK WHEN I finally open my eyes.

Loud footsteps from below wake me from a dreamless sleep and I know Bazur is home. I stretch my stiff arms and rise from the bed. My stomach growls and I think this is the first time I've eagerly been awaiting a bowl of Bazur's weak stew.

The stew smells better than it ever has; perhaps he finally took my suggestion to start seasoning it.

I take a blanket from the bed, wrap it around myself, and make my way down the ladder and into the warm kitchen. The light from the fireplace illuminates the space and my eyes catch on the baskets littering the kitchen table. Dozens of them heaped with meats and cheeses, fruits and vegetables, things I haven't seen in weeks.

"Where did all of this come from?" I ask. Bazur spins around from the stove, his eyes widening. We stare at each other for a moment. The weight of his stare has my heart beating faster in my chest. I break it and walk over to the table and sift through a basket of apples. Their red and green skin is waxy and smooth.

"They're for you." My eyes lift to him once more. "I heard what you did for Jessica and Pardak today. The whole village is talking about it. Being able to have more than one child? It's changed everything for my people."

His stare is heavy again, weighing me down until I sink into the kitchen chair. His eyes trace over me, from my hair to my nose, and linger on my lips. A shiver passes through me and Bazur turns back to the stove, continuing to cook something in a pan.

"This is," I say, picking up another basket filled with fresh bread, "really too kind of them."

"No, it's not. I don't think you understand what you've done."

He's right, I don't understand how this changes things here. I was happy to help Jessica, relieved to save her and her baby. To give her and Pardak the ability to have more children. I remember Lady Myren's face as she told me Targoc was her one and only son. The love in her eyes was so strong but there was sadness there too. Bazur's right: I have changed everything for them.

That idea alone threatens to overwhelm me, and I push the basket aside.

"Is it safe to assume you're an only child as well?" I ask softly. Bazur looks over his shoulder at me before nodding once. He turns back to the stove and we sit in silence, however it's not uncomfortable.

"My case isn't like the others. My mother was an orc. Orc females tend to have better luck then the human women do when it comes to having children."

"Where is your mother now?" I ask. Bazur freezes, his great shoulders hunching over the steam rising from the pan. Just when I think he won't tell me, he does.

"She went to the *Mother of the Mountain* almost twenty years ago."

"I'm sorry," I say. Bazur only grunts as he reaches for a clay plate next him.

"What about your mother, Kaethe?" Bazur asks. I pause for a moment wondering if this is another test. However, just like earlier I don't have it in me to lie today. There's such a genuine quality to his voice that it pulls the truth from my lips.

"She's passed as well."

"Childbirth?" he asks but I shake my head.

"No, she was killed when I was young."

"Your father? Is he still alive?"

"No, he was killed the same night."

"I'm sorry about that, Kaethe. Truly." All I can do is nod as we resume our silence. It's not stew he's preparing tonight; a decadent smell lingers in the air while something continues to sizzle in a pan. "Do you know who killed them?"

I should lie to him, but for some reason, I want him to know. Perhaps it is the grogginess I feel from the day but I want to tell him more about me. So that maybe, finally, he'll understand. Perhaps the truth will take me further with him than a lie ever could.

"Our village was attacked one night. Raiders killed them."

Bazur turns from the stove with a steaming plate in his hand, cooked vegetables and rich sauce coat a large piece of meat. It makes my mouth water as he deposits the food in front of me. There's even a warm roll on the side of the plate. His eyes are soft, gentle, as he nods at what I've just said.

"Humans can be cruel, even to their own kind." He picks up the empty plate beside me. His gaze on my face is so open and honest. An emotion I rarely see grace his rugged features. It's so brutally beautiful that I can't help but let a little more truth slip out.

"Orcs killed my family, Bazur."

A loud shattering sound splits my ears as he snaps the plate in his hands.

CHAPTER 15

BAZUR

KAETHE MOVES TO CLEAN UP the shattered plate.

Before she can bend down though, I grip her upper arms in my hands. I must be scaring her, but I can't stop myself. I have to touch her, I couldn't keep my hands off her now if I tried, but I do restrain myself from crushing her to my chest like I want to.

She wouldn't welcome that, especially not after this confession.

"How long ago?" I growl. Her dark eyes blink up at me. Thankfully she doesn't look fearful of me right now. I don't think I'd be able to stand it if she did.

"A long, long time ago." Her voice is quiet, and my grip on her only tightens.

"Do you know what clan it was?"

She shakes her head, her pink hair tickling my hands. The blanket she wrapped herself in fell off her shoulders when she stood up, leaving the skin of her arms bare. She's so warm, the flesh of her upper arms soft and supple in my grasp. My thumbs graze the soft curves of her breasts. I wish I could savor this, but I'm too angry right now. Angry for her, angry at myself for not recognizing the signs. It's all so obvious to me now.

How many humans have I helped who acted the way she did after being met with the cruelty of my kind? I curse myself.

"I was a child. I barely even remember their faces."

My vision goes red. The longer I touch her, the longer I stare at her gorgeous face and the more the rage inside me grows. I can almost picture it, Kaethe, smaller than she is now, alone and scared. My kind caused her fear. I'm lucky she hasn't tried to kill me. If I was in her position, I don't know if I could resist.

She has every right to hate my kind…so why did she come here? I let go of her arms, but I don't move away. Her neck is craned all the way up to look at me. I'm trying not to show just how angry I am, how much I want to find who hurt her family and make them pay. Make them suffer for scaring her, for making her fearful of me.

For taking away the life she should've had.

"Why have you come here, Kaethe? It makes it all the more reasonable for you to be a spy now that I know about your past." Would a spy really tell me this information? I don't think so. She told me this because she wanted me to know and that warms some dormant part of my heart.

"I have my own motives for coming here." She ducks her head so I can't see her eyes anymore. "My king allowed me to come so I could learn about the *orc's teeth poison*, that is true. But…there is another reason."

I hold my breath. Finally, finally she is going to tell me the truth. All I want to know is why she's here. Maybe it's nothing deceitful at all. Maybe it's something I can even help her with.

"What is it?" I ask gently.

"I've carried around this hatred and fear for so long. And I let it control so many aspects of my life. I realized facing it was the only thing that could help me. Volunteering to come here was the first step in doing that. I have my reasons, ones I can't share yet." Her eyes lift to mind once more and for once I don't want to push her on it. "But more than that I think I wanted to come here to see what you all were really like. There are bad elves and bad orcs and bad humans. I wanted to see for myself that there are good ones too. I needed to see that."

"And have you seen that here?" I ask. Kaethe's smile is small but she nods her head.

"I've lived in fear of that night for too long. It's only since I've been here that I've been able to face my fears instead of being swallowed by my past."

My palms itch to hold her and tell her everything is going to be alright. I can't do that. I can never do that, especially given what I know

now. She may no longer fear my kind, but I doubt she'd welcome one between her thighs.

Humans with stories like Kaethe's take years to accept my kind. I know this firsthand. They certainly don't take them as lovers or mates.

"I'm sorry," I say, crossing my arms so I don't give in to the urge to touch her again. "Raids like that don't happen as much anymore. I've made sure to put a stop to it."

I want to say more but I don't. She has her secrets and I have mine. I'm not ready to reveal everything about this place to her yet.

"You are safe here, Kaethe. I promise."

She laughs softly. "Everyone says that."

"It's true," I plainly state. She takes in my serious expression and nods her head.

Together, we clean up the broken plate, moving in tandem to avoid cutting ourselves on the sharp pieces. After, we tuck into our meal of meat and vegetables. It's been years since I've had food like this. Meals have always just been a way to refuel myself quickly, I've never had much reason to savor them.

But the delight I see on Kaethe's face as she polishes off her plate makes me want to cook like this every night. The silence between us is comfortable. Something sprouted between us last night and now, after her confession, that something is beginning to grow. What exactly is it? I don't know and a part of me is terrified.

Terrified that she'll look up into my eyes as she changes the dressing on my wound and see the truth in my gaze. The truth I will bury until it is rotting and incapable of exposing me.

"You're almost healed," she says surprised.

"Orc skin is thick. Our bones are thicker still." She raises a dark brow at me.

"Even your skulls?"

"Yes, we have very thick skulls," I say matter-of-factly. She snickers as she ties off my bandage and I have the feeling she was making another joke. It matters not: I was the cause of her smile and that makes me happy.

We crawl into bed together, no longer awkward and stilted, but as two people sharing a space. Sharing comfortable silence. After a few minutes pass, the bed creaks as she rolls toward me in her sleep. Her feet gently press against my legs. The moonlight highlights her smooth cheek, her breast pressing against the neckline of her nightgown.

The fact that she can share a bed with me despite what happened to her is amazing. I am grateful she allows me to be this close to her. Even if my skin burns to be closer. I should close my eyes and go to sleep. Allow her sweet scent to lull me to sleep like it did last night.

I should turn away from her sleeping form.

Instead, I prove to myself that I am just a weak male deep down. I roll onto my good side and watch her sleep. Powerless but to count her freckles and tuck a stray piece of magenta hair behind her ear.

In the dark I make a vow. I repeat it to myself over and over, inhaling her scent deeply one last time, before finally allowing sleep to take me.

CHAPTER 16

KAETHE

MORE THANKS ARE BESTOWED UPON me as Bazur and I make our way to Lady Myren's the next morning.

I'm stopped a dozen times by humans and orcs alike. They offer me words of gratitude for saving Jessica and her child and for bringing new knowledge to their village. They all try giving gifts. I have to sidestep an elderly orc female whose yellow eyes glow with reverence as she tries handing me two chicken caracasses midstride.

It's a sweet gesture but I don't need anything else from these people. I'm glad I could help them. If my mission fails, and I am unable to locate my brother, at least I can leave the village knowing I've improved their lives.

My mission.

Yesterday gave me a reprieve but I cannot lose sight of why I'm really here. I didn't help Jessica to earn myself favors from these people, but I would be lying if I said I wasn't going to use their new fondness toward me to my advantage. Someone here must know something about where captured humans go. It sounds like from the few stories I've been told, they all were captives once themselves. If my brother isn't here, there's a good chance someone has an idea about where he might have gone.

Or he never made it out, a small voice whispers to me.

I quickly dismiss it. If I start considering the possibility that my brother perished the night our village was attacked, the motivation I've clung to these last few years will be stripped away. I can't even think about the possibility that my whole life I've been searching for someone who's already gone.

So, I won't. There is much still to be discovered in this village and

I have until summer to do it. I will find my brother; I won't consider any other possibilities.

Bazur is deep in thought as we trudge through the snow in silence. His beard is growing longer, adding an extra layer of protection against the sharp cold on his face. I like it, for some reason. I itch to touch it even though that would be highly inappropriate.

What was never explained to me is how even the smallest things can turn my nipples hard. Why do I grow wet while watching him put on his cloak? Why do I find his corded muscles flexing when he fixes me a bowl of stew so appealing? I know why scientifically, so maybe this reaction would happen with any man or male I spent this amount of time with?

Even if I were willing to let these feelings flourish, what would be the end goal?

I am still leaving once spring comes. As much as I enjoy the people here, I do miss my life in Myrkorvin. I miss Elvie, Breena, and the other alchemists. We were close in our own way. I have a life, research and profession I need to get back to. All reasons to shove these confusing feelings down where Bazur is concerned.

I'd encourage him to do the same if I had even an inkling he felt the same. He has been growling less around me but that doesn't mean much. He called me that name again, *akorzag*, this morning when I accidentally scorched one of the wooden spoons at the stove. He said it with a smile, so perhaps he's beginning to find my annoyance endearing.

That doesn't mean he likes me in a romantic way, I remind myself.

He drops me off at Lady Myren's with his usual farewell. I watch his large form stomp off in the snow and kick myself for enjoying the way his shoulders bunch under his cloak. Perhaps Lady Myren has some sort of sedative she can give me. Or better yet, something to induce nausea so I can train myself to feel sick in his presence instead of this attraction.

Making my way inside, I hang my cloak up on a hook by the door. Looking over to the fireplace, I halt as I see Mornga and Lady Myren's heads together. They are whispering to each other in the *orcish*. Both of them turn their stares on me at once.

"Um, good morning, Lady Myren. Mornga, it's nice to see you

again," I say.

"Good morning, Kaethe. Let's sit at the table, I'll make you a cup of tea."

Unease trickles into my stomach but I nod anyway. I make my way over to the workbench and sit down. Lady Myren sets a chipped teacup down in front of me and slides onto the seat beside me. Mornga lowers herself gracefully across from us, her red eyes appraising me and taking in every hair on my head, noting every freckle on my nose.

I reach for the cup as we sit in silence for a moment. It's not long before Mornga breaks it.

"What you did yesterday was a miracle, Kaethe." I set my mug down, the clay clattering as it rests on the small serving plate. Mornga's gaze is hard and I straighten my spine as I meet it.

"I understand that it may seem like one, but it was just training. Like I told Lady Myren yesterday, I can teach some of the midwives the technique while I'm here." I glance over to Lady Myren who meets my stare before shifting her gaze to Mornga's and nodding once. Something unspoken moves between them and I have the feeling of standing on a precipice.

"It was a miracle," Mornga says firmly. I try to shake my head again and deny it, but she waves me off. "How much do you know about this village?"

My body visibly stiffens at the question. It's asked innocently enough but this could still be a trap. A way to see if I have been using the village's newfound gratitude to spy. I haven't, yet so I answer her honestly.

"Very little."

"But you know about orcs?" Mornga asks with a raised brow. "About the horrors some of them commit?" After telling Bazur the truth about my family last night I don't fear this line of questioning. I have nothing to hide from them, not when it comes to this.

"Yes, I know about that. But I also know not every orc is like that," I add. Mornga nods her scarlet gaze glancing over to Lady Myren. The older woman sets her own cup down and turns towards me on the bench.

"Look," she says, "I know we weren't the most welcoming to you when you first arrived."

You don't say? I want to ask but I simply incline my head.

"There are reasons for that," Lady Myren explains, running her finger around the lip of her teacup. "We can't explain everything to you—it's not our place, but we want you to know that you are safe here."

I let out a frustrated groan. Hearing that statement is getting on my last nerve.

"Everyone says that. You both say it, Jessica said it last week, Bazur says it…why?"

"Because everywhere else on this mountain is unsafe. Especially for humans," Mornga states. She looks out of Lady Myren's front window for a moment; the ice collecting on the glass pain looks like a spider's web. "Bazur is the only general who allows humans to truly live. Here, humans are equals to the orcs that also call this place home. Here, mated couples can live together and start families and live in a community that accepts them."

"Very few humans live in the other villages. The ones who do don't typically last very long," Lady Myren adds. My hands grip the wood of the table. Mind races as I look at the two sitting beside me. What does that mean for my brother? What would that have meant for *me* had I been sent to another village, or gods forbid, stayed at the Keep?

It's on the tip of my tongue to ask but Lady Myren speaks again.

"I was a stray once, living in a village just outside the Keep. All the other humans were gone, and I had a half-orc toddler to provide for. In our sorry state we wouldn't have survived the winter. The general that oversaw that village was particularly cruel. We were on borrowed time with him, especially with no one around to protect us." She swallows, "My mate was…gone."

"Then one day Vorgak's soldiers came and took Targoc and I to the Keep. I knew we were going to be killed. I had heard the stories of the others."

Lady Myren's face has paled a shade as if she is reliving the horrible memory. I can relate to that.

"Luckily, Bazur was there. He had injured himself while on a mission for the king and I was the closest healer. He asked me if there were any other humans with me at the village and I told him it was just me and my son. I was so wary of him, of all of them, just like I can tell you were at first too, Kaethe."

"But you went with him anyways?" I ask.

"Yes," Lady Myren said, "and thank the *Mother of the Mountain* I did. Once we were away from Dread's Keep, Bazur told me the same thing we said to you. That I was safe now. He told me about the other humans who lived here and that they needed a healer urgently. So that's what I came here to do. Bazur gave me safety, a life, a way to earn my keep and provide for my child."

A funny feeling settles in my chest as I think about Bazur. It feels akin to a heart attack, and I have to shake myself before the warmth in my heart spreads any lower.

"But why did—"

"Bazur placates Vorgak," Mornga interrupts. "You live with Bazur. I'm sure you've noticed he's the strongest orc in this village. But he's also the strongest orc on this mountain."

"I've noticed," I say softly, my cheeks flaming. Luckily, neither Mornga or Lady Myren comments on my change in coloring.

"Bazur uses it to his advantage; he appeases Vorgak by fighting his battles for him. Crushing rebellions before they start. Bazur is deadly on the battlefield. The only things he asks in return for his victories is that this place is left alone, and that he can take in stray humans if he finds them."

My mind is racing. This is the truth I wanted to uncover, right? The great secret of this place everyone has been keeping? Now I understand. I understand why I posed such a threat to all of them. Their secret safe haven, taking in an outsider from another kingdom—I wouldn't have trusted me! No matter that Bazur was the one who volunteered to bring me here.

Bazur.

My heart squeezes in my chest. His rage last night at my confession makes more sense. How angry he had been. Not at me, but for me. The things he's done for the humans here and the things he's done for me. Overwhelming emotion crowds my throat, and my breath becomes painful. I want to go to him now. See him and touch him and tell him what I've learned and to tell him all about me as well.

I don't know how long we sit at the table in silence. There's nothing I can think to say. After this revelation, asking about my brother seems tactless and inappropriate. In truth, the person I should be asking is Bazur.

If he secures safe passage for stray humans then maybe he remembers coming across a boy with my brother's description.

More importantly I *want* to ask Bazur if he knows anything about my brother. I want to share that part of myself with him. I need to keep myself busy while I count down the hours until I can ask Bazur about the truth that's just been shared with me.

Sitting by the fire I catalog more seeds for Lady Myren. Although my skin is warmed by the flames this new knowledge has thawed something else inside of me. For the first time, the anger, the sadness, the fear I've carried with me like a second skin melting away.

And when I think of Bazur, what he's made here and all he's sacrificed to keep it safe, an even more dormant part of me begins to melt too. Whatever feelings I have for Bazur, I'm ready to let them flourish.

It's late in the afternoon and I've lost myself to my daily tasks .All day I let my mind ponder the same question :where do I go from here?

I was meant to find my brother and find a way to get him off of the mountain. Yet, I yearn to stay and learn so much more about these people and their way of life.

I'm still dedicated to my mission, but there's a new venture I can follow now. If I can learn about Black Claw Village, perhaps I can get word to Elvie and Arkain and explain to them that the people here need their help. After the Orc Wars, humans were meant to live freely in the orc lands, not cower from fear of death or worse. King Arkain has the power to ease their suffering and offer asylum should they seek it.

It's what I was planning on him offering my brother, but now it's more than just my brother who needs rescuing. Again I find myself unable to idly sit by when I have the means to help. If I can somehow learn how to smuggle my brother out, perhaps I can do the same for the humans trapped in the other villages.

If I approach Bazur with this idea, will he go for it?

There's so much I want to ask him now, and I will the clock to move faster. The initial shock of the revelation has worn off and now I'm just curious. Eager to learn all that I can, eager to see if he knows about my brother. He is my best chance and I trust now he won't turn me over to Vorgak if I confess to him why I came.

Lady Myren's door creaks open, letting the chilly evening air slip inside. She left for the market only a moment ago to restock on low supplies and couldn't possibly be back yet. I slide the last tray of labeled seeds onto the bookshelf and turn, my lips rising into a small smile as I take in the figure at the door.

"I know you've missed me," Zarod chuckles, his tusks curling to the side into a smirk. "And lucky for you, I'm in need of your expert healing once more."

He holds up his bound hand and I see his two middle fingers bent at odd angles. I wrinkle my nose and gesture toward one of the empty cots.

"I'll set those for you," I say, collecting clean linens and a splint from Lady Myren's case.

"Kae: a gift from the *Mother of the Mountain* herself."

I roll my eyes but chuckle along with him. His skin has returned to that healthy, glowing green. And his eyes are clear and no longer fevered. I notice how handsome he is with his short black hair pulled back, but not as handsome as Bazur.

I shuffle around to the side of the cot and brace his hand on a wooden board.

"You look much better than the last time I saw you. Half-dressed and shivering in the snow, smelling like an unwashed wolf." Gripping his fingers, I twist them back into place and he yelps, glaring at me ruefully. I reply with a smirk.

"Hey now…I wasn't half dressed." Zarod snickers as I set the other finger.

"You look well, too. Poison didn't seem to agree with you."

"A male will always look good after bedding his mate for a week straight. Mornga was *lovingly pissed* at me when she found out I almost died. It didn't take much convincing from me to persuade her to celebrate just how alive I am instead of dwelling on my near death." He raises his dark brows and wiggles them at me. Instead of getting flustered or shy I return his smile with one of my own.

A longing sensation makes my chest hurt again. Zarod must read it on my face because a knowing smirk graces his green lips.

"Is it too far for me to presume that only a bath and good sleep have returned your healthy glow, or do we have a certain extremely grumpy, yet very muscular general to thank for that?"

I choke on a laugh, my face heating. Zaord blinks innocent yellow eyes at me. Too bad I don't have another finger of his to twist and reset.

"If you thought that was the case, why didn't you just ask Bazur?"

"Have you met him? He'd have strangled me." He shifts on the cot as I bind his fingers to the splint. "This town hasn't had any good gossip since our baker decided to start taking up with his brother's widow."

"What?" I gasp, my mouth following open. "Really?"

"Oh yeah, it happened two summers ago. You wanna know the strangest part?"

"Of course," I say.

"They were twins." My mouth drops open even wider.

"No way," I say, shaking my head.

"I swear on the *Mother*."

"Oh gods. Well, I hate to disappoint but no village gossip here. It's just sleep that has restored my peachy complexion."

I finish his splint, looping the bandage a few times around his hand to make sure it's secure. When I finish Zarod looks at me, a small smile playing on his lip and I am ready for some sort of bawdy joke but his voice is gentle when he speaks.

"You know Bazur likes you, right?" he asks, but I simply shake my head. Can that really be true? Is it wrong that I want it to be true?

"Bazur doesn't seem to like anything," I say and Zarod barks out a laugh.

"His grumpiness is a part of his charm."

"How long have you two known each other?" I ask, as we rise from the cot.

"Bazy's been gracing me with his surly presence since we were younglings. Both of us were sent to the Keep for soldier training. He was always like this, even as a child. So serious and stoic." Zarod's eyes run over my face, a mysterious expression dancing in them. "He's different with you, though. I noticed it even if he doesn't want to admit it."

My stomach flutters and my face warms. I feel my last reservations toward Bazur slipping away and I'm more eager to return home.

I lead Zarod to the door, helping him into his cloak with his injured hand. He stays still while I tie the laces for him.

"Don't be too hard on Bazy. Given who his father is, it's no surprise he turned out so angry." That causes my brows to lower. Father? Bazur spoke briefly of his mother in the past but never mentioned a father so I had just assumed he had died.

"Who's Bazur's father?" I ask. Zarod frowns at the question.

"He didn't tell you?"

I shake my head and Zarod uses his good hand to rub the back of his neck. "Vorgak is Bazur's father."

CHAPTER 17

KAETHE

I AM QUIET DURING OUR DINNER.

The walk home with Bazur was strange. I thanked Zarod for telling me what he did, and he told me not to mention it to Bazur. He didn't understand why Bazur hadn't shared that with me.

Indeed, it's not a secret. Everyone here knows, so why would he keep that from me? Why would he have kept all of this from me? If I had known what Bazur was to these humans, I could have asked him about my brother a week ago. I was sent as an emissary but things have changed since I first arrived. Could he not have used that time to tell me the truth about this place?

I had been so eager to see him tonight, to expose my truth and to finally share with him how I felt and see if maybe he felt the same. But now, all I am is unsure as I sit in my usual seat at the table.

On one hand there's Bazur, keeper of the human safe haven and protector of humans. On the other there is Bazur, Vorgak's son and follower to the king. They don't look alike; Bazur's eyes have none of his father's cruelty.

He made sure to keep me in the dark and he clearly told the people of this village to do the same. That's not very kind. I have my secrets, but Bazur has plenty of his own. His distrust upset me before, but now it just pisses me off.

How dare he demand my truth when he was holding something like this back?

"Why are you glaring at your green beans?" Bazur asks, his eyes gentle on my face. An expression I would've welcomed just this morning. I can't see past his secret though. His father threatened me. It's clear Bazur doesn't share his father's ideologies on humans, but he still could've told me.

Meeting his gaze, I realize I can't stew on this any longer. He didn't tell me. Maybe he would have eventually but Zarod beat him to it. There has been so much truth today, so much honesty, and I want this secret out in the open.

With the truth out between us perhaps there's still a chance for me to ask for his help in locating my brother. Perhaps even a chance for me to tell him that I like him, even if the thought of doing so makes my knees shake.

"Zarod came to see me today," I say. Bazur grunts and takes a bite of his roast meat.

"The idiot broke them punching a tree."

"Why was he punching a tree?" I ask but Bazur only shrugs as if to say, *It's Zarod.*

I swallow and set my fork down as I look at him. "He told me that Vorgak is your father."

The metal spoon in Bazur's hand bends as he squeezes it. The soft expression on his face is replaced with a fury I've never seen before. I watch as hot rage simpers in his gaze and he rises from the table, his chair clattering to the floor behind him.

"I'm going to fucking kill him," he growls and I scramble in front of him. I brace my hands on his large chest to stop him from moving toward the door. His muscles are so tense and hot under my palms. I feel his heart racing in his chest, the vibrations of it travel up my arm and into my own heart.

"Bazur stop," I grunt, planting my feet to thwart his movements. "Zarod didn't do anything wrong, he just told me the truth."

"He had no right telling you that," he snarls at me, tusks flashing angrily in the firelight. "You didn't need to know." I push him back slightly and he doesn't try to make for the door again. He's still panting, his eyes wild from the sudden adrenaline, but I don't think he'll be beating down Zarod's door at any moment.

I cross my arms over my chest and level a stare at him. "There are a lot of things you don't seem to want me to know."

His eyes narrow but I press on. I'm tired of avoiding the truth, I'm tired of playing these games. The sooner it's all out in the open and he admits to it, the sooner I can start telling him my own secrets. We can start fresh and potentially make something of this with the time I have left.

"Lady Myren and Mornga told me today about what this place is. A sanctuary for humans that you find or rescue from other villages. They told me about the deal you made with Vorgak in order to keep this place safe."

I wait for him to say something, to look relieved. To explain further and say why he did it. For him to see that now that I know the truth I'm staying here and not running off. To finally see that I am no danger to his people and their way of life here. I'll be able to tell him that I have a plan to help the other humans still out there.

But Bazur looks far from relieved. If anything, he looks angrier and more dangerous than I've ever seen him. He huffs a humorless laugh and shakes his head. His honey eyes frost over and make my blood run cold.

"*Mother of the Mountain*, is there anything my villagers didn't tell you today?"

"Is it really so bad that I know some of the truth? Had I known from the beginning what this place was I would've—"

"It is bad," he snaps, shoving his fingers through his hair. "You could still be a spy."

Shock pulls my mouth open. "Really? You honestly still believe that?"

"I don't know anything about you. There's no reason for me to trust you!" His golden eyes pierce me. How can he say that? The only secret I haven't told him is minuscule in comparison to all the others I've shared.

"Yes, you do," I swallow. "Queen Elvie is the only other person I've shared my family history with. I've told no one else save you and her. Ever."

I let him see the truth of that statement in my eyes. But whatever his mindset, anger overcomes him and takes root in his eyes. His expression hardens and makes me shiver. This isn't the Bazur that rescued me from that net. The Bazur who volunteered to take me back to his village, the only place my safety would be truly guaranteed.

I have this wild idea to lay it all out on the table for him. Tell him everything so he can understand. I want to ask him if we can start fresh with no secrets between us. And I would ask him to help me look for my brother, and I would tell him the truth about how I feel about him. Even though I've tried to fight it, I like him. Despite my best efforts not to, I couldn't help it, these feelings for him have grown into something that scares me but also makes me feel alive. And I would tell him all of that, if he was the Bazur who picked me up from Lady Myren's.

But the male in front of me is not him.

He scoffs at me one more time and shakes his head.

"Perhaps another lie. So you can throw me off my guard and get me to reveal more secrets."

My head snaps back and my ears begin ringing as if he has struck me. To think all I wanted today was to be closer to him. But I know now what he really thinks of me. The damage is done and my heart cracks in my chest. To say I would lie about something like that…

"How dare you—"

"Make no mistake, I will keep my people—my village—safe. From any threat. By any means."

That's it then. After all that honesty and openness the last two days, it's amazing how quickly a few words can kill it. I was foolish to believe he cared about me for even a second. It is clear how he sees me. No more than a liar, using the death of her family to steal information and security from him.

I was foolish to think I could ever trust him with my mission. His cruel gaze leaves me with a cold, sinking feeling in my stomach, and I realize he was never going to help me. If I had told him, it would have confirmed his suspicions.

And he would have killed me.

"You sound exactly like your father," I say, my voice rough from the tears threatening to spill down my cheeks. I won't cry in front of him. He doesn't deserve the satisfaction.

My statement must have cracked through his icy rage because his eyes refocus, even soften. It makes my heart break even more. His hand trembles as he reaches for me. Moving quickly, I dodge it and make for the ladder to upstairs, cursing this place for not having any doors. I contemplate going to Lady Myren's but I can't be sure she'd let me in.

She's loyal to Bazur, as is everyone here. I have no allies of my own and for the first time since arriving I feel truly alone. So incredibly alone. I want Elvie. I want to go back to Blackfire castle, and I want to get as far away from Bazur as I possibly can.

"Kaethe," Bazur calls out to me, his voice strange. Raspy and disjointed. I can't hear it. Not when my chest has been ripped open and my secrets thrown back in my face. There's nothing more to be said: he hit me where I'm most vulnerable.

I pause with my foot on the bottom rung, speaking softly and not daring to look back at him.

"Zarod also told me that you liked me, I guess not everything said to me today was the truth after all."

I don't wait for his reply as I climb up the ladder. Once I've reached the top, I can hear him faintly from below, his voice barely above a whisper.

"I'm leaving tomorrow. I'll be gone for a few days."

He sounds utterly devastated.

Good, I want to say but I don't. My hands are numb as I make my way into the washroom. I strip my clothes and turn on the hot water to fill up the bathing pool. I hold on to the anger and the sadness until I sink beneath the clear water. Only then, do I let myself sob. My tears adding to the water around me.

CHAPTER 18

KAETHE

Bazur is gone when I wake in the morning.

His boots and cloak were missing from the door when I came down from the second floor. I am grateful for this time apart, it will give me a chance to think. To process what transpired between us and how we go from here.

My eyes feel puffy and my nose is chapped. I had cried myself to sleep during the early morning hours. Bazur never came to bed and for some reason that made me cry even harder.

I scrubbed my face in the washroom and tried my best to soothe my swollen eyes. If Bazur doesn't trust me, doesn't trust that I'm not here for some nefarious purpose, then he can fuck off. I know my truth, my character. Lady Myren and Mornga knew my character and decided to trust me. If Bazur wants to insist on me being his enemy, then maybe I will be.

Whatever relationship I believed to be growing between us has wilted under his words last night. Only time will tell how successful he was. Last night, as I cried, I still wanted him. This morning, I can't bear to see him.

Would he even apologize? I seriously doubt it.

That is what he thinks of me. What he has always thought of me. I am just an annoying human—probably a spy—here to make his life harder. He won't trust me because I haven't told him enough about me, but at the first opportunity, he takes what I shared with him and calls me a liar.

Real nice.

I'll continue my mission without his help. I'll figure out a way to help the humans still being held against their will to reach safety. I don't need Bazur with his bad attitude and accusations.

My angry thoughts have absorbed so much of my concentration I barely register that I've already made it to Lady Myren's until I'm pushing through the front door. The fire is roaring, and she turns from the bookcase with a soft smile on her face. The moment she sees me I know I did a poor job concealing my crying.

Her eyes soften and I turn away; I don't want her to comment on it. I don't want to explain this fight with Bazur. I clear my throat as I hang up my cloak on the hook.

"I'll start cataloging the last of the seeds Bronwyn dropped off." I walk toward the large bookcase. "Did Targoc leave on the mission with the others?"

Targoc is a good orc male. I'd much rather talk about him this morning than the one whose home I'm living in.

"Yes, I hate when he leaves on these missions, but they'll only be gone for two days," Lady Myren pauses as my whole body goes ridgid. *Two days, that's it?* "Though, I get the sense some people wish it was longer."

Despite myself I smile, falling into my seat at the workbench opposite of Lady Myren.

"Is it that obvious?" I ask as she slides me a steaming cup of tea.

"I've comforted many females after a fight with a male. The signs are easy enough to recognize." I take a sip of the tea and shake my head.

"It's not even like that between Bazur and I. I thought…I thought *maybe* we could have something. An understanding, a friendship, or something more…but last night he made it very clear what he thinks of me." Taking another sip of tea, I swallow down the warm liquid. "He said something that really, *really* hurt me."

"Then he needs to apologize," Lady Myren says simply, "and he needs to mean it. Don't forgive him until he does, or he'll never learn. Males like to speak without thinking, it's their most abhorrent quality."

Chuckling softly into my teacup, I sigh. "I don't think he will apologize."

Why would he if that's what he really thinks?

"Bazur is," Lady Myren hesitates, "a complicated male. But he's a good male nonetheless. He'll fix this."

"I don't even know if it can be fixed."

Lady Myren rounds the table and sits beside me on the bench. It's not until I feel the wetness on my cheeks that I realize I've started crying again. She wraps her arm around me, tucking me into an embrace. The gesture is so kind, so *maternal* that I start audibly crying for a new reason.

"Let me ask you something: do you want him to fix it?" Lady Myren runs another soothing hand up my arm. I nod my head, not trusting my voice. "Then it can be fixed, but only if he apologizes, Kaethe. Remember that."

I laugh and hiccup as I wipe the tears from my eyes. Returning Lady Myren's hug, I inhale her smoky scent. Something about this feels right, a piece of me clicking into place. Lady Myren isn't my mother, can never be my mother. But some small, broken part of me heals during our hug. I lean back and look into her wrinkled gray eyes.

"Call me, Kae," I say softly. Lady Myren's smile is small, and she nods, squeezing me one more time.

"I will, only if you promise to call me Myren." My smile is watery as I squeeze her back.

The next day Myren and I had gone to visit Jessica and her new baby

Both of them were thriving and I spent hours there making sure both of them were as healthy and happy as possible. I stayed there longer than necessary because I wanted to be away from the house with the soldiers returning today. I couldn't stand the possibility of Bazur waiting for me at the bottom of Myren's steps.

After our visit concluded I made the journey back to Bazur's house alone, relieved to find that he was still out. The day had drained me so thoroughly that I had crawled into bed and fell into a deep sleep.

I hadn't been asleep for very long when something tickled my face. My eyes blink open and I notice the lamp beside the bed is still on, illuminating the room in a warm flickering glow.

I look around, wondering what woke me.

It becomes obvious once I see who is sitting at the edge of the bed. I gasp, pulling my knees to my chest and rising into a sitting position. I clutch the blanket to me. Bazur sits motionless, staring off at the wall in front of him. There is a large leather satchel in his hands but it's too dark for me to see what's inside it.

There's a beat of silence before he speaks.

"I wanted" —he coughs, clearing his rough voice— "I wanted to apologize to you, for how I spoke to you before I left. I was wrong to say those things to you…about you. There's no excuse. What I said was appalling and selfish and so wrong. I am so, *so* sorry, Kaethe."

Tears threaten my eyes and I blink several times to keep them at bay. I say nothing. I'm happy he apologized, but he has to do more than say the words. He needs to mean it, like Myren said. So I sit and wait for him to show me he means it.

Another moment of silence passes before he takes a deep breath, his massive figure in the dark deflating with the exhale.

"I should've never, never thrown what happened to your parents back in your face. Knowing you trusted me with that information, and I used it to hurt you…Kaethe, I…" he shudders out another breath, "I am sorry. I can't say that enough. It's inexcusable and you should hate me. *I* hate me for hurting you."

I don't hate him, but I don't say that. I just wait.

"Here I was, wanting to show you there is more to our kind than just cruelty and I go and do that." He looks over his shoulder at me and I barely stop my gasp of shock. The lantern illuminates the harsh planes of his face and he looks horrible. Dark green circles appear like bruises under his eyes, as if he didn't sleep the entire time he was away. His golden eyes are bloodshot, and his hair is in disarray.

Bazur looks at me with wide, devastated eyes and I brace myself for what he's about to say.

"I know what it's like to lose both your parents," he says, gripping the bag in his hands tighter. "Vorgak isn't my father."

My brows furrow in confusion.

"King Bazrik, The Brave was my father. He ruled for over fifty years before I was born. That word that you asked me about, the one Lady Myren and Mornga call me, *prognazoc*, it means prince." The blanket slips from my hands and I slide down the bed closer to him. Prince? Bazur is a prince?

"My family had seized the throne shortly after the Orc Wars had ended. But there was only chaos those first few years. My great-great grandfather during his rule cared more about relocating our people that he didn't pay much attention to how the humans left in our territory were being treated. Humans had been living at the mercy of cruel and malicious orc lords for centuries until my father came to power."

Bazur takes another deep breath, raking a shaking hand through his dark hair.

"As king, my father outlawed the keeping of human servants. Outlawed raiding human villages and taking captives. At first, everything was peaceful. My parents were mated a few years before I was born, and they finally felt like it was time to bring a child into this world. A world they were proud of." He pauses and looks over to the wall again. A deep sadness fills the air, tugging on my heart, as I realize what's coming next.

"But Vorgak decided to rebel. He had been working with some of the lords who were upset by the reforms and they devised a plan to ambush my father. They struck him down in his hall.

"It wasn't a fair fight but our laws are simple. Kill the king, become the king. Vorgak killed my father with an arrow in his back like a coward and took his throne."

"Bazur I—" I stop myself, what can I even say?

"Vorgak took my mother as his bride, declared me his son and successor to the throne. I was young enough then that Vorgak thought he could mold me into a male that stood against everything my father had fought so hard for. His final affront to my father's memory."

Bazur's gaze turns back to me, his eyes are so open and honest, it steals my breath.

"My mother tried to hang on as best she could for me. But the death of a mate does something to you and…she couldn't survive without my father. So, one day she went to the tallest room in the Keep, opened the windows and…"

He lets the sentence hang there and my chest tightens.

"Vorgak was the reason both my parents perished. And he allowed the raids to start happening again, allowed humans to be captured and taken. He would take to the scorched human towns, make me watch as they…took the humans they had caught there. What they did to the survivors, even as a youngling I knew it was wrong."

While Bazur recalls his history, I remember the sights and smells of my own scorched village. To know Vorgak was the reason…

"When I was sixteen, I realized I could do something. I had grown much larger than the other males my age. Faster and stronger, too, and better at fighting than even some of the most experienced soldiers. I had so much anger inside of me that I channeled it into becoming the best soldier and eventually a general, one who would fight for the people who couldn't fight for themselves. I fought Vorgak's battles so he'd let me claim Black Claw Village as my own. The orcs I fought were causing problems for Vorgak. Orcs who would've gladly supported my claim to the throne; but Vorgak had me put them down or else he'd invade this village. I killed my own supporters, all to keep this village protected.

"It is our agreement. I protect him from being overthrown and he leaves my village alone and stops raiding human towns."

My stomach turns and I feel sick. The horrors Bazur has had to inflict on his own people just to keep this place safe. Bazur takes a deep breath. There's so much I want to say but nothing comes out.

"I'm not telling you all of this so you'll forgive me. As much as I want you to, I know there's a real possibility that you won't. And I have to live with that. But knowing I made you cry, that I hurt you like that, Kaethe…" he shudders. "I'm telling you this to show you I do trust you. That's everything, all my secrets laid out. You are safe here, and when the time comes, I will personally escort you back to Myrkorvin.

"And I want you to know I would never report your movements here to Vorgak; I'd rather drive a blade through my heart than betray you. That day at the Keep, I didn't volunteer to take you in solely because you could help my people. I wanted to—no, I needed—you with me, so I could make sure you were safe. Just thinking of you in the hands of someone else…"

I shudder at the memory of the orc who had been eyeing me like his next meal. He really did save me. When I think about what could've happened to me if he hadn't found me, my stomach turns.

"Even when I did consider you a spy, I figured maybe it wouldn't be so bad if you told your king about us. I started wondering if he could be persuaded to aid in my cause and keep this place free. Maybe even help free the humans trapped in the other villages."

My breath catches. That was my plan, before everything blew up. Maybe it can still work with Bazur's help. Together we can put a stop to Vorgak and make him suffer the pain that he's caused here.

"I'm not a spy," I say simply.

"I know," Bazur replies, a ghost of a smile gracing his green lips. "Even if you were, it wouldn't change anything. It wouldn't change how I feel."

"And how do you feel?" *About me*, I want to add. Something in my chest is knitting back together, warm and strong and permanent.

Bazur shakes his head. "Right now I feel…confused, angry at myself. Scared."

His eyes glow in the dim light only making the sensation in my chest spread lower, warming my stomach, and turning my feminine flesh soft and slippery.

Is his fear the same as mine?

"But mostly I feel grateful that you're still here." My cheeks heat and I look away from him.

"Do you want to be king?" I ask.

"I've never wanted to rule over anyone. But Vorgak is growing restless and pretty soon he's going to leave us no choice but to act. My soldiers and I are preparing in case that time comes sooner than we anticipated." His honey eyes find mine, so serious and full of resolve. "I have my people to protect but now I have *you* to protect too. I won't let you get caught up in any of this."

My throat clogs with emotion and I only nod my head as we stare at each other. The silence between us is heavy. What he's shared with me—the things he's gone through. He's broken in the same ways I am. Sure, his edges may be a little sharper than mine but with time he'll be able to smooth them out.

We can work on smoothing them out together.

"Thank you for telling me all of that," I say softly. A part of me screams at my body to go to him where he's huddled at the end of the bed. Turns out he didn't kill what was between us. I feel it in my chest, stronger than it ever was before. I'm no longer upset by what he said, and I understand him now in a way I never could've imagined. He apologized and he meant it, I know it in my heart.

Yet, the last shred of my self-preservation keeps me from moving closer even though my soul is begging me to move closer and submit to this feeling completely.

"I'll never speak to you like that. Ever again. I promise," he vows.

"I know," I say, letting my eyes rest on his handsome face. His large hands twist around the bag on his lap. I had completely forgotten about it until he sets it down gently in my lap.

"These are for you. I hope there's enough of them."

With a furrowed brow, I unzip the bag and dig my hand into it. The scent hits me immediately, so earthy and sweet. My fingers glide along silky petals. There must be fifty? No, a hundred...two hundred at least in this bag! I pull one out and let the light shine on it.

The magenta shade of a *darksky rose* glimmers in the dim light.

That melts the last of my resolve. I let out a squeal and set the bag aside, throwing myself into Bazur's chest. He hesitates for only a moment before his arms envelop me. Pressed against him like this, I can feel his warm skin and I soak it in. I suck down lungfuls of his pine scent. His chest muscles meet my soft flesh, and I appreciate our bodies and their contrast to each other. I feel my nipples harden in my thin nightgown and press against his tough skin. The sensation is pleasant, very pleasant.

In fact, as his large hands trace up and down my spine, I get the same feeling I had at Myren's. A rightness clicking into place. Locked in his arms like this, I feel small and delicate. Protected and cherished. I swallow my moan as his calloused hands continue exploring the planes of my back. The simple touches make my pussy turn wet and I squeeze my thighs together.

Even more moisture slicks out of me when Bazur lets out a groan of his own into the top of my head. *Gods, can he smell my arousal?* A smile tips my lips as I realize I wouldn't mind him knowing. He murmurs something in my hair in his orc language and I pick up that word again, *akorzag*. Maybe I would be annoyed by it if he didn't say it with such reverence. We stayed locked in our embrace for a long time. Not speaking, just enjoying each other's warmth, breathing in each other's scents.

After what feels like an eternity, we finally release each other.

Bazur rises from the bed and stretches his arms above his head with a yawn. It's late and the sun will rise soon. I take the bag of flowers and set it on the floor beside my side of the bed. Footsteps sound as Bazur makes his way to the ladder, and I realize he intends to sleep on the bedroll on the lower level.

I don't want him to sleep down there, I never want him down there again.

"Bazur," I call, and he freezes. Pivoting slowly, he turns to look at me and I drag the blanket down on his side of the bed. I pat the open mattress next to me. He hesitates for a second and then shucks his boots. Then his fur lined coat. Finally, he removes his thin undershirt and my mouth goes dry. He hasn't slept in the bed without his shirt on before.

The light licks the ridges of his stomach and I swear, somehow, he has more abs than the last time I saw him. I find myself a little unfocused as he crosses the room and slips under the blankets beside me.

I extinguish the lantern, plunging the room into darkness. The moon casts everything in a gentle glow and we both lay there, our hands awkward on top of the blankets, our bodies stiff, unsure of what the other is thinking. I wish his arms were still around me, so I can feel that warmth again, but for now, I'll settle for proximity.

Lifting my hand, I slide it along the sheet and under Bazur's. It's much larger than mine and my fingers spread wide as they scrape along his callouses. I trace my thumb along the line of a scar on the back of his hand. Bazur shudders at the contact before giving my hand a gentle squeeze in return.

"Zarod didn't lie," Bazur rumbles at me. "I do like you."

I thank the gods that he can't see my grin in the dark room.

CHAPTER 19

KAETHE

Everything is perfect the next morning.

With most of our secrets laid bare to each other, an unspoken change has declared itself between Bazur and I. He likes me, he admitted to it. I like him too, but I have yet to tell him. I want to, but my depth of feeling goes beyond infatuation. What if that scares him? I won't risk ruining this new relationship between us.

This morning, I woke to find Bazur already awake and staring at me from across the bed. Our fingers were still gripping each other tightly and he squeezed my hand before releasing it so he could go bathe. If I was bolder, I would've asked to join him, but would he have welcomed that? Bazur is serious and literal; if he cared for me in that way he would've said so, wouldn't he?

Not for the first time do I wish Elvie was here. She would know exactly how to navigate this relationship and tell me if I was being ridiculous. She's confident in a way I am not, and I want to kick myself. However, I remind myself this is all new. Bazur and I have plenty of time to figure this out and I don't have to make any decisions or grandiose declarations right now.

We stayed close to each other on our walk to Myren's. My shoulder brushes his arm occasionally and I wonder if the subtle touch makes his stomach flutter like it does mine. He smiles down at me softly, telling me about the fight he had with Zarod while on their mission. I am happy to learn all is well between friends once more.

As Bazur drops me off, Myren comes out to retrieve a few seedlings growing on her front porch. She says good morning to us both, clearly noting the shy looks we kept casting each other. Once inside, I hang up my cloak and she asks me if he apologized. I nod, smiling softly, thinking of that leather bag filled with *darksky roses* back at the house.

"That makes me happy," Myren says before divvying up the day's work. I've started to use some of my alchemist skills. Just last week I showed Myren how I can turn clay pots, which break easily when she crushes up herbs, into steel ones.

With these new steel bowls, we smash twice as many herbs, and their fresh scents tickles my nose. We need to make more of these salves and elixirs with the first frost coming any day now. The two of us work silently through the morning. When the first batch is made, Myren brings me a cup of tea and we sit in front of the fire.

"Bazur told me the truth about this place. The whole truth," I say softly. Myren nods smiling into her cup.

"I figured he would. It was only a matter of time."

"If you don't mind me asking, what was your life like before coming here?"

Myren looks over at me and smiles.

She sets her empty cup of tea down and sighs, sticking her booted feet out toward the fire.

"I was a noblewoman who lived in a large town on the east side of the mountain. When Bazur's father had been in charge things were different. My family sold fur pelts and we often traded with the orcs who passed through our settlement. One day an orc trader stopped by and I fell in love with him. It didn't feel instantaneous at the time but now look-ing back it was. Mating bonds manifest in such interesting ways."

I nod, recalling how it took Elvie nearly dying for her to acknowl-edge hers with Arkain.

"My sweet Rozdan was everything a good male ought to be. Strong, kind, compassionate. Most importantly he was everything I wanted. He told the most amazing stories of his travels and I fell more in love with him each time he would share one. The day when he was set to return back to his own village I went with him, leaving behind my social standing and my life as I knew it. We were a pair, just the two of us going on adventures and falling even deeper in love. He was happy when we found out I was pregnant." Her smile is small, tears shining in her eyes. "Things changed quickly after Vorgak seized power. My Rozdan made his feelings on the new King known. Rozdan wasn't a general but he had influence over the people in his village. Influence that Vorgak saw my Rozdan as a threat so when he came to our town unannounced—it was, barely a year after Targoc was born…we knew what was going to happen."

A tear slips from her green eyes and she wipes it away quickly. "It was hard, so hard that some days I didn't think I could make it without him. But I had our child, I had the proof of our love and I had to live for him."

"I'm so sorry, Myren," I say, reaching out to squeeze her shoulder. She covers my hand with her own.

"Vorgak will get what's coming to him. Bazur will make sure of that. He vowed it to me when I told him what had happened after he rescued Targoc and I from the Keep."

I nod, my stomach flipping at her words. "I do have a question though; how have you managed to keep this place a secret? Humans aren't supposed to live under orc rule, yet we've only heard rumors that a few remain here."

"Vorgak keeps communication between villages weak. The humans that go anywhere else but here don't live long enough to make much noise. The one's here are happy to remain safely behind our gates. Still a few traders and poachers that pass through like to twist and tell stories about things they've seen. Or rather things they haven't seen." Myren raises her dark brows at me. "What were the rumors you heard?"

I swallow. "There was one about a human boy who was found in a raided village. Supposedly he was taken in by the orcs and raised in one of their villages."

Myren frowns. "We have dozens of boys here that fit that story."

"Would a boy with that story be found in any of the other villages?" I ask tentatively. Myren narrows her eyes again, but I quickly add, "Bazur mentioned something to me about trying to rescue humans from other towns."

Myren nods slowly then shrugs. "Possibly, though if he was taken in by one of the other clans, he's likely dead or close to it."

I discreetly wipe my palms on my dress. Our conversation is interrupted when the door opens and an older orc male walks in. He's dressed in simple wool clothes and his skin turning yellow. His long braid is streaked with silver, as is the beard on his face. Using the sleeve of his coat he coughs into it.

A deep, wet cough makes me cringe.

Myren lets out a sigh. "It's starting already?"

The older orc grins sheepishly. "Afraid so."

"Dorlac always gets *Frost Cough* before anyone else. I thought we would have at least a few—" Myren's head snaps up as she looks over to me. "Kae, did you catalog the mint root?"

I lower my brows. "No, Jessica did all the roots over a week and half ago."

"Fuck," Myren says under her breath. "She miscounted them, and we are now woefully understocked. Especially if people are already getting sick."

Unease makes the hairs on the back of my neck stand up.

"Where can we get some more? The frost hasn't come yet so we still have some time," I say. Myren nods and cups her chin with her hand.

"It's about a day's ride up the mountain. It will take a day to collect the amount needed to see us through this winter." Myren clicks her tongue and sighs. "I'm too old to make the journey and I can't leave this place unattended."

I laugh softly. "I can go and collect it for you."

"Oh, would you? That would be wonderful." Myren grabs some of the mashed herbs we worked on earlier and rubs them on the older orc's chest. He sighs in relief before sneezing three times in rapid succession. We're gonna need a lot of medicine.

"We'll tell Bazur about this when he comes for you. He'll need to accompany you." Myren's face grows serious. "The journey up the mountain is very dangerous."

CHAPTER 20

BAZUR

K AETHE REALLY ISN'T BUILT FOR the snow.

She's meant to be inside, reading over herbology books and making sure her *riverheart seeds* are getting enough sun on the front porch. She's meant to sit by the fire and sip tea while smiling softly at me from across the room.

She meant to be warming my bed while I make sure she's covered in thick blankets.

Not on the mountain, where the snow is heavy, cold, and cruel, weighing down on her like an iron anchor beneath a freezing ocean. Still the snow is the reason she's seated firmly between my thighs on the back of my *icewolf* as we make our way up the mountain. There was a snowstorm that blew in a week ago that had made this journey impossible until now.

Luckily, the frost that wipes everything out has yet to come.

A week has passed since my mission, a week since I told her… everything. All of it, every last bit of truth. And she had accepted it. Accepted me and forgave me for making her cry and turn cold. I meant what I said: I'll never, ever speak to her like that again.

Every night this week we have gone to bed together, silently holding hands in the dark. It's become so normal now, I don't think I could fall asleep without it.

I'd give anything to feel her arms around me again. The way the curves of her body fit in my arms just right. Does she think I couldn't feel her nipples harden against me? Does she think I couldn't smell the change in her scent as we hold each other? Or the sweetness of her arousal that floated in the air?

Thankfully she hadn't leaned down any closer on my lap and felt just how hard I was.

Beyond the physical closeness, our relationship has evolved. We talk all the time now. I look forward to dinners when we chat about our days. I've taken to counting down the minutes until I'm done with training so I can rush to get her and share the same space again. I admitted that I liked her, and I want to protect her from everything. I have to distract myself from the fact that she didn't return the sentiment though.

Kaethe is still holding something back from me. It's unsettling. I want to know what she thinks of me; I want to know every thought she's ever had. If only her body desires me, I will be grateful. After the way I spoke to her it's more than I deserve, but that doesn't mean I'm not greedy for the rest.

She leans back into my chest, her pink hair tickling the underside of my chin. She's dressed more appropriately than when I first found her, covered in a thick cloak and traveling clothes. Truth be told, when she came down dressed in her pair of fur-lined trousers that hugged her hips and ass like a second skin I almost came in my own pants. Kaethe is decadent in every sense of the word.

With her so close to me, I try not to think about how I woke up this morning. She had turned toward me during the night, our clasped hands tucked into her chest. My hand was resting against the swells of her breasts. I itched to touch them, bite them, suck them, fuck them. There are so many things I want to do to them…do to Kaethe.

I remember my vow in the dark all those nights ago—I need to stay firm.

Kaethe is beautiful and intelligent. She will make a great wife someday, a great mate even if she is not mine. The thought makes my stomach turn. While I'd love nothing more than to rip off her clothes and shove my cock inside her until we're both sweating and panting, this isn't the type of lust experienced by mates.

I vowed long ago that I would only settle for mine and have that instantaneous love and lust my parents had, that I saw Zarod and Mornga have. Even if the thought of touching anyone besides Kaethe makes me sick. Regardless, I didn't take her from that hunting net I found her in and fuck her into next week as soon as our eyes locked.

No, it was something different than that, something that grew over time. A need to protect her, to care for her, make her and keep her safe. I admit to myself that I do want her, a lot, but it was not the primal need of the mating bond that drew me to her.

It was simply Kaethe herself, and that somehow feels more dangerous. Dangerous enough, that as she leans further into my chest to make me question if a mate is something I even want.

If my mate isn't Kaethe, does having one even matter? A part of me screams it doesn't, because she is mine and I must keep her. There is a reason why I can't stop speaking to her in my language, words she doesn't understand. I've bared my soul to her a hundred times, said words of devotion and ownership while she looks into my eyes. Yet, I'm too afraid to utter these intimacies in a language she knows.

What if she doesn't feel the same?

Even if she felt a fraction of what I did, could I really deprive her of her own mate? The thought of having her now only for her to leave my bed for another's makes my skin heat and red mist settle over my vision. *Mine, mine, mine.* Kaethe *does* want me, but she's never indicated anything beyond physical attraction. I know for a fact she doesn't wake in the middle of the night to count my eyelashes and deep breaths. If she was, she'd catch me doing it to her.

"How many humans have you saved?" Kaethe suddenly asks, taking me out of my thoughts. I clear my throat and flick the reins, urging my *icewolf* to move faster.

"I've lost track. Hundreds, maybe?" I respond. Kaethe grows quiet again and I can almost hear her mind working as she turns over this information.

"Where do you primarily save humans from?"

I sigh, stretching out my neck. "Depends. Sometimes they're already at Dread's Keep, some of them are in other clans. They're a bit trickier to retrieve." I nudge her with my chest. "And sometimes they stumble into my hunting net."

Her head dips under my chin and I know she's trying to fight her smile.

"Why do you ask, Kaethe?" I look down to see her teeth sink into her plump lower lip.

"I was wondering if you recalled rescuing a boy from a raided village." Her shoulders tighten. "Around twenty years ago."

My body stiffens behind her and I realize I've been an idiot; her truth has been staring me in the face this whole time. Why hadn't I considered it before?

"That's why you came here. You're looking for someone."

"Yes," she whispers, seeming to deflate as if a weight has been lifted from her shoulders. "I didn't lie when we first met, I was going to Dread's Keep in the hopes of reuniting with someone. My brother. My older brother, Karth."

"Karth?" The name isn't familiar to me.

"The night the orcs came to my village, my brother and I fled together, only we got separated, I dropped his hand—" Her voice catches, her eyes squeezing shut. "We heard a rumor in Myrkorvin about a man taken in by the orcs as a child. I had to see for myself if it could be him."

"Why didn't you tell me this before?" I ask, even though I know what she's going to say.

"I was afraid. If Vorgak found out my true purpose for coming here, my life would have been endangered even more. Not to mention it would start a conflict with King Arkain, I promised him before I left I would try my best to be discreet." Kaethe's gloved hand covers mine holding the reins. "I know that you won't hurt me or turn me into Vorgak. You're my best hope at finding my brother."

My chest grows warm, emotion clogging my throat, but I clear it. "You've seen all the men in town around your brother's age?"

"Yes," Kaethe says sadly. "Because they spread it the easiest, Myren made all the men between eighteen and thirty come in and be examined now that *Frost Cough* is back."

"A few of the young men have been off scouting with the soldiers. They've been absent since you came here but they should be returning soon." Something jogs my memory. "There's one of the farmers, I found him outside of a village when he was young. He has dark hair like yours. When he first arrived he asked about a sister, but his name is Jaysin. At least…that was the name he gave me when I brought him here."

Kaethe's spine snaps up and she turns in the saddle to look at me, her brown eyes wide.

"Jaysin? That was my father's name." Her brows are raised and her dark eyes bore into mine as her lips part. "How could I have forgotten? My brother was named after my father but we always called him by his middle name to avoid confusion."

There's so much hope shining in her beautiful face it makes my chest hurt.

"When do they return?"

"They're due back with the soldiers in about a week's time. If that's not him, I'll figure out where we go from there."

"Thank you," she whispers, her eyes going glassy again. These are good tears. The only tears I'll ever cause her.

"I swear to you, Kaethe, if your brother still lives, I will find him."

Her cheeks turn pink and she nods. We resume our journey but not before Kaethe snags my arm not holding the reins and wraps it around her waist. The soft curve of her stomach presses into my forearm and I have to swallow my hiss. Especially when she brackets my arm with her own and snuggles back into my chest, my chin resting on top of her head.

"You can call me, Kae you know."

"I prefer, *akorzag.*" She elbows me gently in the chest but I know she's smiling. I shouldn't call her that, but it feels too natural. It's clear she doesn't know what it means or she wouldn't be smiling at me so brightly. That smile does something funny to my chest again but I push it down for now as I urge our beast forward.

"Do I get to call you Bazy?" she asks hopefully. I choke on my laugh and she chuckles, sending vibrations along my arm. With Kae letting me soak in her warmth and sweet scent as the sun shines overhead, I don't think anything could be more perfect.

"Absolutely not."

CHAPTER 21

KAETHE

T HE WEATHER WAS MILD LAST night and we were able to make camp after a long day's journey.

Bazur heated up some stew and we enjoyed it by a small fire. He peppered me with questions about my life in Myrkrovin, my time at the academy, and even shared a bit about his younger years as well.

When the sun had fully set, we crawled into our tent, sprawled out on separate bedrolls and fell asleep holding hands. It would've been so easy to roll over and onto his bedroll, to join his fur blanket with my own, and curl my body into his. I considered it, seeing as the wind blew gently through our tent. After sharing with him my last secret I feel like there's nothing holding me back now. He knows everything about me and he trusts me, and is willing to help me with my mission.

Bazur's vow to help my brother solidified my feelings toward him. As I laid next to him in the tent, his deep breath echoing around me, I vowed I would tell him tonight how I feel. I like him, I more than like him—I crave him. My depth of feeling terrifies me, but I can't miss out on this. I can't miss out on the possibility of *us*.

So that was my plan, and I would've stuck to it.

However, the gods had a different idea.

The weather today has seemed just as mild as last night. Bazur and I worked side by side all day to secure the amount of mint root Myren was needing. I am packing the last containers into my protective case when I peer up at the sky. Bazur is tucking something in his own bag when he lets out a curse. The sparse fluffy clouds have merged together to be dark, ominous masses. Bazur is about fifty feet away from me but I hear his thunderous footsteps sound in the snow as he charges in my direction.

"Kae, we need to—" But he's too late. The sky opens up and soaks us with snow and icy water. My clothes are ruined in an instant. My hair plasters to my head and in another instant, we are pelted with little balls of ice.

Oh gods, how are we going to make it to the tent?

We had to travel a short distance from our campsite to find the roots this morning. We won't survive if we stay out here much longer; my fingers are already going numb from the rain.

Where is Bazur?

My head turns in the direction he was but I don't see him. The wind is whipping the snow around me into a frenzy and I can barely see anything. A familiar panic begins to set in. I can't lose him out here, I won't allow us to be separated.

"Bazur!" I scream, the storm swallowing my voice. "Bazur!"

Godsdammit where are you?

A warm arm wraps around my waist and I'm pulled back against a solid chest. That familiar pine scent fills my lungs and even though we aren't out of the storm yet, I relax a little. Bazur's got me, he won't let anything happen to me.

"Kae, the snow is too deep for you to walk, hold on to me," he shouts. My arm tightens around his hold on my waist as my teeth begin to chatter. Bazur moves quickly in the snow, his long, muscular legs carrying us toward our tent.

"I—I knew y—you—you'd find me," I say, teeth chattering. He grunts his confirmation, and tightens his grip.

The wind stings my cheeks and bites at my nose as we push through it. My clothes are waterlogged as are my boots. We won't be able to make a fire and if I don't get out of these wet clothes…I shudder at the thought. I really, really don't want to lose a finger or toe today.

My body shakes violently as I shiver through our journey. Bazur must be cold too but he holds me through it all, cradling me against his strong chest as we push forward. I must pass out from the cold for a second because I go from being pelted with ice and rain to being inside the tent.

We sealed the tent before leaving this morning so everything in here is dry and preserved from the storm raging just outside. It's dark in here with no fire but I can still see my breath in front of me. I try rubbing my hands together but my fingers are stiff with cold. The tips of my ears hurt from the chill.

"We need to get you out of those clothes," Bazur says behind me. His arm is still wrapped around me, but I can barely move. I have no dry clothes in this tent, but nudity is the least of my concerns. If I don't get out of these wet clothes I will be sick.

"H—help me," I murmur, fingers fumbling with the tie of my cloak. I manage to slip it off my shoulders and toe of my wet boots. My sodden socks go next, followed by my gloves. My fingers can't work the button on my pants but then Bazur is there, ripping it open and helping me shove them down. He does the same with my shirt, whipping it off over my head and tossing it into a pile.

I'm too cold to feel shy. Even though I register how very naked I am right now, I'm more concerned about the blue tinge to my fingers.

Something warm and dry comes down on top of my naked form. It smells so strongly of Bazur that despite myself I let out a small moan. The soft spun wool shirt glides over my damp skin, snagging on my hard nipples, with the hem ending somewhere near my knees.

Gods, he's huge.

"Th—thank you." I turn to look over my shoulder at him. His honey eyes are nearly all black from dilated pupils. He's working the tie on his own soaked cloak. He shucks it off quickly, followed by his shirt and quickly drops his hands to the waistband of his pants. He nods his head at me.

"I need to warm you. Get under my furs, we'll have to use body heat."

Slowly I walk forward and then slide under his fur and onto his large bedroll. It will accommodate us both just fine. We'll need to be close if we want to warm ourselves quickly. Despite my chill, my pussy begins to heat. Liquid arousal pools at the thought of what's to come: Bazur, pressed against me, holding me, while I'm dressed only in his shirt.

I hear his footsteps come round to the other side of me. He's changed into dry linen pants, his dark hair is wet, a few pieces sticking to his cheeks. Pulling back the fur, he slips in next to me, not hesitating for a moment to curl his arm around my frigid body and bring me into his chest. I instantly feel comforted and safe.

Tucked against him like this, my feet hover somewhere around his knees. My body soaks in his warmth. More moisture leaks from me and my nipples tighten painfully against the front of his shirt. My hands press into his chest, feeling his solid muscles and raised scars. This feels right, like I've done it a million times.

I want to stay like this forever.

The realization steals my breath. I don't want to leave in the spring. I want to spend my days helping Myren and the other women of the village. I want to eat Bazur's weak stew. Most of all, I want us to go to bed holding each other like this every night for the rest of my life.

The vision of it is so clear to me.

I'll miss my old life, Elvie especially, but she'll understand. And when Vorgak is no longer a threat, I can take Bazur to visit them. We'll go on adventures and experience new things together. Our future can start right now if I just tell him what I'm feeling. I've put it off long enough. The gods haven't disrupted my plans after all, they've given me a firm push in the right direction.

"Are you warm?" Bazur rumbles against me, turning my center molten.

"Yes. You are very warm," I sigh, snuggling in closer, my leg rises to sling over his hip and bring him even tighter against me. Bazur's whole body tenses as he lets out a hiss. I realize why as my cheeks heat and I feel something hard pressing against my thigh.

He's aroused by me. This is the first time I've felt anything like this pressing against me. I can't help but bite my lip, my hips squirming of their own accord with this new found discovery. Bazur hisses again and I can't help the giggle that escapes me

"Sorry," I say. His hand slips around from my back to curl into my waist. His large fingers dig into my skin. Hands that are rough and so deadly but devastatingly gentle when they hold me.

At this point I'm so wet I may be risking dehydration.

"You sound really sorry," he grumbles.

"It's natural. Scientifically speaking, your body is just reacting to my closeness and as it hasn't been an issue for us before—"

He barks out a laugh, his breath tickling my face.

"You really think this is the first time you've ever made my cock hard?" he asks. My head snaps up, my mouth falling open. His words are rough and coarse and so delicious I want to drink them. His eyes are dark, simpering with enough lust to have my stomach churning.

I swallow as I replay what he said as we stare at each other.

"It's not?" I don't mean to sound naive but I've never noticed. It's never even crossed my mind to check and see if he was aroused. His stare flusters me, to know that he's been hard as well…

"Kaethe, my cock's been hard since the moment I found you in that fucking net." His tongue comes out to wet his bottom lip. My gaze tracks the movement. "I've had to find a way to handle it myself." He grits his teeth and dips his head.

"When you're away from the house or in the bath," he admits.

My heart thunders in my chest and my eyes flutter shut. Oh my gods, I'm so aroused it's almost painful. To know that he desires me that much for this long, I could climax right now.

"I shouldn't have said that," he grunts. "I'm sorry. You're uncomfortable—"

"No, I'm not. I've just never…" I pause. "I've never had that effect on someone before."

Bazur's eyes look down at me and his brows furrow incredulously.

"Believe me, you have. Some of my soldiers can't keep their eyes off of you." My nose crinkles, I've never noticed anyone's stares besides Bazur's. "You're beautiful, I understand their attraction but it doesn't mean I want to smell it."

Bazur lets out a low growl as if the thought is abhorrent to even consider. My mouth goes dry as I blink up at him. Everything around me freezes and as my heart thunders in my chest.

"You think I'm beautiful?" I ask quietly. The warmth in my chest is growing, spreading down to my fingers and toes. I'm warm now, so warm. Bazur looks down at me with confusion, as if I was crazy for asking such a question. It makes my toes curl.

"Kaethe, you're the most beautiful person I've ever seen. Some-times...*Mother of the Mountain* sometimes I can't believe you're real."

I kiss him.

Without giving myself a chance to consider the outcomes or let myself lose my nerve, I just act. I follow instinct, leaning into this primal urge to meet his mouth with my own. My kissing experience is limited and Bazur's tusks prove to be a new challenge. One that makes my pussy grow wetter.

His lips are warm and firm against my mouth. It's a chaste kiss, just a press of our lips together. I'm not sure if I should open my eyes, or what I should do with my own hands but I don't let that worry me. However as the seconds tick by and Bazur doesn't move, apprehension pricks the back of my neck.

I pull back and stare up at him, his pupils blown wide in surprise. Maybe he was put off by my technique? My obvious lack of experience? My stomach starts to sink as he remains frozen.

Oh, no. Oh gods, no. I'm an idiot. A huge fucking idiot. Have I misread this whole thing? I shouldn't have let myself get carried away. Perhaps calling someone beautiful doesn't mean the same thing to orcs as it does to humans.

Embarrassment warms my face.

"Sorry," I blurt out. I remove my leg from around his hip and try to pull away even with his arms still holding me. "I'm sorry, I misunderstood you when you said I was beautiful I didn't mean to—"

Bazur lets out a sound from deep within his chest. Suddenly I'm flat on my back with a very strong, unleashed orc male pinning me down beneath him. His mouth finds mine once more.

This time he's kissing me, really kissing me. It takes a bit of maneuvering with his tusks but he doesn't slow down. His lips tease mine and I return it eagerly, that embarrassment I felt before is wiped away when I feel his hips settle between mine. His hard cock rubs against me and I moan into our kiss.

His tongue licks the seam of my mouth and I open my lips. Large hands tangle in my hair, holding my skull firmly as he plunders my mouth.

His tongue touches mine and I don't know what to do with my own so I let him guide me. I must be doing something right because he lets out his own groan, grinding his hips even harder against my pussy.

The shirt he gave me has risen up and I'm almost completely exposed.

I don't care. I want him to see me. All of me, in a way that no one ever has and never will.

My hands dig into the hard muscles of his back as he plants kisses along my cheeks, my nose, licking the shell of my ear and making me whimper. His tongue then traces a path along my neck, sucking at my pulse and gently biting me there too. I let out a moan, my own hips rising to meet his.

"You didn't misunderstand anything," he growls, his voice more animalistic than I've ever heard it before

My heart glows in my chest and tears threaten my eyes as pure happiness pours through me. He lets out another roar as he buries his head in the juncture of my neck and shoulder. Bazur's whole body is shuddering.

"*Mother of the Mountain*, Kae, if you knew what I wanted to do to you—" He breaks off on a groan as his mouth returns to mine. It's frenzied, like we don't have much time and he has to savor this before it's over.

I whine as his hips lift from mine and I shift to try and get back some of that delicious friction. The muscles under my hands are bunched so tight I'm afraid they're going to snap his bones. Realization dawns on me. He's holding himself back to not scare me. Doesn't he realize the only thing I'm afraid of is stopping?

It dawns on me that I'll have to be the one who takes this to the next level.

I move my hands from his back and press my mouth to his once more. The sleeves of his shirt are so large that they slip off of my shoulders easily. Bazur's eyes go completely black as he watches my movements, his muscled chest rising and failing rapidly.

Pulling the shirt down until my breasts are exposed I look up at him through my lashes.

"Show me what you want to do to me."

Bazur's groan rattles the tent and I watch the last of his restraint break. He falls on me with his mouth open. He devastates my lips while his callous palms cup my breasts. I know they are on the larger side compared to other humans but Bazur's hands hold them perfectly. I'd always thought I'd feel self conscious letting someone see me like this but it's hard to be anything but confident when a powerful male is looking at you like you're a gift from the gods.

Bazur kisses a path down my chest.

"Fuck, Kaethe, these are perfect," he growls, nipping the fleshy swell of my breast. "I could come just from looking at them. They make me want to do bad things."

His mouth closes over one of my hard pink nipples and my back arches. The corresponding tug between my thighs makes me moan. Bazur uses his other hand to roll my other nipple back and forth causing me to pant.

"What kind of bad things?" I ask, losing myself to the pleasure of his touches.

"Kaethe," he warns. I don't want him to hold back, I want to know everything he's thinking. So I have to push him.

"Tell me," I whine as he licks my nipple.

"Fuck!" he shouts, gripping my breasts tighter. "Taste them, like I am now. Watch them bounce as I pound into that little, wet pussy of yours."

"Yes," I moan, the crude words send a shiver down my spine, directly to my pussy making it throb. His mouth suctions over my nipple again as his eyes find mine. It's so erotic, the way his tusks press into the soft skin on the underside of my breast.

"Kaethe, I want to fuck them. To shove my cock in between your breasts and paint them with my seed, cover you in my scent so everyone knows who you belong to," he growls.

I cry out, my pussy clamping around nothing. My hips rise to grind against him. I need him to touch me there, to touch me anywhere. His ownership of me makes my breathing more ragged.

I want him to cover me in his scent, to own me in that primal way. A part of me needs it, craves it above all else.

"Kaethe, I, fuck—" he grits out, shaking himself. "Let me give you what you need. Let me lick that sweet little pussy. Just one taste. That's more than any male deserves."

My mind is fogged with lust but in the haze a bit of apprehension trickles into my belly. Kissing and fondling is one thing, but this is a huge step for me. I want to let him see all of me finally but my nerves threaten to overwhelm me. Still, I manage to nod.

"Say it Kae, I need to hear you say it."

"Please," I murmur, shyness making my voice small. "Lick my pussy, Bazur. I n—need you to."

"Fuck," he curses, kissing down my body. He whips off his shirt that's been bunched around my waist and throws it somewhere into the tent. Bazur's eyes glow dangerously as he takes in my naked body, flushed in the dim light.

I have curves and bumps and rolls and extra padding in places other humans don't. My body is mine and I love it. It saved me that night when my village was raided, it took me through school, and helps me save people's lives. It's what turns Bazur on so much he's practically salivating over me.

That knowledge makes my arms fall to my side and my legs spread wider. I let him see every dimple, every line, every freckle and watch him go feral over them.

"Kae, Kae, Kae" he repeats my name like a prayer. "*Mother of the Mountain*, look at you. Perfect, fucking sweet and soft. Fuck, *akorzag*, I need a taste, I'll die without it." He kisses down the soft slope of my belly, his teeth and tusks sinking into my flesh there.

"You're the only one who's seen me like this. I've never—"

Bazur lets out a groan as he looks up at me from between my thighs. My pale, pink skin in such contrast with his green color. It's perfect.

"You're saving yourself for someone," he says, kissing the soft skin of my thighs. Lust clogs my brain and I nod my head.

I was saving myself for someone, for him. I've never thought my virginity was something that needs safeguarding until my wedding night to prove some complete nonsense about my purity. I just want to give it to the right person, someone I can see a future with, who makes me feel safe and comfortable.

That someone is Bazur. I let him see that confession in my eyes.

"I'm just tasting you tonight, anything more than that and—" He inhales deeply and groans, his hands reaching down to grip my thighs. "I made a vow to myself weeks ago. I swore to keep my hands off of you. I knew what would happen if I—"

His hot breath ghosts over my pussy causing me to moan and thrust my breasts into the air.

"You just had to make me break it. How could I not when you went and rubbed your little pink pussy on my thigh? Soaking me with your sweetness." He kisses along the inside of my thigh, his teeth grazing my sensitive skin. "I want you to soak my face now. Come all over it so that when we return to the village tomorrow all the males will know I had the privilege of tasting your sweet cunt."

He leans down, pressing his nose against my mound one more time before his tongue licks straight up my center.

"Bazur!" I scream, my thighs clamping together around his ears. His giant hands grip me just under my knees, pushing my legs back towards my chest and exposing my untouched, wet flesh to his eyes. Even in the dark tent I can see how wet I am. His groan rings in my ears.

Then he begins to feast on me.

His tongue laps at my clit as his hands continue to hold my legs up and back. I'm unable to move but my hands find his head. My fingers tunnel into the soft, dark strands of his hair pulling on it as he sucks my clit into his mouth. He alternates between flicking it with his tongue and pulling it deep into his mouth.

My breathing is frantic, my hips try and squirm as I try to work myself on his tongue. Bazur pulls back slightly, his mouth curving into a smirk, green lips glistening with my arousal.

Before I can question what he's going to do next he leans down and licks my back entrance. I scream and my thighs tighten against his ears once more. The sensation is obscenely decadent.

"What I wouldn't give to get my cock in this little hole too."

"Bazur," I say, my body starting to shake. I'm not scared of what he's saying, I'm only curious. He makes me feel safe, there's nothing scary about this.

"I'm being too greedy." He shakes himself, his mouth settling over my clit once more.

"Bazur, I—"

"I haven't even made you come yet. I need to taste it." He nips my clit gently with his tusks and my stomach begins to tighten. "Kae?"

"Yes?" My hips are moving on their own accord again trying to seek out his mouth.

"Promise me something."

"Anything," I moan, needing his mouth back on me.

"When you come, scream my name. I can die a happy male having heard it just once." His words confuse me but they become irrelevant a moment later when his mouth is back on me. Licking and sucking, biting and pulling. His mouth attaches to me and my legs go over his shoulders. His muscular forearm pins my hips down so I have no option but to take his attack.

The sensation is everything. I can hear the wet sounds my pussy is making and that causes my thighs to shake. Bazur's eyes lift to mine, looking almost fevered. I feel his tongue prod my entrance and I explode.

My muscles tense, my body locks up, my pussy clenches around this new intrusion. I keep my promise and scream his name. My come leaks out of me and Bazur eagerly laps it up. He kisses my pussy once, then twice, then a third time before removing his arm from my hips. His lips trace up my body before he reaches my mouth.

Bazur kisses me and I can taste myself on his lips. Even after coming so hard my body is primed to go again, more wetness coating my thighs. However, it seems like Bazur has other ideas when he reaches for his shirt and slips it back on over my head.

I'm confused but maybe it's normal to take breaks between each act. I'm basically vibrating with the need to feel him inside of me. Bazur plants a soft kiss on my forehead and pulls me on to his chest. My fingers trace some of the scars there.

He's looking at me funny. His hands smooth over my hair and draw circles along my back. I feel so wonderful, so much lighter than I ever have in my entire life. This is perfect, so unbelievably perfect. I want more of it. I want it forever.

"Bazur, that was…I don't even know what to say." My cheeks warm as I smile into his chest, planting a small kiss there. What is Bazur to me now? My lover? That doesn't sound right. My mate? The thought makes my heart beat faster in my chest.

"It was more than I ever deserved, Kae." He kisses my forehead again.

"Do you want to," I pause. "You know, do you want me to—" He growls but shakes his head.

"Not tonight. I wouldn't be able to stop myself from fucking you." I lift my head off of his chest.

"You don't want to do that with me?" I ask, unease prickling the back of my neck.

"It doesn't matter what I want," he says softly, using his finger to trace over my nose as if memorizing the shape. "You're saving yourself. I understand wanting to wait for your mate."

My head pops up and my eyes are wide. "Bazur that's not what I—" My words catch in my throat and it's like a cold bucket of water has been dumped on me. Dread curdles my stomach as I ask.

"Are you waiting for your mate?" Bazur shudders and can't meet my eyes, his hands pause their movements on my back. I hear what he says next loud and clear. My heart shatters with one sentence.

"It's every orc's dream to find their mate."

His mate. The word hangs heavy between us. In the midst of all this new discovery I hadn't even bothered to take into account that he would be waiting for his mate, the other half of his soul. Someone he believes is not me. Even if a small, ridiculously hopeful part of me thought that he could be mine.

I was incorrect in my assumption that even if I wasn't, I would be enough. He wants me, desires me, lusts for me, but I'll never be his. He won't claim me in that primal, all-consuming way. He can't.

And I'd rather be alone than stay with him knowing he'll eventually leave me for someone else. Even if that means breaking my own heart in the process. It's better to get it over now. The pain will get worse the longer I let this continue.

His eyes narrow as he takes in my rigid posture but before he can say anything I quickly roll off of him and move over to my own bedroll. Somehow I feel more numb than when I first got to this tent. I use this newfound coldness to rebuild my walls, closing myself off to him. Making them thicker and strong enough to hold the bleeding, broken parts of my heart.

"Kaethe." He says my name but I grab my own fur and pull it over myself.

"I'm warm now. We should try and leave after the storm clears. Myren needs these roots as soon as possible." Under the fur, I curl into myself and press my palms into my eyes. I won't cry. Not when I can hear his breathing and still feel his fingers on my thighs.

"Goodnight, Kae," he says softly in the dark. His voice is like a knife, twisting inside my heart. I say nothing and burrow down under the blanket. I let the storm pounding against the tent lull me to sleep and allow the warmth I felt for Bazur freeze over.

CHAPTER 22

BAZUR

THE STORM STOPPED RIGHT AFTER dawn.

After securing the rest of Kaethe's belongings that survived while exposed to the elements, we set off on the back of my wolf. The ride was tense and grueling. There was no time for breaks and Kaethe spent the entire time rigid, barely leaning back against me.

How had the most perfect evening ended like that? I had finally gotten to see her, touch her soft skin, and feast on her delicious body. Kaethe kissed me first. It was such a shock I couldn't even register what was happening. Once I did, something inside me had snapped. Her mouth had been so sweet, her moans even sweeter.

Mother of the Mountain her breasts? Large and round, they filled my hands like they were made just for me. Her flushed skin, her curves, her wide hips, and best of all that little cunt hidden beneath a dusting of dark hair. Kae had been so, *so* wet for me. Her pussy had been silky and juicy and when she came on my face—

I have to swallow down my growl and will my body not to react. I doubt she'd welcome my hard cock now. Kaethe came to me shy and unsure and I watched her blossom in front of my eyes. Confident and in control of herself, all because she saw the truth in my gaze. She finally saw everything that I was dying to say and wanted me to use my body to express it.

But then she said she was saving herself for someone. Not me. That had been a punch to the stomach. She wanted me to fuck her, she was so aroused and willing it was like a gift from *the Mother*. But I couldn't take that from her. It's bad enough that one day she'll find herself in the arms of another. I wouldn't be able to survive if she regretted anything between us.

Even though it looks like she does now. I should've never mentioned the word mate. It shut her down and made her realize what she almost gave to me at the height of lust. If she hadn't scrambled off of me so fast I would've told her that while it's every orc's dream to find their mate, it's no longer mine.

That I'll gladly forsake my bond in order to have her.

Now, I fear last night ruined whatever closeness Kaethe and I had. I miss her being in my arms, I miss her smile, and the way she rolls her eyes when I don't understand a joke of hers. I miss her and she's not even a foot away from me.

It's late afternoon when we cross back into the village. A few people greet us as we return and I lead Kaethe back to our house to unload the supplies. She sits further up on the saddle, removing her warmth from me completely.

I want to tear down this wall of ice between us but I don't know how. Nothing will change the fact that I'm not her mate, not who she's saving herself for. I'd have asked her to forsake her own bond to stay with me but she pulled away.

There's a part of me that is grateful I at least got one taste. Got to hear her call my name as she dripped down my chin. It's more than I ever hoped for. I'd never regret what we did, but if I could go back and change this distance from forming between us I would in a second.

My *icewolf* has barely stopped moving when Kaethe scrambles off the saddle. She unties her bag carrying the containers of mint root and slings it across her body. Her face is so beautiful in the golden sun. Her brown eyes look away from me, cold and distant. Seeing that is like a knife to my heart.

Before I can ask if she's okay she turns away and crunches through the snow murmuring something about getting the roots to Lady Myren at once. I'm not letting her avoid me that easily.

"Kaethe!" I call and she freezes, her shoulders hunching.

"We need to talk about what happened in the tent," I say, crossing my arms over my chest. Kaethe's eyes widen for a second and then I watch with horror as she shakes herself and plasters a smile on her face. Not her real smile filled with warmth and shyness, this one is hard and forced.

"There's nothing to talk about, in fact I think we should just forget it ever happened."

My feet feel unsteady on the ground. "I don't want to forget it happened, Kae."

"Look, we aren't the first two people to ever get carried away. It's mainly my fault. I mean…I kissed you." Her cheeks grow pink, the only genuine thing about her expression. "We can be casual about this. Nothing has to change."

"Everything has changed," I reply. This wall she's erected between us is ten feet high. She's shut me out, I can physically feel it.

"No it hasn't. Finding your mate is important to you, that type of devotion is important to me too. It's obvious we're not mates." The statement makes my stomach turn, but she's right. She's Kaehte, not my mate, and she's mine nonetheless. "I can't do something casual knowing that we're both waiting for someone else."

Her voice is sad, that fake smile slipping and my hands itch to grab her. To crush her to my chest and confess everything. That wouldn't be fair to her, what good would those declarations do when there is a very lucky male out there who will get to have her. Who will bind his soul to hers and see her in his dreams and every thought just like I do.

No matter how much I wish I was that lucky male, I am not. Kaethe deserves more than that.

"I should go," she says quietly. I can only nod as I watch her disappear down the street. I look up towards the house and can't bear to go inside, her scent covers everything. The knowledge that it will fade one day makes my stomach sour. Turning towards town, I walk to try and clear my head.

The first frost is approaching and everyone is preparing. I'm proud of how much this village has grown over the last decade. This is a safe haven my father always envisioned. It will lose something when Kaethe leaves. I've always loved the summers, they felt a reward for surviving a harsh winter. Now I wish this one never comes because it will take Kaethe with it.

I don't realize how far I've wandered until I'm standing outside of the butcher's. The healthy wailings of a baby can be heard from outside and my heart squeezes. My mind immediately pictures Kaethe, swollen with my child. She would be so rosy and gorgeous that my chest tightens at the image. It's so vivid in my mind it's as if I've already seen it.

The front door to the butcher's flies open and Pardak comes lumbering down the stairs. His yellow eyes connect with mine and he gives a surprised smile. He's a few years younger than me, never trained as a soldier, meaning his tusks aren't as pronounced.

"Bazur, what brings you here? We have some *frostelk* meat I can have wrapped up for you. Jessica wanted to make sure Kaethe had enough provisions before the frost hit." I nod at him and try to ignore the crowded feeling in my throat.

"Kaethe has received many gifts. She's set for several winters."

"She deserves it," Pardak says and I nod my head. Kaethe does.

"How is your mate and child?" I ask. Mate, the word tastes different now.

"Wonderful. My Jessica glows with happiness, she was meant to be a mother. My son looks like me, but he has his mother's personality. Both of them are a gift I don't deserve."

"*The Mother of the Mountain* is generous."

"She is, she brought Kaethe to us." *Kaethe, Kaethe, Kaethe.* Her name rings in my head. I look at Pardak so in love and fulfilled. My chest yawns open, the longing there so strong.

"How long have you and Jessica been mated?"

Pardak cups his chin and lowers his brows in thought. "Well, she came to live with my family five years ago, but I didn't realize she was my mate until a few months after that."

My blood freezes, a sharp ringing sounding in my ear.

"You mean…it wasn't instant? I thought mating bonds happened mere moments after meeting?"

Pardak chuckles softly and shakes his head. "Between orcs, yes. Humans don't have mating bonds like we do. There's no primal urge that drives them to mate and claim. It's something softer and it can take longer to form."

I feel the ground shift beneath my feet as I take in his words.

"Bazur are you okay?" Pardak asks, concern lacing his voice.

"What does it feel like? How did you know Jessica was your mate?"

Pardak looks wary but answers me anyway. "I didn't notice much at first. If anything she annoyed me because she was so fragile. I felt like I had to protect her and that irritated me. Soon I realized that I wanted to keep her safe, above all else.

"We were arguing one day over something small and she just kissed me. It was a shock to my system and then I realized how ignorant I'd been to the truth. If I concentrated I could feel the bond between us. I realized it had always been there from the start." He smiles softly. "It's not this overwhelming claiming fever, it's something more delicate and precious. Just like the human female I'm bonded to."

My mind is racing, my hands are sweating and trembling as I try to process what he's saying. "Then you were mates from that point forward? The mating frenzy went into effect?" I ask.

"*Mother*, no. Then I had to convince her to fall in love with me. I had to show her that I was worthy of her. It was only then when I explained to her what I felt, she told me she felt it too. Each day the bond grows a little deeper between us." Pardak's eyes sparkle as they meet mine.

My head is spinning. Pardak asks me if I'm okay again but I mumble a thank you and turn to leave. I'm not okay, I'm so far from okay. Have I been ignorant to what was right in front of me? Have I ruined everything without even realizing?

I stumble back to my house in a daze. This news has changed everything and instead of feeling unsettled I feel…hopeful. A quiet joy lights up my chest at the possibility that I've been so incredibly wrong.

It's late by the time I arrive back home.

There's a bowl of cold stew sitting out for me and my heart warms at the gesture. The second floor is dark and as I climb up the stairs I can see Kaethe's sleeping form underneath the blankets.

Stripping down to my undershirt and pants, I slide into bed beside her and take a deep breath. Pardak's words float back to me. *That if I concentrated on it I could feel the bond between us.* I shut my eyes and let my mind clear, focusing on my heart, my body, my soul. Everything that I am is filled with Kaethe, her face imprinted on every part of me.

Even as I try to center myself I can't stop myself from recalling her smiles, her smell, her moans of pleasure as I licked her cunt. How perfect she is, how much I want to protect her from harm. How I will give anything to get rid of this separation—

There in the dark I feel it. It's a tiny thing, just like her, but it's there. I can see it in my mind, a shining, glowing string that's tying my soul to the one next to me. Exhilaration flows through me, this new knowledge overwhelms my senses.

Kaethe is mine. Mine.

She always has been. Every moment with her replays in my head. From me finding her in my hunting net, to riding on my *icewolf* together, to me giving her my cloak so she would be warm. Walks to Lady Myren's, eating stew together, and falling asleep holding hands. Her jokes, her smiles, her body, her face, everything is right there and I can feel it, taste it, and my body screams at me to claim her.

It's why I said those words to her in my language. It was my soul trying to push me towards her, my heart realizing the truth before I did. She is my most precious one, my only one.

And I get to keep her, I get to have her…if I can convince her I deserve her. My Kae needs to know that I'll do anything to prove myself worthy of her. There is no one else for either of us. I am the only male who gets to claim her. She's mine.

I know exactly what I need to do.

Silently, I slip from the bed and make my way downstairs. My body hates being so far away from her but this is worth it. I grab some parchment and a pen, not even bothering with a coat and head towards where we keep our messenger ravens. There are consequences for what I am about to do, but I don't care.

Kaethe is more than worth the risk.

CHAPTER 23

KAETHE

B AZUR ISN'T AT HOME WHEN I wake up in the morning.

I felt him come to bed late last night and left moments after climbing in beside me. I don't know where he's gone, all I know is that I miss him terribly. Maybe I was too rash in saying I didn't want something casual. It will hurt me when he eventually leaves me for his mate but nothing can be more unbearable then the pain I am experiencing now.

His marks on my thighs have faded and that made me sob softly as I dressed this morning. I want them back, I want to be back in his arms.

With time perhaps his wants will change. Maybe his affections towards me will grow and he'll no longer desire to find his mate. My chest felt so hollow yesterday but it glows again for him, even more so now. I should've told him the truth about what I felt. Despite what I said before, I'm not waiting for anyone else.

Bazur is it for me and I'm done pretending that he's not. I'd rather him break my heart knowing everything than let him believe he doesn't mean anything to me.

I'm late walking into Myren's. Mornga is there, her smile is warm in greeting. I nod to both her and Myren as I hang up my cloak by the door. A steaming cup of tea is already waiting for me.

The two women speak in *orcish*. They're speaking about an old…man… something to do with his door? No his son, something to do with his son.

"Do you think you could teach me *orcish?*" I ask, taking a sip of tea. "I've picked up a few words here and there, already."

Mornga looks surprised as does Myren.

"You want to learn?" Mornga asks, she breathes in through her nose and her eyes widen in surprise as she stares at me.

"It would be easier to communicate with the younger patients who come in," I explain. Most of them speak the elven language but the younger ones aren't fluent yet. It hasn't been a real problem but it could become a big one as I plan on staying.

Because I am staying.

"Which words have you picked up?" Myren asks, taking a sip of her own tea.

I list off the few *orcish* words that I know and the two females both nod.

"*Akorzag* means annoying or something like that, right?" Curiosity got the better of me, even though I'm not sure I want the answer.

Myren's head snaps up and Mornga freezes where she stands. I shift uncomfortably under their stares. Their reactions make the hairs on the back of my neck stand up.

"Where did you hear that word?" Myren asks, her hands trembling slightly.

"Bazur calls me it all the time," I say softly. Myren almost drops her teacup and Mornga stands next to me, making me crane my neck up to look at her.

"Technically, it's a name for a jewel that was found deep within the mountain. Its direct translation is *'my precious one'*." My heart beats quickly in my chest. My palms turn sweaty and I set my teacup down before I, too, almost drop it.

"More commonly it's used for—"

"It's used as a term of endearment between mates." Myren interrupts, her green eyes are serious as they bore into mine. "My precious one, my *only* one."

My hands begin to tremble. All this time, that's what he's been calling me? I thought it meant annoying, to find out…He called me it that very first night by the fire. This whole time the truth has been right there.

The icy walls I've built crack as I realize he's not waiting for anyone else either. The two of us have been so foolish. Me most of all.

I've kept too many secrets and I've withheld too much from him. I think back to the last time he called me that name. It was in the tent, right before he licked my pussy. I have so many questions for him, but more than anything I need to see him. Now. I rise from my seat in a daze. "I—I have to go."

"Yes, you do," Mornga agrees. I put on my cloak with numb fingers and make my way down the snowy street, not registering the world around me. My feet trudge quickly through the snow. People greet me as I pass but they're just a blur, I'm focused on one thing.

Bazur.

I'm at the training yard and I don't see him. He's larger than the others he should be easy to spot. I spy Zarod and he winks at me before sauntering over to where I am by the fence.

"Visiting me at work, Kae? What would Bazy say?" he chuckles, abruptly stopping when he sees my face. "What's wrong?"

"Bazur," I murmur. "Where is Bazur?"

Zarod lowers his brows and gestures over to Bazur's house. "At home, said he received something important—"

I stomp off without a goodbye. I'll apologize for my rudeness later but I don't have time. My need for Bazur grows with each passing moment. I push open the door, immediately greeted by the warmth from the roaring fireplace. Standing over the kitchen table is Bazur.

My knees almost buckle as he looks over at me, a soft smile on his face. "Bazur—"

"I wrote to the other generals about your brother. I didn't give away your connection to him, but I asked around. A few of them can be trusted but they'll want some form of payment to turn over their humans."

"Bazur," I try saying again, my heart filling with warmth and affection. Standing next to him at the table I can see the countless messages all written in *orcish.*

"There's still a chance the man I told you about is him, but if he's not I'll pay whatever these other generals want. I'll find him for you, challenge the other generals if I have to."

The icy walls I built shatter, as if they were never there.

"Bazur."

"If that doesn't work then I'll go to your village, Kaethe. I'll ask if anyone knows where he could be and I'll leave no stone unturned until I can get you answers."

I put my hand on his forearm and his gaze meets mine.

"Bazur," I say softly.

"I'll do anything to make you happy, Kaethe. I'll do whatever I can to help you. You're important to me." He covers my hand with his large one. "You're *the* most important thing to me."

My laugh is watery and I smile up at him, tears blurring my vision. I cup his cheek, my thumb tracing the line of his beard. He's so brutally handsome my nipples harden against the front of my gown.

It's time, no more hiding from the truth.

"Bazur, I know what *akorzag* means." Bazur lets out a breath and it tickles my face. Pushing up onto my toes I place a gentle kiss on his lips. "This whole time, that's what you've been calling me. Your precious one, your—"

"If you weren't my mate I didn't want one, I never should've let you think otherwise. There's no one more perfect in this entire world for me. You're beautiful, smart, compassionate, and so, *so* brave. I hate that I was too much of a coward to not just tell you. I hate that I made you question what you meant to me. You mean everything to me." He takes another shuddering breath and I feel tears slip down my cheeks.

"It's obvious what you are to me. I feel it in my heart, in my soul; it's always been there tying you to me. Your mine, you've always been mine."

"I've been a fool too," I say, pressing up to kiss his lips again. "I kept things to myself when I should've just told you the truth. I was so scared of the possibility that you would leave me for someone else."

Bazur lets out a low growl and I kiss him again.

"There will never be anyone else for me, Kaethe. What else can I do to show you all that you mean to me?"

"What you've done for me Bazur, the risks you've taken to help find my brother…I never should've doubted you. I never should've doubted what I felt. You're mine too." I reach for the tie of my cloak and let it slide to the floor behind me while smiling up at him. "I think we both know a way for you to show me what I mean to you."

Bazur lets out a groan and scoops me up in his arms. He climbs the ladder in seconds and then my back hits the bed. His massive body comes down on top of me. Bazur's mouth lands on mine and a part of my soul is freed. My hands snake up his back into his hair and tug. He growls, his own hands skating across my body.

His warm tongue slips past my lips and my pussy grows even wetter, my nipples achingly hard. My legs fall open and he slides between them, I can feel his hard cock pressing against me.

Bazur lets out a snarl as his hands grip the top of my gown.

"I'll buy you more." It's my only warning before he rips the fabric in half. I moan as his finger circles my nipple through the thin material of my shift. The sun is shining from the skylight above, there's no hiding from this. He kisses my mouth once more before he gives my shift the same treatment as my dress. I help kick off my boots until I'm left in only my knee-high wool socks.

Shuffling down the bed, Bazur sits back and picks up one of my feet, gently pulling off the gray sock. I squirm as he places a kiss on my shin, then my ankle, and then the top of my foot. Letting out a squeal when he nips my toes with his tusks, I use my other foot to push against his chest.

"Stop! Not my toes," I giggle. His hand snags my other foot and gives my other leg the same treatment.

"Everything about you is delicious, *akorzag*." My pussy gets drenched at the use of that word. "Don't deny me any part of this feast."

"I want to feast on you too," I say, watching as his whole body tenses. He lets go of my feet and my thighs rub together. My arousal slips down my legs and Bazur shudders as he inhales deeply. Rising from the bed he begins removing his own clothes with brutal efficiency. I lean up on my elbows to get a better look at him undressing

"Fuck, Kae, I want to savor this but I'm dangerously close to coming just from looking at you." I blush and bite my lip. "Never wanted anyone this fucking much."

"Me neither," I say, my cheeks getting even warmer. "I mean you know I've never been with anyone else but still…"

"Kae." Bazur's hands freeze at the lacing of his pants. He leans down onto the bed, his hands bracing on either side of my body as he presses a gentle kiss to my forehead. "You're safe with me, we'll go slow. I've never been with a human before, in a way this is both of our first times."

My smile is small as I nod. "I like the idea of that."

Lifting his hand from the bed, he uses his thumb to pull down my bottom lip before his hand coasts lower, wrapping around my neck.

"Your pussy is mine. And now I'm going to claim it. Other males will smell you and know exactly who owns you." His voice turns dangerously soft. "And what will happen if they try to take you from me."

There's so much cold violence in his voice that I should be scared. I most definitely shouldn't be turning even more aroused. I let out a sigh as he gives my throat a light squeeze before dropping his hand.

He moves back to the end of the bed and finishes undoing the laces of his pants. My eyes widen as I take in what I'm staring at. I don't think cocks are supposed to be that large. Like his amount of abs, the size of his cock seems completely, medically unnecessary. The shaft is the same green as the rest of his body, with the head being a few shades darker. Dark veins decorate the sides and…my eyes narrow on this newly revealed body part. *Are those ridges?*

I need to explore this new discovery for science, of course.

Squirming on the bed, I watch him pad over to me. His cock is so long and hard it bounces with each step, pointing straight up to rest against his stomach. Bazur kneels on the bed and now it points at me like an accusation. Gods, it must be almost as long as my forearm, almost as big around as my fist.

How is that going to fit inside me?

Bazur chuckles and I realize I just said that outloud. "I need to get you nice and wet first, *akorzag*. Don't be scared of it, my cock's only purpose is to pleasure you."

His lips curl into a smile. Bazur is gruff and stoic but in bed he's the opposite.

"It's massive."

"You can take it." He crawls on top of me again, our naked skin grazing each other. His hand comes up to untie my braided hair, letting it fall down my back in a pink wave. "You'll be taking it every day for the rest of your life."

I whimper over his declaration.

"Tell me you want that," he commands me but I see the earnest plea in his eyes, hear the uncertainty in his voice. There's no going back from this and I want to embrace it fully, with everything that I am.

"I want that. I want you."

His mouth finds mine again. His tusks pressing against my mouth as his tongue dances with my own. My hands tangle in his hair, pulling it from his own leather band and raking my hands through the shoulder length strands. Bazur moans into my mouth before his lips leave mine.

A warm, wet tongue glides up the length of my neck and I shudder. My pussy throbs as he leaves kisses along my jaw and nips at the soft underside of my chin. Pushing me down gently onto my back, he settles between my splayed thighs.

Bazur kisses in between my breasts and mutters something in *orcish* before shaking himself. Squeezing one breast, he sucks the other into his mouth, working my nipple into a tight peak. With a pop, he releases it.

I groan, my hands tangling into his hair. With one last squeeze, he kisses down my stomach, licking into my navel before his breath ghosts over my pussy.

"A day is too long to be away from this little cunt." I squirm as he runs a finger through my wetness before sucking it into his mouth. "So fucking sweet. No one should be this sweet, not even you. Have a taste."

Bazur runs a thick finger through my pussy again, my arousal making it glisten in the light. He holds it towards me, I hesitate before opening my mouth. I taste myself and Bazur's eyes grow wild. I guess I taste sweet? All I know is that when I suck his finger more firmly into the warm cavern of my mouth he groans.

"I need you to do that to my cock." I giggle and nip at the tip of his finger. "*Mother of the Mountain*, I need you to do *that* to my cock even more."

His finger leaves my mouth and he squeezes my breast once more before bracing his hands back on my thighs. I bite my lip and look down at him. Taking him into my mouth excites me. I'm not scared or nervous, I welcome these new experiences and I can't wait to try them all with him.

Bazur's fingers dig into the soft skin of my inner thighs and holds them open as he stares down at my pussy. His breathing is heavy and his eyes are wild as he looks up at me.

"This little cunt is so fucking pretty. It was mine as soon as I licked it. It was mine from the moment we met." Bazur spits down onto my sex, I watch as his saliva slips down my slit. It's crude and erotic, it makes my hips begin to rise of their own accord. "You like that?"

"Yes," I moan.

"I've figured you out." Bazur bends down to run his tongue up my center. "The blushing, shy alchemist is what you portray to the world, but in our bed, I see the real you. You're a greedy girl. My greedy girl, who's going to grind her little pussy against my tongue until she comes. Aren't you?"

I'm panting but I nod my head. Bazur isn't lying, that's how I usually am but not when we are together like this. This side of me was always there; he was just the one that had to unlock it.

Bazur latches on to my clit making me scream. His hands hold my legs open as they try to lock around his head. My pussy clenching down around nothing. I move my hips against his mouth and he's right, I do grind for my orgasm. He growls against me, the vibrations rattling along my nerve endings.

One of his hands leaves my legs and dips into my opening. I tense up at the intrusion but Bazur soothes me by giving my clit another thorough lick. The tip of his finger slides into me. I feel so full I don't know how I'm about to take his cock inside of me.

"So fucking tight," Bazur growls, his finger retreating slowly then pushing back in. He does it over and over again, his assault on my clit causing my muscles to loosen. My climax is close, I can feel release warming my stomach. Without warning Bazur adds another finger inside of me and I'm done for.

My pussy clamps around his fingers so hard I feel like I might break them. He licks me feverishly through my climax. My back arching clean off the bed and my thighs trembling. The sensation spreads throughout my body, settling in my chest and making itself at home. I shudder again as I watch Bazur pull his fingers from my entrance and lick them clean. His chin shiny with my come.

We stare at each other for a long moment. There's such a look of devotion in his eyes but instead of making me shy I grow bolder. I want him to see just how much I've flourished with his attention. This male is obsessed with me and I want him to know it's very much mutual.

Bazur crawls up the bed towards me once more, the fur blanket beneath me tickles my extra sensitive skin. He swoops down to kiss me but I move my head at the last moment with a giggle. His eyes narrow as he tries again but I dodge his kiss once more.

"What are you playing at, Kaethe?" I bat my eyelashes innocently and wait for him to try and kiss me again. When he moves quickly to ensnare my mouth, I move faster. Using the element of surprise to lock my legs around his middle and flip him on his back. He laughs into my mouth, his hands coming up to rest on my ass. Kneading the supple mounds in his massive hands, he gives one a light smack and I squeal.

"I love your ass." He spanks the other cheek just as lightly. I kiss him again before sliding down his body. His tough skin scrapes against my nipples and I sigh at the sensation. I know how much he loves my breasts so I rub them along his front, dragging them against the rigid planes of his chest.

From this position, his cock pushes against my stomach and I make sure to squirm on it as well. Extending my tongue I run it over each one of his abs, they are flexed in response to my movements. His massive chest is rising and falling, his pupils blown wide. I bite my lip again and press soft kisses to his stomach before going lower.

"Kaethe," he hisses, "you want me in your mouth?"

My lips graze the head of his cock. Its bulbous tip is warm as I press a gentle kiss to it and nod my head. I have no frame of reference when it comes to this but like with any good experiment I'll just gauge his responses. He fists the sheets at his sides as I give his cock another kiss.

An excellent reaction in my humble opinion.

I give the dark green head of his cock one more kiss and am rewarded by a little bead of moisture at the tip. Sticking out my tongue,

I lick up his seed, his salty flavor explodes on my tongue. His eyes flutter shut and then snap back open, as if the sensation is too much but he can't miss a moment of what's happening.

"*Mother of the Mountain*," he growls.

I swirl my tongue around the head of his cock, licking up more seed that leaks from him. Like I did with his finger before, I suck him fully into my mouth. His hands shred the blankets at his sides as he sits up. This is the strongest reaction so far and it urges me to keep going. I suck him deeper into my mouth, using some of my saliva to help me pump him with my hand. It takes me a few tries to get the rhythm right but once I do Bazur's groans fill the air.

"Perfect," he growls.

I brush my tongue along those ridges I spied early and wonder how they'll feel inside of me. Gently, I graze the sides of his cock with my teeth and he groans.

"You do that again, Kae, and I won't be able to stop from fucking your mouth."

I moan and feel more moisture leak out of my pussy. His hands spear into my hair as he grips my skull. There's a part of me that craves his dominance and authority. I don't want him to hold back with me.

With that thought spurring me on, I graze him with my teeth again.

"You love robbing me of my fucking control, don't you?" I nod my head on his cock, saliva dribbling down my chin. His fingers tighten on my scalp and he holds my head still and lifts his hips to meet my mouth.

This is deeper than I've taken him and his cock nudges the back of my throat making my eyes water. I don't stop him, I know that I can if it gets too much. I want him to lose control and push me past my limits. I work him with my hand as he goes deeper into my mouth, over and over again.

His ab muscles tense and he curses. "Fuck, Kae, I'm going to come. I wanted the first time to be in your cunt but your mouth is too good. Fuck."

I squeeze his thigh and his grip on my head loosens. Sliding him out of my mouth, I pump him in my fist.

"Wait—"

"Did I hurt you?" Bazur is immediately reaching for me. "I was too rough, I knew I was. You're so tiny, compared to me Kaethe. I'm sorry, I—"

"Bazur," I cut him off, "you didn't hurt me. I was going to ask if you wanted to do what you said before in the tent."

His brows lower and I run my tongue along his cock again. "Don't you want to come on my breasts?"

Bazur stops breathing, another spurt of seed leaks from the tip of cock, covering my fingers that grip him. I slip off the bed, my knees sink into the soft carpet as I motion him to sit on the edge. Even from this angle my head is just level with his cock. Taking him in my hand again, I give the underside of cock a kiss and then lick up the seam of his balls.

"Well?" I ask, batting my eyelashes again. How had I ever been shy before? I feel capable, like I do when I'm healing someone. I feel in charge and sure of myself.

"Kaethe, *akorzag,* I can't believe you're going to let me do this." He grits his teeth as I continue to jerk him. "Next time, it's all going in your cunt."

I nod and lick his cock once more. He's so handsome and powerful, my fingers dig into the hard muscles of his corded thighs. My teeth graze his balls and he curses.

"Fuck, I'm coming," he growls and I nod encouragingly.

"Get some on my face, I want to taste it." He tenses and then his hand is on top of mine as we pump him together. His face contorts in pleasure and the first spray of his seed lands across my nose, followed by another one that decorates my lips. Together we aim his cock lower and I press up onto my knees so the next spurt hits my chest. The white, sticky substance is warm as it lands on my skin. There's so much of it that a few more jets land on my chin and cheeks.

Bazur shudders as the last of it leaves his cock. Looking him in the eye, I lick my lips as I swallow it down. His eyes are fevered as he watches me, his massive chest rising and falling. I run a finger through the come on my chest and suck it clean in my mouth.

"You taste sweet too," I say. Bazur stares at me so tenderly and lifts me from the floor. I'm sticky and satisfied but I don't want to stop, not yet. I watch his cock harden again before my eyes and smile.

Picking up one of the shredded blankets on the bed, Bazur mops at my skin.

"Do you need anything, *akorzag*?" Bazur asks, placing a kiss on my temple.

"Could you bring me the trunk with my herbs please?" I ask. Bazur looks confused but nods, retrieving it for me quickly while I admire his naked backside. He sets the truck down beside me and I pop open the top.

"What are you looking for?" My fingers find the jar I need and pluck it from the trunk and set it down beside me. Myren and I made these last week and I'm so happy I snagged one.

"This." I hold the jar of cream out towards him.

"What is it?"

"Something that will help you ease your way inside of me." I watch him twist off the cap and stick a finger into the milky substance. "It'll still hurt at first but this should help considerably."

Bazur's eyes widen and he twists the lid back on.

"*Akorzag*, I don't want to hurt you. If you're too small for my cock then we'll figure something else out." I kiss his cheek, his genuine concern is sweet. It makes me want him inside of me even more.

"I'm a virgin, Bazur. It's going to hurt the first time regardless. This will help that." He still looks unsure and I sigh. "If you aren't inside of me in the next five minutes I'm going to run naked through the training yard."

The wind is almost knocked out of me as he flips me onto my back.

"Where does this go?" he asks, unscrewing the top.

"Put some inside me," I urge him. He scoops out a decent amount on his finger and spreads it all over my opening, tucking his finger just into my entrance to smear some in there. I moan at the contact, the cream mixing with my own arousal makes an obscenely sloppy sound. "Now put a lot on that monstrous cock of yours."

He chuckles and shakes his head sending the black strands of his hair scattering around his shoulders. Using his hand, he uses a lot to coat all sides of his cock. The cream makes it shiny and he hands me back the jar to set on the nightstand. I have a feeling we will be needing this quite a lot.

"Now?" he asks. I smile and spread my legs as far as they will go. Letting his gaze lick over every part of me and watch his eyes darken even further.

"I need you inside of me, Bazur."

His shoulders rise with the force of his inhale as he shuffles towards me. With our size difference, he grabs a pillow beside me and shoves it under my hips, raising me so that his cock is level with my pussy.

Bazur leans down, nudging my entrance with his massive cock. The cream has made us both slick enough that the head breeches me with very little effort. Already I feel full and the anticipation is making me shiver.

My hands cup his cheeks as I bring his mouth to mine. His kiss is devastatingly soft. He feeds me another inch of his cock before he feels resistance.

"Kaethe I—"

"Claim me, Bazur. You said you owned my pussy, now own it."

With a growl into my mouth he gently pushes past the barrier of my virginity. There is a pinch and tug inside of me; I squirm at the pressure. The cream has definitely helped him but he's huge, there's no way to avoid the discomfort.

"Are you okay?" he asks me but I am too lost in the sensation to respond. "Kaethe."

My eyes blink open at him and I nod. With one great shuddering breath he pushes the rest of the way inside of me, those ridges on the side of his cock drag along the walls of my pussy. He stills inside of me, both of us trying to catch our breath.

The pressure builds and builds and then it stops. The discomfort dulls and I realize the pain reliever herbs inside the cream are working. Thank the gods.

After a few minutes the pain is gone and now all I want is to feel him move inside me.

"Move. Please move, Bazur, I want to feel you."

"Fuck, your pretty little pussy is squeezing me so tight, Kae. So fucking tight it's making my headspin."

"Fuck me, please. Fuck me." Bazur lets out a growl and grips my hips in his hands, and then, oh gods, *oh gods*…

He's slow at first, a quick retreat of his hips before snapping them forward, before he starts to really move. His thighs flex with the force of his thrusts as he pounds into me. Our skin slaps together echoing around the room.

We moan in time with each other, his hands holding my waist are firm as he fucks me onto his length. My breasts bounce in rhythm with his thrusts and my eyes start to close. The sensation is too much, too good. His scent wraps around me, dragging me higher and higher towards bliss. Those ridges inside of me only amplify the pleasure, while his cock hits a pleasurable spot deep inside of me.

"Give me your eyes, Kaethe. I need to see them as I fuck you." He grits his teeth as he continues to power into me. Sweat glides down the hard muscles of his chest. "My pussy, my Kaethe. I'm the only one who's had this pussy. You kept it for me until I could find you. Good girl."

His praise warms my body, making my muscles tighten. Another part of me is unlocked and my pussy flutters around his cock. The muscles in my thighs burn as they stay open wide to accommodate his massive frame.

"It's yours, you're the only one who gets to have it," I pant.

His mouth crashes down on mine as he swallows my moan.

"That's right. Your pussy is mine, your body is mine, your soul is mine." His chest rumbles with another growl. "Mine. Mine. *Mine.*"

"Yours!" I scream.

"This sweet pussy needs protection at all times, *akorzag*. Males want it, so I have to guard you even more now. It's not enough," he pants. "It's not enough just to protect you. I want to keep you all to myself so no one can see you. I want you so wrapped up in me there's no separating us."

My pussy clenches and I scream as the force of my orgasm hits me. His claiming words sent me right over the edge and my pussy pulses around him.

"Fuck, Kae. Fuck, so tight, *too* fucking tight." Licking the pad of his thumb, he begins to rub tight circles on my clit and until my body is hurtling towards another climax.

"You liked the sound of that? Of me being so fucking obsessed over you that I'm no better than an animal."

"Yes," I sob, the pleasure he's causing me is almost painful. Fire licks along my body, my hands grip the top of the headboard. The force of his thrusts make the old wood bed creak and I'm certain we're going to break it. Not now but very soon.

"I need another one, Kae. Need you coming on my cock while I fill you with my seed." Bazur rubs me even harder, my breasts bounce in time with his thrusts. It's the edge of the pain that tips me over. I scream his name as my body clenches down on him. His muscles lock and his thrusts become jerky. Throwing his head back, I watch as Bazur finds his own release.

The muscles in his neck are tense as he comes, filling me with a hot rush of his seed. There's so much of it that it leaks out between us and soaks on to the sheets. Even as he's coming down, he still thrusts into me making sure that my pussy gets every last drop of his come.

My throat is sore, I'm not going to be able to walk tomorrow, but I've never been happier. Bazur pulls out of me, a rush of come coats the insides of my thighs. He presses me into the mattress and kisses my lips, my eyes, my nose.

Rising from the bed, Bazur disappears into the washroom and I hear the faucet turn on. Moments later, he returns holding a warm, wet cloth and gently cleans between my legs. My cheeks warm as he wipes away the come and blood.

It's so intimate I can't help it.

"After all we just did together, you can still blush?" he asks, tossing the cloth aside and gathering me to his chest.

"I'm still me," I reply primly and his soft laugh vibrates against my side.

"You are. I wouldn't change a thing about you, you're perfect." I duck my head and hide my smile into his neck. "Are you okay?"

"I'm wonderful," I murmur. We grow silent and I sigh tracing along a scar on his shoulder.

"What is it?" His hand slides under my chin and tips my face up to look at him. As if he can sense what I'm feeling before I can.

"Kaethe," he prompts.

"It's just that, I can't help feeling like I robbed us of time together. If I had just told you how I felt, the moment I started feeling it, we could've been together like this so much sooner." Bazur presses a kiss to my mouth.

"*Akorzag*, everything that happened led to this right now. Led to you laying naked in my arms after I just fucked you full of my seed." I giggle and try to dip my head again. He holds my chin in his grasp so I have to meet his stare.

"We have forever to make up for lost time," he says.

Tears threaten to spill from my eyes but I kiss him instead, pouring everything I am into it. Letting the kiss absolve me from my guilt over wasting time and allow it to weave together our souls and hearts. When I open my eyes into Bazur's honey colored ones I see that he's done the same. I snuggle into his warmth and feel a peace I've never known.

"Forever."

CHAPTER 24

BAZUR

"Bazur!" Kaethe squeals. "Myren is expecting me!"

Her protests are cut off when my tongue flicks against her tight asshole. Then she starts squirming for a different reason. I feel a smile curl my lips. I think I've smiled more in the past twelve hours than I have in the last thirty years.

Mother of the Mountain, I am so lucky.

To have Kaethe as my mate, to hear her say she's mine, and to get to gorge myself on her body for the rest of my days. Last night we dozed in each other's arms until the early afternoon when Kaethe's stomach began to growl. I made her sit on my lap completely naked as I fed her bread and an assortment of cheeses. As her eyes began to droop, I carried her back to bed.

I was content to let her rest but as I settled her against me her kisses became more frequent, her touches more exploratory until I was reaching for that cream on the nightstand and pushing inside of her wet cunt once more. I filled her with more of my seed then I bathed her in the washroom, her skin soft glowing from the multiple orgasms and warm water.

When I finally tucked her into the fresh sheets I put on the bed she looked like a goddess. We huddled together before sleep claimed us once more. It wasn't long until I woke up with her leg over my hip, her nipples rubbing against my chest, and heard her soft pleas for me to come inside her again.

What would any male do in my situation?

I move my tongue from her back entrance to her sweet pussy. Kae is on her hands and knees in the middle of our bed, that gorgeous ass of hers thrust towards my face. I deliver a sharp smack to one cheek and watch the color bloom on her fair skin. Her body shakes and shudders, she's close to coming again. Every bounce and jiggle of her body makes my mouth water.

Sex in the past had been fulfilling. A way to work off energy and find mutual release. With Kaethe it's something else. Within minutes of exploding inside of her I'm dying to be back in her body. To be as close to her as possible so that I can feel our souls fusing together.

How could I have thought for even a moment she wasn't my mate?

"Are you close, *akorzag*?" I ask, pushing two fingers inside of her. I scissor them in a way that makes her thighs clench. Rising from behind her, I trail kisses down her spine making her whimper. She nods, looking over her shoulder at me, her dark eyes wild with lust.

Pulling my fingers from her, I take her hips in my hands and line my cock up with her entrance. She moans as I push fully inside of her. With her ass pressed to my abs I reach over her hip to play with her clit.

"This is going to be fast, Kae."

"Bazur," she sighs, "you're so deep." I thrust into her mercilessly, her ass providing enough cushion and absorbing the impact. Kaethe can take what I give her, she craves it as much as I do.

I'm the only one who gets to see her like this, gets to hold her, provide for her, and worship her. That knowledge spurns me to fuck her faster, harder so that our bond brings us even closer. Her pussy is tight and so wet her arousal smears all over my cock.

She clenches down on me, her cunt squeezing me like a fist, as I rub her clit faster.

"Bazur—" Her voice catches and her legs begin to tremble.

"Come, *akorzag*. Come for me, soak me with your sweetness."

Her scream catches in her throat and she does, fingers digging into the bed as she climaxes. My own release follows suit. The base of my spine tingles before locking straight up and I feel my seed flood her, soaking her in my own release as well.

Pulling out, I watch as our mingling come slides down the insides of her thighs. With a satisfied groan Kaethe collapses onto the bed face first.

Coming down beside her, I roll her onto her back and kiss her lips gently.

"Myren is gonna be mad at me," Kae cringes, wrinkling that adorable nose of hers.

"No she won't. She'll smell me on your skin and understand how greedy a male like me can be." Our scents have merged and it makes me swell with pleasure. My mate, my Kaethe, my *akorzag*. Mine, Mine, *Mine*.

I wouldn't be surprised if her name was carved into my heart.

As my hand traces along her body, I narrow my eyes at something I hadn't noticed yesterday. My finger snags on a few pink and purplish lines on Kae's stomach, on the sides of her breasts. Some are light, as if faded over time, while others are dark, newer. Running my thumb along a particularly dark one around her navel I catch her eyes.

"What are these?" I ask. Her smile is soft, her cheeks turn a delicate pink.

"Stretch marks. They just mean parts of me grew too fast or got bigger." I trace a fainter one on her hip.

"I like them." She giggles and shakes her head.

"Well that's good because they're not going anywhere."

"You'll get more of them when you grow round with my child." The thought of her pregnant makes my cock harden, demanding I make it a reality. Kaethe giggles and shakes her head, playfully shoving at my chest.

"We fuck a handful of times and you can't stop talking about me being pregnant." As much as I want that, we agreed she'd start taking the contraceptive herbs this morning.

"It's true now isn't the best time to bring a child into the world." Even if it's what I desire most in the world, I need to be assured of her safety. Even if I wanted to keep our mating a secret, which I don't, everyone can smell me on her. It won't be long until word reaches Vorgak and he'll try to use our bond against me. "But when the time is right I want lots of children."

Pure joy shines on her face.

"Do you know when things will be safer?" she asks softly. This openness between us is new. I can tell all of my plans, and we can solve things together. The strategy I have in place to safeguard our future together has never been more important.

"The humans and soldiers that are away aren't just scouting for new farmland," I hedge. Kaethe lifts her face to look at me. "They're trying to find support within smaller territories to back my claim to the throne."

"I thought you didn't want to rule?"

"I don't but Vorgak's becoming restless. We've heard whispers that he's mounting an offensive. He's grown tired of peace and he'll strike here first." I kiss the top of her head, gathering her to me. "You're here now Kaethe and I'm not hiding you. Vorgak will learn what you are to me soon enough and he'll try to come for you. I'll kill him before he gets the chance to hurt you."

"You'll keep me safe. You'll keep us all safe." Her confidence in me makes my heart pound. "What is your plan?"

I sigh. "There's a kingdom to the east we haven't heard from in a long time. We've made contact with them and they have something that will help us kill Vorgak."

"Can you not just challenge him to fight? A duel for the throne?"

"Vorgak would never agree to it. He knows that in a fair fight I'd kill him easily." I curl a lock of her pink hair around my finger. "He's heavily guarded at all times. Do you remember the armor he was wearing when we were at Dread's Keep?"

"Yes," she says.

"It's made from some magical element one of his alchemists discovered. No blade or arrow can piece through it and he never takes it off. His healers have guarded him against every type of poison so that's not even an option. We'll have to plan an ambush in order to take him down."

Kaethe burrows into my chest and holds me tightly against her.

"You can't get hurt." Her voice is muffled. "I just found you."

"*The Mother of the Mountain* couldn't take me from you, *akorzag*. But I will do what I have to in order to keep you safe." Her grip on me tightens as she nods into my chest.

"When things are safe, I'll ask King Arkain to send some of his royal surgeons to train the midwives on how to do the incision births." Her delicate brows furrow. "What's the kingdom to the east you have contact with?"

"It's an old kingdom, one that is shrouded in myth and mystery. It's said the hundred foot walls that surround the city are there to keep the creatures living there from ravaging the land. The stories of what happens to people entering their kingdom are horrible enough to keep even the most curious away."

Kaethe's body snaps up so quickly her head almost smacks into my jaw.

"Wait," she says, disbelief in her eyes, "are you trying to tell me you made an alliance with the *vampires?*"

CHAPTER 25

KAETHE

Anticipation makes my palm sweat inside Bazur's hand.

The humans have returned with the soldiers and I am going to see if one of them is my brother. There's excitement mixed with trepidation. I'm trying not to let myself get too carried away. Bazur and I slowly approach the crowd that's gathered to welcome them home.

I note with a small smile how sore I am between my legs as we walk through town. Bazur and I can barely keep our hands off of each other. It's been almost a week since our first time, and the hunger we feel for each other has only gotten more intense.

When he leaves to train the soldiers and I go off to help Myren, we hardly make the walk back to our home without ripping each other's clothes off. Each time we come together, the power of our connection grows stronger. It's all consuming and filled with so much love.

Love. My depth of feeling for Bazur should scare me, but it doesn't. It means what we have is real and permanent. He's seen me, all of me and he wants every broken piece.

Just like I want all of his.

"That's him, in the blue wool coat," Bazur whispers in my ear. My chest feels tight as I survey the crowd for the item in question. My eyes land a threadbare blue coat and I stumble forward. My brother was eight when I last saw him, but I know that I'll recognize him after all this time. This man is tall like my father was. My boots crunch through the snow as I get closer.

The hair is dark like my mother's, like my own natural color. The man in the blue coat turns. This is it, could it really be him? My mouth opens to call his name, my father's name—

I glimpse his face. With a sinking feeling I know he's not my brother. His eyes are a pale green with a mole above his brow my brother never had. His eyes catch mine and I try to hide my disappointment with a polite smile. Quickly, I turn and walk back to where Bazur is standing.

He raises his brows in question but I simply shake my head and return to his side.

His arms wrap around me as he kisses my forehead. "Don't lose hope. We'll find him."

I nod, soaking up his warmth. Clasping my hand in his, we make the short walk back to our house. The weather is getting colder. Several times Bazur has had to catch me as my feet slide on newly formed ice.

"What are your plans today?" he asks, I shrug.

"I don't know. Myren doesn't need me so I think I'll just try and find something to keep me busy at home. My *riverheart seeds* should be ready, I'll bring them in from the porch before the frost comes."

"I have to debrief with the soldiers who just came back, but I shouldn't be too long. Then I'll keep you company." I blush at his offer. Keeping me company involves both of us naked in bed, sweating and panting. That actually sounds like a perfect way to spend my afternoon. It will make the perfect set up for what I have planned this evening.

"Tonight, I'm going to cook for you," I say, giving his hand a squeeze. His eyes widen and his steps fumble. "Mornga asked me if I had done it last week after she smelled me."

It's a ritual between mates, one that will cement another part of our bond.

We stop out front of our house and Bazur's grin is infectious. He leans down and presses his lips to mine. There's so much passion in our kiss that by the time he pulls back I'm breathless. It's on the tip of my tongue to ask him if he has time to get inside of me before his debrief when a shrill whistle sounds behind us. Zarod is smirking, tusks glinting mischievously in the morning light.

"Bazy, in public? Who knew you were such an exhibitionist?"

"An exh-what?" Bazur asks, pulling me close to his chest. Even in Zarod's presence, the most vocal male about being mated, Bazur needs to show that I am his.

"What does that make you for watching us?" I quip.

"Aroused." I choke on a laugh while Bazur growls at him. "What? Bazy, somehow you're even more growly than before. I'd always thought it was sexual frustration but given the scent coming off Kaethe—"

"Okay," I interrupt, a vein in Bazur's neck is twitching which is never a good sign. I press up on my toes to kiss his cheek. "I'm going inside, try not to kill each other."

Bazur catches me around the waist before I can get too far away and kisses me again.

"You two are worse than me and Mornga." Bazur lets out another growl from deep within his chest. "See! So much more growly now."

"I like him growly," I admit, before turning to make my way up the house.

"Oh I bet you d—okay, *okay* relax, Bazy!" Zarod's laughter follows me into the house. Leaving the front door open, I move to collect some of my gardening supplies. I'll start the fire as I catalog my seeds so the house is nice and warm when Bazur returns.

This task will also let me distract myself from my disappointment earlier. I'm upset that the young farmer wasn't my brother but the usual hopelessness that would've plagued me isn't there. Bazur is helping me, he's already reached out to other clans. One of them has to know something.

From inside the house I can hear Zarod and Bazur chatting in the *orcish*. Targoc's voice joins theirs as I collect my clay bowl to harvest my seeds. I double check to make sure I have enough clean jars to store them in since this is my last chance to grow them before the soil freezes.

Another voice joins the males out front, one I don't recognize. Probably one of the soldiers who's been out scouting these other territories. His voice stands out from the others due to his hint of an accent. How strange.

I take my clay bowl with me as I head out to my flower bed on the front porch. My seedlings have sprouted nicely, their bright blue seeds glimmering in the morning sun. Looking up from the porch my eyes immediately land on Bazur as he talks with the other soldiers. Right now, he's every bit the general. A powerful male with absolute authority.

A shiver runs down my spine, heating my pussy.

I'm about to turn back to my seeds when my eyes land on something. In the small cluster of soldiers one stands out as different from the rest. Not just because he doesn't have black hair though that's a big part. My hands gripping the bowl start to shake.

His hair is dark blonde in color, I assumed with time it would've gotten darker, but our father's always remained golden. From my perch, I can see the soft rays of sun illuminating his face. My father's face. I knew him as a skinny eight year old but this man is tall with a muscular build. Those dark brown eyes glow in the sun and are just like our mother's, just like mine.

This soldier…it's him. My brother.

The clay bowl slips from my hands and hits the porch with a thunderous crash. My heart is beating rapidly in my chest, my knees are beginning to shake. I'd almost think it was my imagination if his head didn't snap up with the other's upon hearing the bowl shatter. His eyes widen and he turns as white as the snow.

"Kaethe, are you alright?" Bazur calls out but my eyes stay locked on my brother's. As if in daze I stumble a step forward.

"Karth?" I choke out. The soldier—my brother—Karth swallows.

Zarod's eyes dart between us. "Who's Karth?"

I ignore him and take another step forward. My brother blinks rapidly and shakes himself.

"Thea?"

That name, no one's called me that name since I was a girl. It's him, it's really him. A sob wrenches from my chest and I'm flying down the steps, into the snow below. He moves like lightning and then we're in front of each other. Hesitating for only a moment until my arms encircle his neck and I bury my face against him. Karth's arms band around my back as he lifts me off the ground, burying his head against me as well.

Tears spill from my eyes. My brother is alive and in my arms. He's safe, he's safe, *he's safe*. We both survived and now we're together again here, beating all the odds.

"You're alive," I sob.

"You're alive," he echoes. His voice is deep and raspy, nothing like the child he was.

I pull back slightly and he drops me back to the ground. We stare at each other for a moment both not knowing where to start.

"I've been looking for you, all this time I never gave up hope that you survived."

"I've been searching for you too. I went back to our village countless times and tried to find where you'd gone," he explains. "I got close and found out some of the survivors relocated upstream. By the time I got there, the older couple you lived with had already passed and no one could tell me where you'd gone."

"I was in Myrkorvin," I breathe. "I'm an alchemist. I went to the academy there and I work directly for King Arkain."

Karth whistles and shakes his head. "You were always smart. I remember that. How'd you manage to get yourself here?"

"King Arkain," I admit. "We heard a rumor of a man living amongst the orcs who had been taken in as a child. I'm friends with his queen and she persuaded him to let me come here and investigate. I was meant to stay at Dread's Keep but Bazur found me and well..."

I look over to Bazur, his eyes are wide as he takes in me and Karth. Targoc and Zarod watch us too in disbelief.

"Bazur is both of our rescuers then," Karth chuckles, turning his head towards my male and nodding. "After we had gotten separated, I fled into the woods. I was bleeding and close to death. Bazur found me and brought me here."

Snow crunches next to us as Bazur approaches slowly. My smile is massive as I take him in. He saved my brother. He's the reason he lived and was kept safe for all of these years. Bazur's honey eyes lock with mine, Karth pulls back from me and glances between us.

"So the dark elf king sent you here as a royal emissary? That doesn't explain why you're living in Bazur's house." He narrows his dark eyes at me. "Or why you smell like him, Kaethe."

Bazur waits for me to decide how to explain this. The choice is simple. There's no room for any more lies. I take a few steps towards Bazur and grab his hand, locking our fingers together.

"Karth, Bazur is my mate."

The male at my side inhales sharply. It's the first time I've called him that outloud. I'm ready to embrace us in every way. He is mine and I am his and I want everyone to know.

Karth looks at us in shock, his eyes moving between our two faces. Before long he breaks out into a wide grin and chuckles.

"Well, would you fucking look at that."

I giggle and squeeze Bazur's hand, curling into his side.

"Is someone going to explain what the fuck is going on?" Zarod asks. Bazur growls at him and I smile even harder. Yes, in time, I'll explain everything to everyone. Right now, I need some alone time with my brother.

CHAPTER 26

KAETHE

KARTH AND I SIT AT Bazur's kitchen table and watch each other carefully.

Two steaming cups of tea sit next to us. It's strange, I pictured our reunion many times in my head but the real thing feels different. Not in a bad way, but I just always thought it would be more grandiose. Instead, it's a bit awkward.

It's easy enough to understand why.

We're both adults, it's been two decades since we last saw each other. I remember my brother, but I don't *know* my brother. I doubt that his favorite things to do are skipping rocks across the river and tying sticks into my hair. His face isn't as scarred as Bazur's but from the crooked set to his nose I can tell it's been broken. The wraps on his hands do very little to hide the callouses and cuts along his knuckles.

Whatever life he's had it hasn't been a peaceful one.

The silence presses down on us and I can feel Karth's leg bouncing under the table. This is ridiculous. One of us needs to be brave enough to say the first word. I clear my throat and pick up my mug of tea as a way to keep my hands busy.

"Karth," I say at the same time he says, "Kaethe."

We both laugh shyly and he shakes his head. "I've thought about this a million times and now that it's happening I don't know what to say," he confesses.

"Me neither," I agree. "Karth, that night…I'm so sorry. If I hadn't let go of you then maybe—"

"Thea," his voice is sharp, "don't apologize. Nothing about that night was your fault. We were kids, it's easy to forget just how young we were when it happened. The orcs that attacked us are at fault." His dark eyes go distant and his mouth flattens into a line. I'm not sure I want to know but I ask anyway.

"What happened to you after we were separated?"

Karth takes a deep shuddering breath. When his eyes meet mine again I have to stop myself from looking away. The terror in them is still there, even after all these years.

"The orc that was chasing us, the one who killed the blacksmith, you remember?" I nod my head feeling my palms beginning to sweat. "He caught up to me in the forest after I had lost you. I tried to run but he was faster. He hit me over the head with that hammer from the forge."

My hand shoots out and covers his. We are quiet for another moment until he continues. Karth gives a humorless laugh.

"The blow knocked me unconscious, I think he believed me to be dead so he left me there bleeding. I don't remember much beyond being kicked awake the next morning.

"Vorgak was there, the raid had been issued by him after a trader from our village had slighted his orcs on fur pelts. Next to him was a cart full of the bodies of our townspeople. And one of them, Kaethe, one of them had brown hair like yours and I thought…I thought…"

Tears well in my eyes and I try my best to blink them away.

"Vorgak yelled at his males for leaving one alive. I can still remember the feel of his blade on my neck. My head was throbbing, I could barely feel my legs. I couldn't fight or do anything to stop my impending death. Then Bazur was there. He stepped out of the treeline and yelled something at Vorgak that had him pausing before he could deliver the death blow. Bazur was a lot younger then but about the same size he is now.

"He scared me when I first saw him. I tried to fight him as he picked me up and put me on a wagon. Before long I felt the wagon begin to move. Except we didn't follow the other orcs there, we went in the opposite direction up towards the mountain."

"He brought you here," I answer and Karth nods.

"Once we were away from the other's Bazur told me I was safe, that he had a healer who could help me. He asked me if there were any members of my family left and in my state I could only shake my head no. Even if you were still alive, I didn't trust that this wasn't another trap. One I wouldn't drag you into.

"I even gave him a fake name, Mika. That's why Zarod asked who Karth was, I've never used that name here. It took years for me to finally realize I was safe. No matter how many times Bazur repeated it to me. Or how many times Lady Myren told me while she was healing me. I carried so much anger and rage for not being able to protect you like I promised mom."

"Karth, it's not your fault either."

"It should've never happened. That's why I've been helping Bazur make sure it doesn't to anyone else. He saw my restlessness when I first arrived and kept making trouble. When I finally told him about my rage, Bazur said there was a way for me to channel it. I trained with him to become a soldier. He gave me purpose, a way to avenge what happened to our family."

Bazur, my heart warms as I think of him.

"As I grew I kept remembering that cart I saw. The memories faded and then I couldn't remember if her hair had been brown like yours, or red. Maybe even blonde. Once I was old enough to leave the village on missions I started scouting. They were all dead ends until I found that village that you last stayed in." Karth smiles softly. "The last place I ever would've checked was Myrkorvin. Don't tell Mornga, but dark elves really fucking scare me. The eyes—"

Karth breaks off in a shudder and I can't help but chuckle.

"You get used to it. I never gave going to Myrkorvin a second thought. If I had I would've been in that village when you came to visit. We would've reunited."

"Thea, you can't let what-if's rule your life." His eyes are serious as they bore into mine. "I replayed that night over and over again, wishing I could change a dozen different things. I wore myself ragged doing that. Kaethe, look what you accomplished, look at the life you lived. I wish more than anything I could've been a part of it, that you could've been a part of mine but we didn't get a choice."

"But now we can be," I say firmly.

"Now we can be." Karth swallows and averts his gaze. "Do you… remember them?"

I know who he's referring to and my heart gives a tight squeeze. This isn't something I like to think about.

"Bits and pieces, I was so young. I remember mother's pies, she was the best cook, told the best bedtime stories too."

"You loved that mermaid one, drove me crazy how many times you made her tell it to us," Karth grumbles, though his smile is soft as he looks at me.

"I remember…father's laugh, it shook the whole house. He was always so happy." I give his hand another squeeze. "I remember how much they loved us."

Karth squeezes my hand back. "They did."

"Bazur will make Vorgak pay for what he did to us and to so many others."

Karth nods. "Things are bad now, Thea. I don't know how much Bazur has told you but—"

The front door to the cottage squeaks open and Bazur is there, looking serious and handsome. His eyes sweep over me as if to make sure no harm has come to me while he's been away. The floorboards creak as he walks over to us and stands at my side. Reaching down, he runs a hand through my hair and I shiver, my nipples tightening painfully.

I pull my hand away from Karth's and capture Bazur's in my hair. Interlocking our fingers, I bring his hand to my lips and kiss the back of it. We stare at each other so lost in our own world that it isn't until my brother clears his throat that I remember we aren't alone.

My cheeks warm and I look away sheepishly.

"Did you get what we need from our contact in the east, Karth?" Bazur asks, turning his stare towards my brother. Karth winces at the use of his real name but nods anyway. My brother opens his mouth but shuts it, eyeing my warily. I almost offer to leave in case this is some secret I'm not privy to but Bazur waves his hand. "Kaethe is my mate, I trust her. Whatever you have to report can be shared with her."

His authoritative tone makes my thighs grow damp. Bazur obviously smells it as his eyes darken when he turns his gaze back on me. I give his hand a squeeze as if to say, *Later.*

Karth digs around in the bag at his hip before pulling out a small metal box. He extends it to Bazur who pops it open and takes out the contents. It's a small glass vial filled with some bright green liquid. Bazur lowers his eyes questioningly.

"It's a special elixir they make. It'll cut through any metal, any steel, even Vorgak's armor." Karth rubs a hand against his lightly stumbled jaw. "We have the support of a few northern generals. They advised us that Vorgak is mounting an offensive. They say he's planning to strike here any day now."

"We'll be ready. It's more important than ever to keep our village safe." Bazur's tender honey gaze traces over my face. I want him so badly, I want him all the time. We stare at each other, everything around us becomes unfocused. Karth's kitchen chair scrapes along the floor as he rises.

"As much as you're a worthy male, Bazur, the way you keep staring at my sister is making me very uncomfortable." My mate growls but I only giggle, blushing terribly as I rise too.

"We'll talk more tomorrow, I have a feeling that whatever you two are about to discuss I don't need to be here for. And could you please wait until I'm a few houses away to start *discussing*," Karth pleads.

"No promises," Bazur grits out as I playfully swat at his chest. Leading my brother to the door we hug on the threshold saying our goodbyes. There is so much to learn about each other and today was a good start.

Now I just want to be alone with my mate.

Bazur and I stand in the doorway until Karth is out of eyesight. Silently, I close the door and turn to snuggle into Bazur's chest. His wool shirt is cold against my cheek as I feel his arms wrap tightly around my back.

"I never considered him to be your brother. He told me his name was Mika and that his family was all dead." His grip on me tightens. "That village I saved him from was yours. To think all those years ago you were so close to me and I just missed you."

"I wonder what would've happened had you found us together. What our life would've been like."

Bazur places a kiss to the top of my head. "As much as I would've loved to have known you sooner, I'm glad you escaped. You've had experiences you never would've gotten the chance to have here. There's no point in wishing for things to be different when I wouldn't change anything about the outcome."

"My brother said something similar." Bazur cups my chin and makes my eyes meet his.

"How are you feeling?"

"I feel…happy. We're strangers, we've been apart longer than we were ever together but he's my family. We're both alive. We're both here thanks to you. How could I be anything besides happy?" I pull back from Bazur's chest and smile up at him. "Now I want to take care of you."

Leading him by the hand, we climb the ladder and walk into the washroom. I turn the handles on the bathing pool and watch the deep tub fill up with steaming water. Along the sides of it sit various soaps and creams that I've made at Myren's for my hair. Bazur told me he didn't understand the need for so many things to wash oneself as if I wouldn't notice him smelling like my lavender hair treatment four nights ago.

Kicking off my boots and unlacing my gown, Bazur matches my movements until we are both naked. This bath was built for someone of his size. He grips me around my waist and gently places me along the edge since my feet don't touch the bottom. My mate climbs in behind me and pulls me against his muscular chest. I sigh as his hard cock begins to press against the cheeks of my ass.

The water makes our bodies slick and Bazur traces his large, calloused hands along my neck and arms. Goosebumps break out and I sigh into his touch as he begins to massage the base of my skull. His thick fingers dig into my scalp, the sensation making my toes curl.

"Can I wash your hair, *akorzag*?" His voice is barely more than a growl. I nod and he reaches for one of my hair cleansing tonics. Pouring some on my head he continues digging his hands into my hair until the mixture becomes foamy. He pours clean water over my head from a pitcher, before grabbing my lavender hair conditioning cream and spreading it throughout the ends of my hair.

I never taught him my bathing routine but he's mastered it nonetheless.

After he rinses the cream from my hair, he begins to soap my body.

His hand wanders down between my legs. He groans at the wetness he finds there. With his fingers pressing into my clit I throw my head back against his shoulders. He works me until my legs begin to tremble and as much as I don't want to stop, this bath is for him.

Turning in his arms, I rub my nipples along his chest and he shudders.

"I want to wash you now." He barely nods as I take the soap from his hands, sudsing it up before rubbing it all over his body. My fingers dig into the muscles of his arms, trace along every scar and cut. My hand trails lower, over the muscles packed on top of each other that make up his stomach. They go lower still as I grip his cock in my hands, fingers dancing over his ridges and giving him a gentle tug.

"Does my mate like it when I hold him in my hand?" I purr in his ear, giving him another tug. Bazur's eyes are wide and his mouth pops open. I trail kisses along his neck.

"You mean so much to me, Bazur. After hearing what you did for my brother, knowing what you did for me. Knowing what you are willing to risk to keep me safe, how could I not feel this way about you?"

I give his cock one more jerk and nip at his pulse.

"I love you, Bazur."

There's a thunderous sound as I'm yanked out of the bath. I giggle as my wet body is thrown down on the bed and Bazur is wild above me. His hips pin mine to the bed and his hands tangle with my own, holding them above my head.

"Love isn't a strong enough word for what I feel for you, Kaethe. My mate, my *akorzag*. I'm obsessed, I'll do anything, kill anyone for you." His lips rain kiss all over my face as my wet pussy grinds against his cock, those ridgids digging into my clit. "I love you. I'm going to marry you, give us a family. I'm going to give you everything. Everything."

"You already have."

"Once it's safe, if you want to return to Myrkorvin I'll go too. I don't care where I am so long as we're together." I shake my head underneath him. I've already said goodbye to my life in Myrkrovin, I belong here with Bazur.

"I don't want to go back to my old life, I want to stay right here with you."

Bazur's mouth attacks mine, his tongue slipping inside to tease my own. A hand trails down my body before he sticks two of his fingers inside of me. He twists his wrist and hooks his fingers just the way I like to hit that spot inside of me. Just when I'm about ready, Bazur grabs the jar off the nightstand and coats his length in the cream.

Slipping inside of me with a satisfied groan, my legs cinch around his hips. Bazur moves slowly, as if to savor this. His hands touch every part of me from my breasts to my hips to my stomach. The touches are reverent and exploratory and so loving I could come right now.

I hold off on that and let his body work itself inside of mine. The thread tying us together grows stronger. I can feel our souls knitting together with each thrust. There were so many heartbreaks along the way, so many things that I wish I could change but none of that matters now.

Bazur is right, there's no point in wishing for something different when the outcome is this perfect.

"My mate is so beautiful. You're a blessing from *The Mother of the Mountain*."

"Bazur, my love, my mate. Make me come," I pant.

Bazur's thrusts become harder. I feel my release barreling down on me, my pussy begins to tighten as Bazur's thumb works my clit. My pussy clamps down around his cock and I'm coming. My back arches clean off the bed and my hands tangle in his silky hair.

Bazur follows me over the edge and I sigh as his warm seed begins to fill me.

Gathering me to his chest, there's a routine comfort in this sensation. Bazur's hands trace up and down my arms, both of us sharing breath and not speaking. My chest is warm and everything feels right.

There's just one last thing for me to do.

Pressing a kiss to his cheek, I rise from the bed and wrap a blanket around myself. His seed slips down my leg as we head into the kitchen. I motion him to sit at the table and I get to work.

I roast vegetables in the oven and fry a large piece of *frostelk* meat. Seasoning and garnishing it with a sauce I made from the drippings, I plate it and present it to Bazur. He gathers me on his lap and the blanket slips off my shoulder baring my breasts. He kisses the side of one making me squirm before slicing off a chunk of meat and eating it. He groans as he chews and swallows.

Our bond locks inside my chest and Bazur presses a hand to his own heart.

We smile softly at each other and he feeds me a piece of meat, the flavor exploding on my taste buds. We polish off the plate together as the custom dictates. Bazur holds my hips in his hands, gently rubbing them up and down my sides.

"My mate is a wonderful cook. Teach me so I can make this for you. I'm sorry you had to put up with my bland stews for so long." His fingers graze the underside of my breast and I moan, leaning my head back against his shoulder.

"Your huge cock makes up for what you lack in the kitchen." His hand closes around my breast, gently squeezes my nipple as his tongue licks up the side of my neck. It's not long before we are back in bed and he's showing me just what that cock of his can do.

CHAPTER 27

KAETHE

The next week passes in a blur.

After feeding Bazur that meal we've entered a mating frenzy. Which has led to us rutting like animals at all hours of the day. We only break so I can help Myren and he can train the soldiers. The moment we are sharing space again, he's inside of me.

On a few of our walks home, he's pulled me into a dark alcove and fucked me against the wall, muffling my screams with his mouth.

It's heady stuff. Even now as we sit at the table, I catch the looks he's giving me. We do this every morning as well. My mate wakes me up with his mouth on my pussy until I come on his tongue. He then fucks me quickly in bed until I come again and then once more in the bath. My legs feel wobbly but some mornings, especially when he's told me training is going to run long into the evening, I let him take me one more time before we leave for the day.

"I'm taking a few of the soldiers into the surrounding woods for terrain battle training. I'll be home late." My pussy heats, making some of his seed still inside of me slide out. I bite my lip, no longer interested in my breakfast as lust fills my stomach.

"Really? How late?" I ask, my chest rising and falling as my nipples pebble against my gown.

"Late," Bazur breathes, leaning forward. Our lips are just a hair apart when the front door creaks open. It's Karth. In the short time since being reunited with my brother our relationship has grown tremendously. The more we learn about each other the more similar we realize we are. With time our relationship will only get stronger.

With a quick peck to Bazur's lips I pull back.

Karth's face is serious as he approaches us. "We've just gotten a report from one of our scouts. There are orcs coming here from the west. They wear Vorgak's crest."

Bazur curses and rises from the table. I do the same and look up into his face.

"Ready the soldiers. We will ride out to put down the threat before it reaches us." Bazur wraps his arms around me and pulls me to his chest. Pressing up on my toes, our lips connect and our tongues tangle together. His hand cups the back of my head and I pour everything into our kiss. "Be on your guard until I have you back in my arms."

"Be safe," I say, pulling back from our kiss. "I can't lose you."

"You won't, my mate." Bazur presses another kiss to the top of my head. "Wait for me to return at Myren's."

We both walk towards my brother and I wrap my arms around him next. "You be safe too, I just got you back."

Karth returns my hug and promises me he will be. I lead them both to the door, with one last squeeze to Bazur's hand they make their way towards the barracks and I let the tears burning my eyes flow freely. *He will be fine*, I assure myself.

Giving myself a few minutes to cry, I wash my face and run a comb through my hair. Myren needs my help today and that will distract me from my worry for the next few hours. Gathering my things, I head out into the snow towards the healer's house.

Pushing in the front door I see Myren by the fire and an angry Targoc next to her.

"I heard what happened," Myren says, rushing over to me. I can only nod. My eyes glance toward Targoc in a question and Myren sighs. "He was left behind. The general told him he's to stay back and protect the village."

"It's not fair!" Targoc cries. "I should be with them."

"I don't like being left behind either, Targoc," I say, my smile sympathetic. Myren looks conflicted and I understand. Targoc wants a chance to prove himself and being left behind wounds his pride. I don't want him feeling like that, maybe we can both try and take our mind off of today. "I came to help collect *winterberries* for those fever elixirs."

"Yes, we do need those. I was able to grow a few bushels out by the front gates." Lady Myren nods. "Targoc, why don't you help Kaethe. You can protect the general's mate while he is away."

"I would love the company," I say, trying to coax the young male. Targoc's nod is reluctant but he rises nonetheless and comes to my side. "We shouldn't be gone long."

The morning sun is bright overhead as we make our way towards the front of town. The village is quiet, word has spread of where the soldiers have gone. A few people nod at Targoc and I as we pass. I will time to move quickly today. I need to be back in Bazur's arms where I can assure myself he is safe and unharmed.

We stop in front of the old wooden gate. It's open slightly letting in a stream of light. Kneeling down in the snow off to the side I pluck a few dark red colored berries and begin placing them in my basket. The berries smell sweet and are good for lowering body temperature and reducing swelling.

"I wish there were more of these," I say to Targoc who's remained sullen at my side. Placing the last shiny red berry in my basket I sigh.

"We'll only have enough for a few more elixirs."

Targoc's eyes are narrowed until he perks up.

"I saw these berries yesterday, when Bazur took us training out front. A whole bunch of them had grown at the base of an evergreen tree. Here it's right outside the gate," Targoc babbles, excitedly. As pleased as I am he isn't sad anymore, venturing outside the gates makes me apprehensive.

"I don't think that's a good idea. When the other soldiers are back maybe—"

"Come on, Kaethe! It's less than fifty feet away, the frost could come at any time and they'll all be killed by then." He does have a point. Still, I don't feel right about this.

Targoc doesn't give me much of a choice as he slips between the crack in the gate and enters the other side. With a curse, I stand wiping the snow off my knees and follow him through. The gate opens out onto the tree line path. The sun makes me squint my eyes, it's eerily quiet out here.

"Over here, Kaethe!" Targoc calls. He is waving at me from under a nearby tree, the red berries sparkling in the sun. I sigh, I'll make this quick so we can head back inside. I stomp over to him and kneel down to collect the *winterberries*.

"That's strange," Tarogc says, I look up to see his dark brows furrowed.

"What?"

"Where are the guards that patrol the gate?" he asks, pointing a finger to the empty watchtowers along the side. Dread curdles my stomach as I rise to take in the scene. There's a blood red stain coating the bottom steps and trailing off into the snow.

Something is very wrong.

"We need to go," I say, tugging on Targoc's sleeve.

"We should—"

It all happens too fast for me to register. Hulking figures, dressed in *icewolf* fur make them impossible to see in the snow. Orcs. Two of them creep up on us from a snow mound and before I can even let out a scream, Targoc's head is rammed into the trunk of the evergreen tree.

His face makes a crunching sound and my stomach turns.

Targoc falls into the snow unmoving, his nose clearly broken. Adrenaline makes me drop my basket and run. The orcs move faster, easily overpowering me. I try to let out a scream but a hand wraps around my mouth. I'm hauled back against one of them. He twists me in his grip, his skin a yellow-green, his eyes bloodshot and beady. A scar runs through his eyebrow and he's wearing the crest I've only seen once before at Dread's Keep.

I thrash in his grip to try and break free but it's useless.

"Vorgak wants to see you," he snarls into my face. The other orc stands over his shoulder wearing a lecherous grin. I can't allow myself to be taken. I need to get help for Targoc, to warn the village. I escaped orcs once before, I can do it again.

I bite down into the tough skin of his palm. The orc curses, his grip on me loosening enough for me to break his hold and run as fast as I can through the snow. I let out a scream but it is of no use. My arms are grabbed and I'm spun around. The one with the scar through his eye backhands me, making my ears ring.

"Bitch," he spits, before slamming his forehead into mine, sending me plumenting straight into an unending darkness.

CHAPTER 28

BAZUR

THE SUN IS JUST BEGINNING to set as we return to the village.

Today was a waste of time. Our scouts had been wrong or at least whatever orcs had been seen coming had hidden their tracks well enough that we couldn't locate them. We will be on guard at all times and make sure our defenses are fortified until Vorgak's plans have been defeated.

I have Kaethe to protect.

I urge my *icewolf* to move faster. I missed my mate all day and now I need to be back in her arms. To feel the warm press of her body, to lick her little wet pussy, and plant myself inside of her so our souls can join. She's getting it rough once I'm back, I need to focus this frustration in a better way.

Making her come until she passes out seems like the best use for it.

We crest the hill until the gates come into view. My blood runs cold as I see them ajar with the watchtowers empty. I glance over at Zarod to my left, his own expression wary. Urging my beast faster, we rush through the gates, my stomach is in knots as I race towards Lady Myren's house.

I need to find Kaethe, to assure myself that she's okay, that there's an explanation for—

The sight before me makes my knees buckle and I barely stop myself from collapsing on Lady Myren's threshold. She's bent over a bleeding and broken Targoc. His nose is shattered, one of his fledgling tusks is chipped, and there's a cut along his cheek.

I can hear his chest rattling with every faint breath. Myren weeps over him softly. Mornga is there, rising from a chair and coming over to us. Zarod pulls her against him and I need to do the same with my mate.

"What happened?" I growl out. "Where is Kaethe?"

Mornga pales under my stare.

"We tried to send riders out to find you but no one knew where you'd gone," she says carefully. I brace myself for the blow that's about to happen. "We don't know how many were here but Vorgak's soldiers snuck in, killed the guards at the gate without us knowing. They would've raided the village but—" Mornga swallows audibly.

"But what?"

"Who they were looking for went outside the gate." Lady Myren rises from Targoc's side and comes to stand before me.

"Kaethe and Targoc went to collect *winterberries*. They had been gone for a while and I got suspicious. I saw the gate ajar and remembered Targoc telling me he had found more berries while he was training yesterday. I found him out there like this, barely alive—"

"Where is Kaethe?" I growl, my vision darkening and the room around me spinning.

"They took her," Mornga whispers.

I let out a roar that shakes the floorboards of Lady Myren's house. A red haze goes over my vision. Kaethe taken by Vorgak's males. My mate, scared and alone and hurt. She needs me, I will find her. I will kill whoever laid their hands on her.

The door to Lady Myren's pushes open.

"Bazur, where's my sister? She's not at your house—" Karth stops talking when he takes in the scene. His inhale is sharp as he registers the look on my face.

I am nothing without her, if she is killed…

I growl again. I won't consider the possibility. Vorgak is dead. I will kill him where he stands, that's the price for daring to hurt my mate.

"Ready the males, we set out now. Vorgak will be dead by this time tomorrow." Both Zarod and Karth nod. Karth departs to deliver my orders.

Kaethe is alive, I can still feel our bond, it thunders in my chest like a second heartbeat. My mind whirls with images of her. From the very first time I saw her, shivering in that hunting net, to the last time I was inside her this morning, her dark eyes warm with love. I will get her back, I will save her. She's mine to protect, mine to keep, mine to love.

Karth returns a few moments later, his face furious and severe.

"The males are ready to leave when you are." Zarod kisses Mornga and they speak quietly before he is at my back. Stomping down Lady Myren's front steps I see my soldiers all assembled on their *icewolves*.

"Vorgak, has taken my mate," I say to them, gasps ring out. "This sunrise will be his last." I mount my beast and nudge its sides. We shoot back into the snow and ride fast and hard. I speak into our bond and pray that she hears me and that she knows I'll be with her soon.

Hold on for me, Kaethe, I'm coming for you.

CHAPTER 29

KAETHE

THE FIRST TIME I AWOKE my head was throbbing uncontrollably.

I stirred long enough to realize I was tied down in the back of a wagon. I could do nothing but shiver against the cold wind. The pain in my head was so intense that I barely stayed conscious for a minute before I was out again.

This time when I wake, I am in chains in a cell. A bowl of stew is placed next to me with a moldy piece of bread. I'd rather starve than eat that. My feet are bare but thankfully my clothes remain in place and I don't feel touched in any way. Sending up thanks to the gods, I press a hand to my face, it's tender, a bruise already forming.

I pull my knees up to my chest and shiver in the cold cell. It's quiet save for a small trickling sound of water. I almost doze off again when I hear the sound of loud footsteps approaching. I tense as two male orcs appear in front of my cell.

Kicking out my feet, I try my best to fight them but they over power me. They unsnap the shackles at my wrists and grip my arms tightly as they drag me out of my cell. They talk in *orcish*. Both Mornga and Bazur have been teaching me so I can just pick up parts of what they're saying.

"Vorgak is mad she arrived almost frozen," the one with a chipped tusk says. "He wants to be the one to kill her."

The other one nods and says something too quickly for me to make out. They drag me through the hallway, my naked feet catching on the raised stone of the floor. Torches light up the hallway, the energy here is awful and oppressive. It reeks of death.

We push through a set of wooden doors and then I'm thrown down in the middle of the throne room. Sconces and torches illuminate the space, while long tapered candles drip wax onto the floor. Vorgak sits on his throne of bones, draped in his armor. His clawed hand rests on the skull with the circlet on its head and my stomach turns as I realize whose skull that this.

Bazur's father. The one who wanted peace for his people. A rage like I've never known flares to life inside of me. I'm going to kill him, I'll find a way. Vorgak must register it on my face, his smirk deepening.

"I'm glad to see you made it through the journey," he growls, licking over his tusks. "That will make this next part so much more fun."

"Fuck you!" I spit at him.

He chuckles at my outburst. I need to find a weapon, something to fight him with. It's clear he doesn't see me as a threat since he's left me unshackled. I'll make sure he regrets it.

"I never trusted you. Didn't trust your bastard of a king either," he says.

I need to keep him talking so I can figure out a plan of attack.

"Then why not just send me back as soon as I got here? Why not have me killed that first day?" I ask, my eyes scanning around the room. Vorgak laughs again, his tusks twisting into a frightening smile.

"The way Bazur was looking at you made me realize you would prove more useful the longer you remained in his company. I've seen males become entranced by pussy, it makes them sloppy, weak." His grin is all teeth as he flashes it at me. "And that's exactly what you did to Bazur. Now I have his mate."

My stomach sinks and my hands begin to shake. No, I won't let fear control me. I survived before and I will survive again. Bazur is coming, I know he is. I just have to wait for him. I need to keep Vorgak distracted long enough for my mate to reach me.

"How did you learn I was his mate?"

"You think anything happens in that village I don't know about? I let Bazur keep it, for now, because he's deadly on the battlefield. Killing his own supporters who back his claim? No better way to make sure he remains in his place." Vorgak lifts a hand, motioning to the orcs around him. "I have spies watch over it. It was fascinating to learn that not only are you Bazur's mate, but your brother has been living in that village as a soldier all this time."

"You're horrible," I say.

"Maybe, but I'm at least an orc of my word." His grin grows even wider. "Do you remember what I said if I found out you were here for any other reason beyond what was in your king's letter?"

Bile rises up in my throat.

"Sending Bazur your head will take the fight right out of him. Just like it did his mother." My hands begin to shake and my stomach flips.

"It will surely quell whatever uprising he's been planning," Vorgak says.

A shocked gasp leaves my lips, but Vorgak only shakes his head.

"Come now, you really think I didn't know about that?" Vorgak motions for an orc behind him to come forward. My stomach sinks even further as I take in those heinous features before me. "You remember Mazgark, don't you? He was very angry Bazur took you away from him."

Mazgark's gaze travels down my body and my spine locks. Unsheathing the sword from his hip, he approaches me with it extended. This is it. I didn't stall long enough, Bazur didn't have enough time to reach me. The thought of him finding my body makes my chest tighten. I've come all this way, met all of these people, found love…just to meet the same fate as my parents.

I love you, Bazur, I say to our bond and I hope he hears me. Mazgark places the blade at my throat and I close my eyes and brace myself. The blade pulls back from my skin and—

The blow never comes. Instead, I hear a grunt then a clattering sound as the sword falls to the stone floor. I peek open my eyes and see Mazgark is still standing in front of me.

Only this time he has an arrow protruding from his skull.

Chaos erupts. Vorgak shouts and slides on his helmet. His special armor glimmers in the firelight. More arrows come raining down, each one hitting their mark and delivering killing blows to Vorgak's guards. My mind is spinning trying to take in what I'm seeing.

The door to the throne room flies open and…he's there. Bazur is leading the charge, his eyes wild as they land on me. His eyes focus on the bruise forming on my face and he lets out a roar. My heart beats in my chest and I rise on shaking legs to go towards him.

He came for me. I knew he would, I love him, I love him, I—

The cold press of steel against my neck has my movements stopping. Vorgak's chest comes to rest against my back as he presses the blade along my throat. Bazur's eyes darken even further as he takes in the scene. His muscles bunch and his fingers wrap around the hilt of his own sword.

"One move from you and I cleave her head from her shoulders."

An arrow whizzes by and is deflected off of Vorgak's armor with a snap.

"I cannot be killed while wearing this," he chuckles. Bazur's eyes find mine and he nods slowly. I follow his eyes as they move above my head. I dip my chin in the briefest of acknowledgements.

"Anything can be killed," Bazur growls. Vorgak's eyes lock with my mate's and I use the distraction to subtly move away from his sword. I lean my head off of his chest, creating a small opening where his heart is.

Enough of an opening for Karth to fire a green-tipped arrow right into Vorgak's chest from the tunnel above.

There is a sizzling sound as the arrow pierces through the metal and embeds itself in his breast. Vorgak's grip loosens and I push away running towards Bazur who's already halfway to me. Bazur holds my arms and surveys the damage. With a curse, he turns to the king, on his knees with an arrow sticking out of his chest.

Bazur rips off Vorgak's helmet and brandishes his own sword. Vorgak begins to breathe heavily, beseeching Bazur to be merciful.

"This is for my father and my mother," he spits down at him. "But most of all this is for hurting my mate."

With one clean, powerful strike Vorgak's head is removed from his shoulders. Blood sprays as it tumbles away, Vorgak's eyes open and unseeing. Bazur's own sword falls to the ground as he turns to look at me.

His arms engulf me as we sink onto the cold stone floor. Our knees press into the unforgiving ground but I don't care. I sob quietly into his chest as his hands run over my back, my arms, my head. I pull back to peer into his face and he growls softly, touching my bruised face.

"I wish I could kill him again," Bazur murmurs but I only shake my head. "Are you alright?"

"You saved me, I knew you would." His arms wrap tighter around me.

"You're safe with me, I'll kill anyone who threatens that." Our mouths meet and I pour everything into our kiss. The fear, the pain, all of it until my soul is wiped clean and there is only us. Kneeling on the floor of Dread's Keep, with Vorgak's blood cooling on the stones next to us, Bazur becomes king. We hold each other while the world around us changes.

CHAPTER 30

BAZUR

We survey the damages and take the rest of Vorgak's soldiers as prisoners.

There will be many changes now that Vorgak is dead. Most importantly, Kaethe is safe. My beautiful mate. She's so brave and strong. Once this is done I will spend hours enjoying the fact that we both survived today.

My soldiers who pass me in the hall nod respectively. I had to threaten them all not to bow in my presence. I am king now, but the formalities of the title don't appeal to me. All this new title has done is given me the power to ensure peace for my village and help the other humans spread across Brokenbone Mountain. It means I now have the power to keep my mate safe, that's the most important thing.

There's so much to do, so many decisions to make but I can't bring myself to do any of them right now. I speak with my soldiers and with some of Vorgak's healers and alchemists that have crept out from the tunnels. Messenger ravens have been sent out to the other clans to inform them of the shift in power. More will need to be sent in the coming days to tell the other kingdoms.

It's late, my soldiers and I are exhausted. I need my Kae.

Climbing the old stone steps I make my way up to where I left Kaethe earlier. A long, long time ago it was my room as a youngling. It has been left untouched. That's another thing we'll have to figure out: where we are going to live.

We'll solve it all in the morning.

Right now, as I push through the door and find her sitting on the bed in a towel with wet hair, all I care about is us. Her smile is soft as I sit on the bed beside her. My hands skim over the soft skin of her arms, along the delicate slope of her nose, and over each round cheek. A growl is pulled from chest as I take in the bruise along her forehead, the split to her lip.

I don't even realize how much I'm shaking until Kaethe's hand cups my own.

"Don't think about how bad things could've gone. We're both alive and safe." She leans in and touches her soft, plump lips to mine. "What happens now?"

Letting out a shuddering breath, I trace her lips with my thumb.

"That depends. I have the power now to order all human captives to be set free. With Vorgak's arsenal of weapons we can easily put down any uprisings. There's a hundred things that need to be done."

Kaethe nods. "What do you want to do?"

"The same thing I always do," I answer, untucking her towel from around her and letting it pool at her waist. Her beautiful breasts are illuminated by the soft light in the room. I thumb her nipple and she moans into my touch. "I want to get you naked and stuff you full of my cock."

My mate giggles and smacks at my chest but she doesn't pull away.

I grow serious as I look into her dark eyes. "You know what me becoming king means? As my mate, you're queen now."

"Are you okay with that? With being king?" Her hands skim up my own arm to tangle in my hair.

"I never wanted power, never wanted to rule. I've only ever wanted to keep people safe."

"Then it sounds like you're the perfect orc to be king."

"Are you okay with it?" I ask, curling a piece of her pink hair around my finger.

"As long as we're together, the rest is just details." Kaethe leans in and presses her lips against mine again. I groan brokenly into the kiss and suddenly I'm flattening her to the bed. Her soft body cradles mine as I settle between her legs. Her arms go around my neck as she sucks my tongue into her mouth.

We work together to shed my clothes and I love the way her eyes glaze over as she takes in my chest. I flex my muscles for her and she sighs, pressing her hands to my back and pulling me down on top of her. The old bed we are on rattles and creaks. It was made for me when I was child, so my feet hang over the edge and there's barely enough room for Kaethe to lay flat in it.

"If we are planning on living here we're gonna need a bigger bed," Kaethe says as I kiss my way down her neck. I nip at her pulse, then suck along her collar bone. My hands knead her breasts until she's squirming against me.

"I'll build you the biggest bed ever made."

I kiss my way down her body, leaving nips and kisses all over her soft skin, before hooking her legs over my shoulder. Her little pussy is drenched, so pink and pretty. I press my nose against her and salivate over her sweet scent.

"Bazur," she moans as I enjoy my feast.

My tongue works her clit as my fingers slip into her entrance. She's so slick and hot, it's not long before her juices are running down to her back entrance. Pulling my fingers from her cunt and making sure they're slick from her arousal, I gently prod that untouched hole. I get to the first knuckle before she lets out a shriek.

"What are you doing?" she asks, her head thrashing against the pillow. My finger presses farther into her ass while I slip my tongue inside her pussy. I fuck both of her holes with my tongue and finger until her hips start grinding against my face.

I push my finger all the way inside of her ass and she screams, rewarding me with a rush of her come on my tongue. I drink it all down and pull my finger out. Her eyes are unfocused and her chest rises and falls as she watches me loom over her.

"One day soon, my cock will go in that hole too." I bite the fleshy swell of her breast, her hips tilt up to try and guide my cock into her. Reaching down, I position myself at her entrance, her thighs being hoisted up by my hands.

"We'll need lots of my special cream for that," she says, breaking off on a moan as I fill her in one thrust.

"So tight, *akorzag*." Her cunt squeezes me and I move slowly within her for a moment. It's not long before she starts whining, pressing her feet into my ass and urging me to take her harder. I'm not one to deny my queen.

The headboard of the old bed rattles as it slams into the stone wall. Her breasts bounce and her legs cinch tighter around my waist. Without warning, my mate uses all of her strength to try and flip me onto my back. I chuckle as I help her accomplish the task.

Kaethe straddles my thighs and I position a pillow beneath my head so I can take in all of her. She is so gorgeous. Her fair skin is covered in a fine sheen of sweat, her cheeks and knees are both pink. She places her small hands on my chest and I watch as she begins to move on my cock.

Her movements are slow and disjointed but as she gets more comfortable being on top, she starts slamming down on me in more precise movements. I watch her delicious body bounce and jiggle with each downward thrust of her hips. Over and over again, until my own breathing grows ragged. My hands slide up her stomach until I am able to cup her breasts, pinching her pink nipples.

Kaethe's hands cover my own and she leans down to kiss me, her hips beginning to grind in circles while she's stuffed with my cock.

"Do you want to come on my breasts this time?" she asks innocently. My body jerks and my hands fly to her hips.

Mother of the Mountain, spare me.

"*Akorzag,*" I groan and she kisses me again.

"Because you can." Her teeth sink into her bottom lip as her legs on either side of me squeeze tighter. She hoists her hips higher until I am barely inside of her and then slams them back down. Over and over again she does it until I'm panting.

My finger finds her little clit and I rub tight circles on it causing her back to arch.

"I'm not coming anywhere but in this tight pussy," I growl. Kaethe leans off of my chest and places her hands behind her on my thighs. She raises her body again, showing me all of her and I have to close my eyes because it's almost too decadent to bear.

"I knew you'd say that." Her eyes are hazy with lust but her smile is mischievous. My restraint snaps with what she says next. "Come inside me, mate. I need my king's come."

I let out a roar and suddenly I'm in control again. I rip her off of my cock and throw her face down on the bed. My tongue runs from her clit to her asshole and then I'm slamming myself inside her tight pussy again. My hips smack against her ass as she frantically claws at the sheets.

"My mate's pussy is gripping me so good. Are you going to come, Kaethe?" I say into her ear, sinking my teeth into her shoulder. Her hips move back against me so she can fuck herself on my length.

"Please, make me come."

"Then tell me what I want to hear." I lick my thumb and hover it just over her clit. One press of it and she's done for. Kaethe's eyes are filled with so much lust as she glances over her shoulder and holds my gaze.

"I love you," she sighs and I thumb her clit. Her climax claims her as her pussy clamps down on my cock. I fuck her hard, once, twice, three more times before I'm flooding her little cunt with my seed. She gets all of it and one day, one day very soon it'll make our first child.

That thought stays with me as I pull out of her and hold her tight against me. On this narrow bed, over half her body lays on my chest and I don't mind it. In fact, I'm rethinking the whole, bigger bed idea. I like being this close to her, our bond so strong between us and tying our souls together.

"Think we can make this place into a home?" Kaethe asks softly into my chest.

"My home is wherever you are." I kiss her brow and she snuggles even deeper into me. I hold her hand on top of my chest. It's so tiny and delicate yet it holds my entire heart in its palm.

"Forever," she says, even as her eyes begin to close and yawn sneaks up on her.

"Forever," I agree, draping a heavy blanket over us. Tomorrow the work starts, but right now there is only Kaethe. I have everything I have ever wanted right here in my arms. I welcome these new challenges knowing my mate and I will face them together.

EPILOGUE

KAETHE
SIX MONTHS LATER

THE DRESSMAKER WAS A LIAR.

Well maybe not a liar, but royal purple didn't *highlight my features*, like she insisted. Truthfully, I would've been happier greeting our guests in one of my wool gowns. Bazur isn't dressing up, he wears his wool shirts and fur cloak and no one says anything because he is the king. Me on the other hand? I need to be primped and polished whenever we hold court.

The old dressmaker told me it was tradition. It's not as if I want to disrespect their customs but could the royal color be something other than purple. It doesn't suit my hair and makes my skin look sick. This latest creation has puffy sleeves and gold thread. I look like a rotten cupcake instead of a queen. I sigh and tuck some of my curled pink hair behind my ear.

Bazur walks in and his eyes immediately light up. I try not to sulk over seeing him in his regular clothes. The king's room we share is completely renovated. The stone walls are polished, decorated with tapestries that tell the tales of Bazur's father and Bazur's own bravery. There's even a royal portrait of us done by one of the people from Black Claw Village. We try to go back at least once a month but it's been tricky.

Being a royal is so much work that I look forward to when we can make the journey back. When we are in the village it's like nothing has changed. I help Myren with the sick and wounded, teaching the midwives the incision births to do in my absence. Bazur and I enjoy dinner at his small kitchen table and make love underneath the skylight. It's perfect. It's what I want us to return to but that will take time. Until then, I will be patient and suffer through this contraption of a dress.

"You look beautiful, *akorzag*," Bazur says, coming up behind me and kissing my neck. His hands squeeze my breasts that have been pushed up by the lacing of this gown. Bazur would think I looked beautiful in a wool sheet. The thought has my pussy turning wet but I still manage to shake my head.

"I look ridiculous, I can't see why I'm not allowed to wear my regular clothes like you."

His dark brows furrow. "Who says you can't?"

I sigh and lean back against his chest, both of us staring at our reflection in the large mirror.

"The dressmaker told me it's tradition for the queen to wear these formal gowns whenever we have visitors. Practically passed out when I told her I was more comfortable in my own simple gowns." I let out a groan. "I don't want to be ungrateful but I feel uncomfortable like this."

Bazur nods. "Then tell her you won't wear them."

"I can't do that, I'll seem rude," I say, my cheeks turning pink. "It's fine, it's only for an evening."

My mate's lips return to my neck as his hands skim up my front. He's insatiable for me. There's always a frenzy the first time we come together and then a second time follows that's softer, more emotional. I love both versions of our fucking and as much as I would love him to take me now, we can't.

My palms sweat as my nerves kick in.

"Bazur," I hiss, "we're needed in the throne room."

"I am the king, they wait for us," he says, running his tongue along my exposed shoulder. His hands tangle in the front of my gown before he rips it clear down the center. I gasp, my eyes flying open as my breasts are exposed. Bazur reaches inside my shredded gown and kneads one gently.

"Bazur!" I scream.

"You're welcome, my mate, now wear a dress that you like." He kisses my lips and helps me take off the ruined gown. I slip into one of my regular ones, it's pale gray and hugs my body like a second skin. Instantly I feel better and more relaxed.

Bazur and I lock hands just as the dressmaker enters the room carrying a gossamer train I was supposed to attach to the dress. *Whoops.* The ancient orc's eyes go to the dress on the floor then back up to me in my plain gown. Her graying braid whips at her back with the force of her head moving.

"Your Majesty, why are you not dressed? The guests are arriving—"

"That would be my fault," Bazur interrupts, his hand possessively curling around my waist. "I couldn't keep my hands off of her, your gown was the unfortunate victim. I hope you understand."

"Of course, my king, of course," the dressmaker bows and my cheeks color.

Without another word Bazur pulls me from the room and I giggle, pressing myself into his side. Gods, I love him. These past six months have only solidified that. Every day with him is an adventure, an opportunity to sink deeper into our feelings for one another. Sure we fight sometimes, but no male knows how to apologize better than Bazur.

"Can you rip all of my dresses?" I ask as we make our way down to the throne room.

"I prefer you naked anyways." His smile is beaming and so beautiful it takes my breath away. This life is wonderful and perfect. Now it's time for me to reconnect with my old one.

The throne room has been redecorated in our time here. On the dais no longer sits that horrible throne of bones. We had it destroyed, the bones comprising it were given proper burials. In its place are two identical stone thrones. Simple and efficient, just like the type of rulers Bazur and I are. It's still a shock that I am a ruler.

Mainly I oversee healing and science, helping those humans who were recently freed get an education and learn new skills. Bazur rules firmly but fairly and only has had to deal with a couple generals who were resistant to the new changes. Whatever trouble comes our way, Bazur will keep me safe. He always does.

The throne room is filled with humans and orcs alike as we take our seats on the throne. My brother steps into the center of the room and hush falls over the crowd. Bazur and I don't wear crowns but our authority is there regardless.

My brother's beard is longer. He's been away these last two months to meet with our liaison in the east. I've missed him. Before he left our relationship had progressed so much that we started sharing *I love you's* and have made new memories together.

"How was your trip, brother?" I ask. Bazur captures my hand and kisses the back of my palm. My mate feels extra possessive with so many other people in the room. As much as I know he would never do it, a part of him is deadly serious about keeping me confined to the bedroom all day so that no one gets to see me.

Perhaps, I'll grant that wish as his name's day gift next month.

"Uneventful, but our vampire contact has sent the prince's regards and recognizes you both as the new King and Queen of the Orcs." Karth grimaces but goes on. "The Vampire Prince of Windgate Castle, is old and mean but fair. I don't think we'll be hearing much from him now that he has what he asked for."

Bazur and I both nod. I can't help the shiver that runs down my spine as I recall what it was exactly he wanted in exchange for that elixir. What could someone possibly need with that much poison? I hope we never find out and whatever he's planning to use it for stays confined to the Walled City.

Karth bows and steps back. My leg bounces as we wait. Bazur squeezes my hand and offers me a reassuring smile. I've been anticipating this day eagerly. Now that it's only moments away I don't know how I'm going to handle it.

"Don't be nervous, everything will be fine."

Faintly I can hear the sound of hooves, they get louder and louder as each moment passes by. My heart is beating wildly as the sounds get closer. Hooves give way to thunderous footsteps that clank with the armor the guards are wearing. My throat closes as I watch them file into the throne room.

A legion of dark elf royal guards come through the door. They keep perfect unity as they march toward us. A few of the orc's eyes go wide as do the humans. The dark elf guards are armed with swords, their gray skin and red eyes are lit by the torches lining the walls. They form parallel lines and face the center.

Then, in the doorway they appear. King Arkain and Queen Elveena of Myrkorvin, wearing their matching black pointed crowns, dressed in their royal black and red. King Arkain looks as severe as ever but Elvie's silver eyes are alight with mischief as they walk down the path their guards created towards us.

Bazur and I rise and step down from the dais to greet them at the bottom. Elvie, my friend who I haven't seen in so long. Will things be awkward? The last time we had contact was when I was in Moonbourne. That had been around Yule.

Just over nine months since we last saw each other. Has that time made us strangers?

The moment is tense as Arkain and Elvie approach. Standing in front of each other, Arkain and Bazur size one another up, both placing protective hands on us, their mates. They're the same height and build and assess each other for a potential threat.

We are silent for a moment, Elvie and I just staring at each other. My friend looks the same but something is different. There's a new mature glow about her. Whatever it is I don't get to study it for long as she bursts into a giggle and throws her arms around me. I do the same, laughing and crying into her neck. She's so much taller than me, her chin rests on top of my head.

"I've missed you, Kae," she says, holding me tighter.

"I've missed you too. Much has happened."

"I can tell that from your scent alone." Her eyes dance with amusement as we pull apart from each other. "Which is why, I convinced Arkain to let us stay for a week."

Arkain rolls his eyes but pulls her into his side. "I can deny you nothing, my mate, you know that."

"I do, that's why you get my mouth on your cock so often." Arakin makes a choking sound and lightly swats her ass. I snicker and Bazur's eyes meet mine with alarm. I shrug as if to say, *That's just Elvie*. My friend's eyes turn back to me.

"I can't believe it, Kae. An orc mate, becoming a queen, finding your brother? Is there anything you haven't done in these past few months?"

"It's surreal." I cover Bazur's hand resting on my hip and give it a squeeze. "It's love."

Elvie and Arkain share a look and smile softly at each other. Bazur kisses the top of my head and my chest feels like it's going to burst, overflowing with so much emotion.

"First the official business," Elvie says and nods to her mate. Arkain clears his throat and speaks loud and clear.

"As King and Queen of the Dark Elves, Elveena and I officially recognize your ascension to the throne and proclaim that you have our full backing and support as leaders of the orcs, King Bazur and Queen Kaethe." Applause breaks out around the room and we nod our thanks to them.

"Now, the fun business," Elvie says even as Arkain tenses beside her. She looks over her shoulder to one of her ladies-in-waiting and nods. They scurry off only to return a few moments later with something wrapped in a blanket. The dark elf female bounces the bundle gently and bows as she hands it over to Elvie.

I narrow my eyes and let out a gasp as I see what was retrieved. Not a what, a who.

There nestled in that black blanket stitched with the Myrkorvin crest is a beautiful baby. Its skin is a very light gray, with white hair just a few shades lighter than Elvie's. Its silver eyes are the same color as my friend's. Elvie cradles the child in her arms and Arkain tickles its chubby cheek with a clawed finger.

"Elvie…you never said," I trail off.

"It all happened so fast, there was no way to get word to you." The baby lets out a soft coo and pure happiness shines on Elvie's face. She looks perfect holding her baby. Arakin and Elvie stare down at their child, both smiling softly. It makes me look up at Bazur and see what I'm feeling reflected back on his face.

One day, that will be us. One day very soon.

"Would you like to hold her?" Elvie asks. My heart turns over in my chest and I nod, taking the soft bundle from her arms. "Kaethe, I'd like you to meet Princess Miralyn Kae of the Dark Elves, our daughter."

Tears slip down my cheeks and my laugh is watery, I'm touched by their kindness. To name their daughter after me? I have no words, I tell them as much.

"We were hoping," Elvie says, "that you two would agree to be her godsparents."

My eyes fly to Bazur whose smile is soft. Looking towards the King and Queen of Myrkrovin, my friends, I nod my head frantically.

"Of course, we would be honored."

I look down into Miralyn's tiny face. Her big eyes close and she's asleep within seconds. She's so tiny and perfect. I thought I wanted time with Bazur all to myself but this feeling of holding a child in my arms makes me realize what I truly desire. A family, Bazur's and mine.

Tickling her babysoft cheek, I'm certain and ready to take this next step with my mate.

Our dinner with Elvie and Arkain ran late into the night.

It was just like old times, sharing stories and telling jokes. There was so much love and laughter. Not to mention I think Arkain and Bazur could be great friends, they're both so serious and surly. They talked about hunting which made me and Elvie groan with disinterest.

We parted a few minutes ago with hugs and promises to spend time together tomorrow without our mates. I love Bazur, but sometimes you just need time with a female friend. Besides, I'm hoping Elvie can help me with a few techniques I've been meaning to try out with my male.

If her and Arkain's screams of pleasure that used to shake the castle are anything to go by, she definitely knows what she's doing in the bedroom. Bazur and I have been known to scandalize a few castle guards ourselves. I'm curious about what all is out there and I'm looking forward to talking to someone else who understands.

Back in our chambers, Bazur helps me get out of my gown, placing soft kisses against the back of my neck. I sigh as he strips me down, before I turn and crawl on the bed naked. I look over my shoulder and see his eyes locked on the sway of my ass.

"Did you have a good day, *akorzag*?" he asks me, knowing what effect that word has on my pussy. I roll onto my back as the fur on the bed tickles my sensitive skin.

"It was one of the best days," I say. "I've missed Elvie so much. It's baffling how much both of our lives have changed since we last saw each other."

Bazur is naked soon too and crawls up the bed towards me. His monstrous cock bobs before he settles his body between my splayed thighs. Kissing me until I'm breathless, his fingers skimming up my sides.

"You looked perfect holding their baby." My stomach flutters as he presses a kiss to my chest. "I can't wait until it's our baby in your arms."

"Me neither," I confess, taking his face in my hands. "Bazur, I love you. From the moment you captured me in your net, until right now, this love for you has only grown. You promised to make me safe and you have. I know I said I wanted to wait but I'm ready. Both of our families got taken away from us. I want us to make our own and do everything to keep it safe."

Bazur groans and slams his mouth into mine. Our kisses are frantic, consuming, and taste like love. His hands squeeze my breasts, my hips, my ass, touching everywhere he possibly can. His hand trails down to my pussy and feels how wet I am. I urge him to sink inside of me by pressing my feet to his backside.

"I love you so much, Kaethe. As long as I have you everything is perfect."

I kiss him again, feeling our souls knit together. My life was ruled by fear and loss. Now there is only this, only us. This is the right time, whatever happens next Bazur is with me and that is all I need.

"I love you too," I say, reaching between us and guiding his cock to my entrance. "Now come inside of me."

THE END

ACKNOWLEDGEMENTS

This book was a journey in every sense of the word. I knew when I first sat down to write this book that the story I had planned for Kaethe was a deeply personal one. Elvie is who I want to be, but Kaethe is who I am. Kaethe is a lot of us and I hope her story made you feel seen in some way. I'm still searching for my grumpy orc general, still looking for love even when I think my time for it has passed. It hasn't. It's never too late for any of us to find the love we deserve and there's nothing wrong with waiting until you do.

Next, I want to say thank you to the people who helped make this book possible. The map and interior formatting done by Qamber Designs & Media went beyond my wildest dreams. Magdalena Pietrzak (@barn-swallow.art) for creating the most beautiful cover I have ever seen, and Haya from Haya Designs putting the finishing touches on it to make it look like an actual cover. I also want to thank Taylor from A Taylor(ed) Edit for helping me so much with the editing process! This book needed all of your tender love and care.

Thank you so much to my beta and ARC readers. You all go above and beyond for me! From putting out my first book in October of 2022 until now the immense support you all have shown me has blown me away. Never in my wildest dreams did I think so many of you would enjoy my work but here you are! I am so thankful to each and everyone of you.

I can't wait for you all to read book three…sexy vampires anyone?

MEET THE AUTHOR

CHARLOTTE SWAN is a twenty-four year old, living in Chicago. When she is not dreaming about being whisked away to a world filled with magic and sexy monsters, she is busy being a freelance social media marketer and full-time smut lover. To hear about her upcoming projects or to connect with her on social media please find her at her website or by scanning the code below.

www.authorcharlotteswan.com